THE
MEDUSA COIN

Also by Lou Paduano

Signs of Portents

Tales from Portents

THE MEDUSA COIN

Greystone Book Three

Lou Paduano

Eleven Ten Publishing LLC

GRAND ISLAND, NEW YORK

Eleven Ten Publishing LLC
282 Fareway Lane
Grand Island, NY 14072

Printed in the United States of America
Edited by Kristen Corrects, Inc.
Cover art design by Kit Foster Design

First edition published 2017

Library of Congress Cataloguing in Publication Data
Paduano, Lou
The Medusa Coin / Lou Paduano

LCCN: 2017909036
ISBN-13: 978-1-944965-52-5 (hardcover)
ISBN-13: 978-1-944965-06-8 (paperback)
ISBN-13: 978-1-944965-07-5 (eBook)

For Gam

Truly immortal for she will never be forgotten.

PROLOGUE ONE

The lightning struck.

Fast and free, splitting the sky, it shattered the windows of the apartment, careening for its target. The ravenous beast, lusting for innocent blood roared, its end reflected in the single bolt of electricity. Her victim raced for the door, trying to escape an unforgettable nightmare. The lightning was justice. Pure. Simple. Controlled.

The vampire shrieked, her final moment met with nothing more than terror. One instant present and the next vaporized in the aftermath of the directed storm. The perfect climax to Soriya Greystone's first night back on the job. Life continued in the city of Portents with her protector back on the streets. Until the lightning struck.

Then everything changed.

There was no control in the blast. The lightning, once channeled to perfection through the rune cast on the Greystone's face, hit with such terrible fury that the room exploded with the force of a thousand shockwaves. The creature of the night felt nothing in the instant of her death. Soriya, however, took the brunt of the aftermath, ejected from the room by the lightning.

She felt weightless. Wind whipped around her, the seconds lost in confusion and fear. The city blurred, the lights below blinding. Instinct took over. Seven floors up, there was little time for decision making. Even less time for her better judgment, not that it had a role in anything anymore.

For Soriya, only survival mattered. The ribbons of Kali shot out from her left arm, catching the railing on a fourth floor balcony across the street. Her body jerked, reeled in by the gift of the Hindu death goddess. The arc was steep, her momentum from both the blast and the change in direction too quick to maintain.

She landed hard in the street, her breath leaving her at once. The ribbons retracted, snapping back to her skin. Soriya rolled from the impact, skirting two lanes of highway.

Bright lights beamed through closed eyelids. Headlights bearing down on her. Horns blared. Shouts from aggressive drivers and delivery trucks worried about accident reports more than the life of the woman crumpled on the road. Soriya tucked down, rolling between vehicles, watching the rush of traffic speed over her compressed frame before she inched meticulously to the roadside.

Blood coated her knees and elbows. Standing was agony but Soriya found her footing with the help of the corner mailbox. Screams continued to ring out and she worried that more cars headed her way, that the danger had yet to pass.

She was only half right.

The screams echoed, not from the dizzying evening traffic, but from the apartment building across the street. Screams that melded into the blaring alarms. The symphony created by the fire consumed the southeast corner of the ten-story structure.

"No," Soriya muttered. She fell to the sidewalk, the orange and red flames filling her wide eyes.

Sirens blared, flashing lights coming from all directions. Dozens of people flooded the street, onlookers curious about the destruction. Those who came from the building itself wore looks of worry and devastation. Their lives had changed in an instant.

Firefighters set to work immediately. Exits were opened on all ends, families escorted out with trails of smoke close behind. The flames already consumed three floors of the building, and were spreading mercilessly to the rest. If not the heat, then the smoke, filling every hall, clouding every window.

The victims, their homes destroyed, cried out from down the block. Their safety meant little to the losses suffered.

Because of a single act.

A few onlookers moved to help, lending a hand to those in need. Jackets offered due to the cool night air. A smile and a friend. Emergency crews did the rest, rushing into the devastation to help where they could while others contained the spreading flames.

Soriya Greystone did nothing but watch it all unfold. Her breath caught in her throat, her heart unable to calm. The stone rested in her palms, the light upon its surface long since gone.

What have I done?

The young woman settled into the shadows, the sorrow of the innocent ringing in her ears. Innocence the stone should have protected. That she should have kept safe. Their cries followed her fleeing steps, carrying her broken frame deeper into the night.

PROLOGUE TWO

Loren quit drinking a year ago. Thirty-six years old now and he hadn't tasted a drop of alcohol in the last twelve months. In fact, he had never cared for the stuff. It was the convenience of the product, the idea of its effectiveness in pulling one out of the doldrums, out of life itself and making the world more acceptable for a time.

Until nothing was acceptable. Not the drink. And not Loren. Drinking never brought out feelings of joy or created a distance between reality and fantasy. It simply made Loren angrier, a gift passed down from his father.

That much was fact from the moment of his first drink. Seventeen and his neighborhood friend, Cliff—he wanted to change his name to Logan like the hairy guy from *X-Men*—handed him his first beer. *Swill* was an understatement. The stuff was poison wrapped in aluminum and something Loren downed with four more of its brethren, not that he noticed the count after the second. All he remembered was blood on his fist and Cliff crying very un-Logan-like tears. Whatever the argument mattered little in the long haul, much like their future friendship (of which none existed after that night). Loren quit drinking after that, his first attempt of many over the years, but everything eventually circled around and it did the same for him.

When Beth fell. Only at the end of the day it was Loren that fell, lost in anger and mistakes.

Which made his entrance to McDuffie's Pub that much more peculiar. He slipped inside the dive bar tucked in the shadow of Evans Tower, shifting between patrons celebrating the approaching summer season with drinks and smokes on the patio.

Damn, I miss smoking.

Loren slipped a stick of gum from his pocket then tucked it away. His latest nasty habit could wait. He needed to celebrate and McDuffie's was the place he remembered. Not exactly the best of memories considering what followed—his brawl with Standish and subsequent suspension from the force.

Loren took a seat at the bar, fighting for comfort on the stool. Small glances flitted his way, but Loren ignored them. He reached into his pocket and removed the small metallic item behind the need for some celebration.

His badge.

The meeting with Ruiz went very well, beyond his own expectations. His sister continued to avoid his calls, the "I told you so" mentality spanning the silence between them, though Loren knew this was the smart move. Portents never faded into the background as he had hoped with his departure. Those were the dreams of a man looking to run away and keep running. They were the words of a kid unable to control a situation. He was an adult and it was time to face the world rather than ignore it.

No matter the bridges burned and the pain endured.

Or the mysteries left open.

"I've seen that look before." A shadow fell over the badge resting on the bar in front of Loren and a voice pulled him from his musings. The man behind the deep voice smiled, his teeth unnaturally white against his dark skin. He ran a rag over a pint glass. "Usually with someone a little younger. No offense. But definitely that look."

"Which one is that?"

The bartender put the glass down and pointed to the badge. "Awestruck. Like finding a jewel at the bottom of the ocean by chance."

Loren nodded. "That's not far off, actually."

"Late bloomer?"

"Reinstatement," Loren said, clearing his throat. He picked up the badge and ran his thumb along the embossed shield at its center. "And a long story."

"Any way you spin it, sounds like there should be some celebrating involved." The bartender lifted the glass and tilted it to Loren, waiting for a reply.

Loren waved the glass down. "I don't drink. Not anymore."

"Strange place to plant yourself then."

"Familiar ground," Loren replied.

The bartender nodded, looking around. "Comforting."

"Instinct."

The man left and returned, Loren following his movements. There were a number of patrons waiting for refills but all deferred to the tall black man behind the bar. When the bartender came back, a glass settled on a coaster in front of the detective.

"Water for the man in blue," he said with a smile. "Always on the house."

Loren lifted the glass. "Water? How generous."

"I am a kind-hearted soul." Reaching beneath the bar, the man retrieved his own glass of water and held it up. "To new beginnings."

"Cheers." Loren took a long sip, every drop satisfying him.

"Can I get a table set for you?" the man asked, looking around for space. "How many are joining you?"

Loren hesitated, the satisfaction of the moment fleeting. He looked around at the strangers in the bar. Dozens of people he had never seen before tonight and would never see again. None were alone; all were with some companionship for the night. Laughing. Loving. Together.

"I'll be fine."

The bartender read his face, and knocked on the bar. "Congrats again."

Loren held up the water. "And thanks again—"

"Dominic." The man extended his hand. Loren took it and gave a hard shake. "Here every day."

"Living the dream."

Dominic smiled, heading to a group of waiting customers. "Aren't we all?"

Loren stared at the badge on the bar. He certainly could not argue against the sentiment. As Dominic left for the far end of the bar, Loren sipped at his drink, thinking over the events leading to this night. Nathaniel Evans. The loss of Mentor. Soriya and the Greystone. The Night of the Lights.

Portents was changing.

More than he wanted to admit, it seemed. Watching Dominic pour a pitcher for the waiting customers, he realized the bartender wore an unseasonably thick sweater over a shirt with a high collar. Surrounded by young men in shorts and women in considerably less than socially accepted outfits, Dominic stood out as the odd man in the room.

Then he saw them. Tucked under the collar, pulled low by the man's sweater, small slits ran up the bartender's neck. After handing the pitcher to the group, Dominic downed his glass of water, then filled another before swiftly dispatching it without pause. The small slits flared along his neck, like tiny lips cooing with contentment.

Gills.

Dominic caught the detective's stare, finding the sunken point on the collar and fixing it expediently. He grinned to the man at the center of the bar, a finger to his lips. Loren nodded, half astonished.

Portents was changing and he sat right in the middle of it all now. Right where he asked to be. The hidden city out in plain sight. Everywhere around them.

Loren laughed, finishing his water.

Outside, sirens blared. Emergency vehicles including fire and ambulances rushed down Evans heading west. Trouble. But not his. Not tonight.

He was celebrating.

Loren peered around the room at the strangers among him. None glanced over. Not at the flashing lights or the city's booming noise. And not at the lone man in the center of the room. They were lost in their own lives, content in the moment.

The city was changing but some things stayed the same.

Loren turned back to the bar, a fresh water in front of him. Alone. He lifted the glass, eyes on the badge. His fresh start. His new beginning.

"Bottoms up."

CHAPTER ONE
Three Months Later

A storm was coming. Rushing wind crashed, sending shutters slamming against the faded veneer of the old home. Neglected over the last few years, the Victorian-style domicile on the Upper East Side of Portents stood in complete shadow apart from the neighborhood. Overgrowth from trees surrounding the property kept it hidden from the world.

Perfect for Henry's needs.

He coughed, blood mixing with spittle against his clenched fist. The candle, the only light down the long second floor hallway, shook in his grasp. He tried to find his balance, the blood and saliva mixture spreading against the wall from outstretched fingers. His vision blurred from the sweat dripping off his brow.

He was getting worse, the old feelings of pain and sickness filling him from head to toe. Time grew short. His world was collapsing and had been for the last three years, since his first fall.

It came at work. Long hours and intense study were the excuses of the day but it was more than that. He pressed on until his body demanded an answer to its screams. When he fell outside his office, there was little choice but to find out the truth.

Doctors poked and prodded. Appointments stretched weeks and months, tests never explained unless the questions were direct and thorough, something he prided himself on being, thankfully. Unfortunately, the answers didn't work in his favor, joining the uncomfortable looks and apologies every time a health community member entered the room.

"Henry," they would say, always staring at a computer screen or clipboard. Never catching his wary eyes. "I'm sorry to have to…"

Their apologies ended his listening. Apologies amounted to nothing but a waste of time. The test results spoke for themselves. They gave their statement on his life, on his existence culminating in a final diagnosis confirmed with a single word by dozens of professionals in lab coats.

Terminal.

The first time he heard it, Henry wept for a week straight. He had controlled every aspect of his life. His relationships. His professionalism. Every piece of his world was finely tuned, from his place of residence to his selection of careers. Everything lined up for him. He controlled it all and everything served the greater good; his legacy, his contributions to the world.

All washed away in a single word.

Terminal.

"How long?" Henry asked after a time, when emotions were lost and apologies faded behind cold, hard truth.

Each professional mumbled their reply, always looking away, their focus never on the patient before them. "There's no way to know for certain. Some patients—"

"How. Long."

"Six months. Maybe a year."

Always the same response, with the disease so virulent throughout his system. He felt it with each breath, with each sudden movement, the striking pain rising up his legs and into his chest. He could have collapsed at the diagnosis, the timeline set by men seemingly smarter than him. For a time he did, all sense lost in that single word.

He dropped everything and left his job. He cut himself off from the world and devoted every waking moment to curing the illness within. Chemo left him weak, his body aging decades in only three short years, two and a half more than anyone predicted at the start. Pain, once sudden and sharp, became a way of life. Doctor appointments riddled his schedule, his own time little more than sleep on top of naps on top of light meals that ended up vacating one way or the other. His once controlled world was no longer his anymore.

Everything was taken from him.

All for nothing.

Treatments failed. One by one, all avenues toward any form of cure dissolved, evaporated with the middle-aged man's every hope and dream. Holistic solutions came and went more than traditional methods, failing at every turn.

The less traveled roads became the only ones left. As a younger man, Henry learned of them all. He saw things uniquely, his mind open to different possibilities. He filled his waking hours, which were becoming fewer and fewer, with tomes seldom seen. He shopped on the Internet, spending every last cent earned over a lifetime of study and perseverance. Another thing lost—his financial security joining the rest of his life. All went toward one goal.

Survival.

His need outweighed all sacrifices, fighting against all pain and the ravaged waste that had become his body. All proving futile, the books and alternative solutions proving every bit as useless as the rest.

Until one presented itself.

Henry woke from a deep dream, one plaguing his thoughts for days. A woman in a blue dress with hair as black as night. She danced along his thoughts until her smile turned to screams.

The sudden shift startled him awake. Most nights this led to tossing and turning but tonight was different.

Something was waiting for him under the dim light of his nightstand lamp. A single sheet of paper and a round object resting upon it.

A coin.

Confused and uncertain, Henry's withered hand reached for it. It slipped between his fingers, jolting him awake with its touch. Shivers raced through his body, feeling and sensation long since abandoned due to the raging disease. His breathing did not cause sharp pains in his chest.

Creaking wood alerted him to another presence—a shadow in the doorway. Henry held up the coin, the ghoulish face on its front sneering at him.

"What is this?" he called into the darkness.

The shadow chuckled. "An opportunity."

Henry understood it as something more. A *miracle*.

Overnight, blurred vision and failing function turned around. Henry rushed from his bed able to stand and walk and even dance as if the illness had been nothing more than a dream. A three-year nightmare that ripped the world from him. That took control from him.

Never again.

"Full remission," the doctors said, flummoxed. Henry held tight to the coin and smiled at each question the doctors asked. No answers would come their way, the same as they shared with him for so long. Except to their final inquiry before returning Henry to the world at large. "What are you going to do now?"

"Live."

Forever.

The truth of the coin unwrapped itself in the manuscripts accumulated during his frantic search. He used the knowledge to reclaim his old position, to start again, though his worldview had shifted. Still, the coin remained a priority. He took his time to study it, examining every last word, and every last instance of the coin in history.

Until time began to run out once more.

The initial effects, while staggering and life altering, began to fade. To lessen. To dissipate.

His illness was returning, the disease ripping through him even more fiercely.

Leading him to this moment.

The candle continued to flicker as he closed the door to his private study, tucked from view from the rest of the home. His bloodied hand ran along his side, staining his already discolored shirt. The room came to light from the thin flame. In the center was a circle, more candles placed around the chalk marring the floorboards.

It was time to reclaim his life, to fully control his destiny for the first time in years. And never relinquish it again. The coin sat in the center of the circle, the list of names beneath. Weeks of inquiry, of bribes with the last of his funds, had made the meaning behind the list clear.

As well as its purpose to what lay ahead.

Henry entered the circle and sat before the coin. He lit the candles around him then blew out the thin wick of the first. Slipping his hand into his pocket, it returned with a small knife. He took the coin into his other hand and nicked the end of his finger. Blood dropped on the coin's surface, the sneering face obstructed.

Until the coin absorbed the blood.

Henry closed his eyes and breathed deep, pain filling his lungs. He recalled the words, studied them and recited them for days in preparation. He feared the result, the consequences of his actions, what would be unleashed by his request.

Survival won out.

"Σας καλούν. Λάβουν σοβαρά υπόψη την έκκλησή μου."

The words were soft but carried along the wind, a growing maelstrom emulating the storm outside the Victorian style domicile. They grew in the telling, like the legend behind the coin, the power it held over the creature being summoned. The creature that would save Henry from fate, placing it back where it belonged: under his control. Forever.

"Σας καλούν. Λάβουν σοβαρά υπόψη την έκκλησή μου." Louder now, the wind swirling in the study. The candles went out, dropping the room into darkness. More than that, the shadows appeared to grow in the corner. They gained shape and form, reaching from the darkness of some other space.

Announcing the arrival of the beast.

"Σας καλούν. Λάβουν σοβαρά υπόψη την έκκλησή μου."

It exited the shadows, howling at the words, screeching at the coin in the man's hand. Henry tried to look away, drawn to the sight of the monster. Black tangles of hair escaped the cloak covering most of its enlarged form. The hair cascaded over the beast's desiccated face, unable to block the hollowed-out sockets where eyes once lay. Oversized arms protruded from the cloak, fingers of bone and sinew stretching out and ripping the air. Unable to penetrate the circle. Unable to fight against the coin held tight in Henry's grasp.

The creature cowered before the coin. This was not the path Henry chose, not the one he wanted after a lifetime of study and hard work, of sacrifice and patience, of control. It was, however, life he was after. And life he would attain once more.

Forever.

He held the list before the creature's sightless face, the power of the coin pulsating through him. He knew what was to come, the price to be paid. A small price for the reward to come.

"There is work to be done."

CHAPTER TWO

Saint Sebastian's Church sat on the corner of the Knoll, its arches visible from as far north as the coves and as far south as Tolliver's Grove. Built in 1902, one of the first from the famous Walker Company, which constructed many landmarks over the city's beginnings including the second Evans Tower after fire consumed the original structure. They staged the construction in three waves, one for the church's main body and one for the bell towers that rang in the start of each new day for Portents. Walker's words at the dedication ceremony were inscribed on a plaque garnishing the front vestibule.

These bells will signal the departure of any shadows that may fall over Portents and ring in the return of the light for all.

At the time of its inception, little else surrounded the church. Roadways were few; motorcars decades away from making it into the mainstream, though city planners had the foresight to build the growing number of avenues and streets wider.

Portents grew, and with it did Saint Sebastian's as its ecumenical center. Other elaborately constructed churches cropped up in the expansion days when the city co-opted the northern coves and the southern border stretched into the next county. Walker himself was pulled back into the work, but even he failed to live up to the pageantry of that first landmark.

Downtown built up around the church, the residential neighborhoods pushed farther and farther away, the map dominated by too much business for too few people. Despite the distance necessary to attend, Saint Sebastian's Church kept its core audience over the decades, generations following their ancestors under its arched roof and perfectly preserved stained glass windows.

Alejo Ruiz was a second-generation member of the church. His mother brought him no less than three times each week, knees bent between the pews, his head bowed. Thought and prayer for a child amounted to little but the experience marked him for life. It grounded him in his day-to-day as a captain of the Portents Police Department.

It kept him rooted to the city.

The days of multiple visits passed when his mother left this world, but Ruiz made a vow to continue the practice of her faith, dropping everything to attend a weekend service. Work did its best to interfere, as it did with all things of importance in his life, but faith won out more often than not.

Today was almost a "than not" day, the Ruiz family struggling to get out the door. His fault, as usual. Even with the ringing of one functional bell tower every morning, the shadows of Portents clung over the city, demanding the weary captain's attention. Saturday blinked away from him under a mountain of backed-up reports and briefings, all which continued straight through Sunday morning, giving him the evening mass to make it up to the impatient Ruiz women.

Still, he almost missed the deadline, racing to meet Michelle and the girls at the church directly rather than share a ride from home. His loving wife of twenty years understood, but the hurt look on her face always brought the cost of his dedication to the forefront. It brought their distance front and center for all to see, especially their daughters.

"Does it help?"

Ruiz looked down, the confessional line before mass short but unmoving. Angela Ruiz held his left hand and played with her skirt, her impatience in conflict with her desire to spend time with her wayward father. Always smiling, the little girl of six swung from his hand, her shoes squeaking along the floor.

"Huh?" Ruiz turned around. Michelle sat on the far side of the church, eyes down in prayer. She prayed for him, though he wasn't supposed to know. He caught her whispering beside their bed most nights he made it home. He understood her concerns. He shared most of them.

The line shifted forward and Angela pulled him along. Smiles broke out from the patrons behind them, and Ruiz threw a wave with his right hand. Smiles faded into concern as churchgoers caught a glimpse of the scars running up Ruiz's wrist and the vague indentations of a hand imprinted on his forearm. Ruiz lowered his sleeve, tucking his arm in front of his midsection.

"What did you say, Angel, baby?"

Angela rolled her eyes. "Daaaaad."

He laughed, clearing his throat dramatically. "Sorry. Angela, young lady?"

She was the spitting image of her mother, head to toe. Attitude as well, though Ruiz did his best to ignore that fact.

When Angela was born, Ruiz promised a lighter workload. No more dreams of advancement, those days long since passed. His office on the second floor of the Rath Building took enough of his life away from everyone and everything he cared about. Now Angela stood six years older, like time suddenly blinked away.

He held her hand tighter, hoping to keep it locked in his for a few more years. A little longer, always a little longer, to keep his world in place. Wishful thinking that could never stop the clock. Angela was already discovering friends and the wider world they provided. Church became their final respite, thanks to his burdening workload.

His endless work.

"Does it help?" Angela asked again.

Ruiz leaned closer, eyes forward as they inched to their destination. "Does what help?"

"Confession."

"Sometimes." His smile broadened. Only six years old with the attention span of one yet attuned to the world around her. Seeing things much more clearly than the adults in the room. "Everyone needs to be able to talk to someone about certain things."

"I talk to you and Mommy."

"And that's good. You should always talk to your mom and me about anything."

"Can't you?"

Ruiz looked back to his wife. He wondered if the question was prompted, knowing better. Angela had always been smart. Intuitive.

"I do," Ruiz said softly. "We talk, Angel."

"Not this morning."

She was right, of course. The silence at breakfast was awkward. He came home late last night, as usual. Endless paperwork demanded more time and the clock sped away without care. A two hour reprieve for his family would never be enough to win his wife's favor or that of his middle daughter, Teresa, who had plans for the evening, now broken plans to shift their visit to church around. Family won out except in his case.

Not that they understood. Crime was up in the city. An uptick in open cases, including murders, though the department happily downplayed that statistic. With the election only a year away, the mayor remained a fixture at the station, demanding answers to questions not yet discovered. The district attorney's office had stepped up the pressure on the department as well, requiring more with less and less resources at their disposal.

The demands fell on him. Always him.

The silence at the breakfast table was deserved. The same silence he returned in kind for so many years. But worse since the Night of the Lights. Since Evans Tower. The event that left his right arm scarred was the tipping point. His injuries kept him awake, his sleep fitful and pained. Michelle wanted to help. He pushed her away, fearing the explanation behind the pain, the crimson eyes peeking out from the darkness.

Church was reconciliation for them. A place of belonging and a way to turn the day around for Ruiz and his family. Promises of a meal out were offered, the bribery working on the children but Michelle remained silent, reticent over what had become a string of broken vows.

For too long.

"You're right," Ruiz whispered, crouching next to his daughter. "Sometimes adults have a lot on their mind. I was just thinking is all."

"About your arm?"

He tucked his right arm closer at its mention, feeling the heat through his shirt. "My arm?"

"Is that what you talk about in there?" She reached for his right hand and he pulled it back, distracting her with a smile. "You never say anything about it."

"It's nothing to talk about, baby. I'm fine."

Angela threw her hands to her hips. "Mom doesn't think so. She says it hurts still. That you're being brave."

"Your mom's a smart lady."

"She also says you're being stupid."

Ruiz laughed, drawing attention from the couple behind them. "I sometimes am. And now you've heard my confession."

"Daaaad."

Ruiz shook his head, standing. "No more 'Daaad,' Angel, baby. Are you going to wait here or head back to Mom?"

"Here," she said, her feet stamping the floor.

Ruiz held her close. "Don't con these people into stealing you. You're stuck with me."

He threw a careful look to the couple behind them and the woman smiled. "She'll be fine."

"Thanks." Ruiz headed for the confessional. Beyond the door was a wide hallway leading to the rectory including the offices of church officials and the Sunday school no longer in operation. The hall was dark and quiet. Strange considering the time of day but Ruiz ignored the distraction, stepping into the confessional.

He knelt before the screen separating him from the priest on the other side. He prepared himself for the ritual, the holy rite that seemed easier somehow than everything else. Relationships. Family. Ruiz thought of his mother and the silence that split his parents after so many years of marriage.

Silence stemming from secrets and lies.

The great divide.

"In the name of the Father, the Son, and the Holy Spirit. It's been…" Ruiz sighed, unsure anymore.

His sigh was returned from the other side of the screen. "You never remember."

Ruiz smiled. "I tried to find an app for that, Father."

"*Father.* You can barely say that with a straight face still."

"Confession to my childhood friend isn't easy, Edgar," Ruiz said. Edgar Rusch remained a friend, despite their years apart. There was the academy first. Then dating. Edgar's decision to join the seminary was a shocker considering their unruly youth breaking windows from mobile games of stickball through the streets of Portents, but Ruiz always respected his dedication to their faith and to their friendship over the years. It bound them. When Edgar returned to take over their family church, Ruiz stood at the front of the line to greet him.

"Quit sinning so much," Edgar joked. "You're a great dad and a wonderful husband, Alejo. But when you come, all I hear is the burden. Work?"

"Some of it," Ruiz said. "Michelle's pissed as usual."

"Should she be?"

"Probably," Ruiz replied. He pinched the bridge of his nose. "Definitely."

"I can recommend a florist."

Ruiz smiled. "No Hail Mary's?"

"Will they help?"

Ruiz chuffed. "Point."

Edgar moved, his shadow shifting along the screen. Ruiz sighed. Only so much could be shared, so much to confess without crossing the line. Details only brought knowledge of what really sat in the darkness of Portents. No one needed that knowledge.

"What about—?" Edgar stopped, interrupted by the sound of creaking wood at the back of the small booth. Ruiz leaned closer, the room drowning in thickening black.

"Edgar?"

"My God."

Intense light grew, temporarily blinding Ruiz, who stumbled back against the wall. The light, bold and bright, showered over him and he strained to see two forms through the screen.

Then darkness returned. "Edgar? What is it?"

No reply.

"Edgar!" Ruiz rushed for the door. Those waiting in line, including his daughter, jumped at his panicked return.

"Daddy?" Angela moved for his hand.

"Go to your mother," Ruiz ordered, inching for the confessional's other side. "Go now."

She started to back off and he turned to the confessional door. Slipping his hand under his jacket, he drew his sidearm. Another compromise made over the years. Church was meant to be his safe place, the last safe place in Portents. But ever since Evans Tower, since the reeling pain running up his arm, the gun stayed with him.

"Give me some room," he commanded, reaching for the handle. Shocked looks at the gun were the response, yet fear eventually motivated everyone to shift away from the confessional.

"Edgar?" Ruiz opened the door. Darkness reached out for him and he jumped away from the frame. Edgar Rusch tumbled through to the floor of the church to audible gasps filling the hall.

"Daddy!" Angela cried. He waved her back once again, this time catching sight of Michelle running over. Edgar didn't move, didn't shift.

Didn't breathe.

The confessional was empty apart from Edgar. Ruiz crouched, tucking the gun away. His hand fell on Edgar's back, hot to the touch.

"Come on, buddy. Don't joke around about—"

Ruiz turned his friend over and stumbled back from the sight. Screams rang out from the throng of parishioners surrounding the body. All were pulled in by the fallen body of Edgar Rusch, Ruiz's friend for almost four decades.

And the two smoking craters where his eyes once were.

CHAPTER THREE

Deep below the city there was a wellspring of light. Caught in the heart of Portents, beneath spire and monument, lurked a hidden place. A secret room and within the secret, a glimpse at every answer imaginable.

The junction off the C line from Evans Station remained clear of the spider webs of its brethren. The handle, worn from age and use, turned compared to the rusted-over wheels on the others. There were no signs of the door, no great light beaming from above or across for any wandering soul to stumble upon in their travels.

Beyond the door and the deep metal staircase, creaking and moaning with each footfall, the chamber opened. Forty feet tall with four columns of white surrounding the middle. Each engraved with the languages of worlds both past and present. Those dead and forgotten resided next to their replacements. They were keys, access points, and protectors locking the chamber's contents in place.

Keeping the Bypass at its center.

The chamber's lone occupant, the gatekeeper of the secrets buried beneath the city, kept her distance. One foot remained on the thin carpet; the other felt the cool concrete of the larger space and the glow from the orb at its center. Warm and inviting, yet speckled in shadow, the Bypass shifted and shimmered.

The shadows started small. A flick of black along the surface, dancing within the endless echoes of the past inside the crossroads hidden inside the floating orb of light. Thin streams of darkness turned to waves of shadow along the surface, fluctuations building larger and more violent with each passing day.

Since the Greystone fell out of control.

Three months. That was how long inaction held its tight grip on Soriya Greystone. Since the lightning struck the apartment complex. Since the stone turned against its bearer, raging with boundless defiance. Three months of trying to find answers.

And failing.

The stone stayed hidden now, buried in the hand-sewn pouch tied to her right side. Even with it out of play, Soriya did her best to keep an eye on the city above. Afraid to act, but more afraid to step away completely, she tried to protect the city. Ultimately, it was another failure.

The Bypass was changing.

Mentor would understand it. He would know what was happening. Her teacher found answers in all things without hesitation. Without the doubts that plagued her every thought.

Balance. Balance is the key.

The Greystone and the Bypass. The key and the door. Two pieces of the same system. Both out of sync. Both a mystery she could not solve, could not understand.

Soriya tucked close to the bedroom that once served her teacher. Months since his passing and his presence lingered in the confined space. Texts filled the right wall. His cot lay along the left. The map hanging in front of her with the city was dotted with areas of interest. Circles of shadows.

More mysteries. Never explained by Mentor. Like so many other things in their relationship.

Soriya tried to ignore that fact. After what happened at Evans Tower, Soriya believed everything had changed. That *she* had changed. Plagued with loss and doubt, she took hold of her life and embraced her role as the Greystone, the way Mentor would have wanted. She saved the city and returned the Bypass to its rightful home. Yet it all continued to slip away.

Was she unworthy of the task? Could she ever truly measure up to her teacher and father figure? More answers never to come. Soriya held up the image of Mentor, the photo taken from his former life—Christopher Eckhart's life. He kept it secret from her, his former existence. Unlike her own, lost to the fiery crash that took her family. One life forfeited by choice and one by circumstance.

One still missing by the choices of another. Never her own. For the good of the city.

Soriya squeezed the frame, three months of frustration vacating her in an instant. The thin slice of glass covering the image cracked at the pressure points before shattering. She let the pieces scatter on the ground. Broken. Like so many other things around her.

His face carried the same grin, the one he always wore during their time together. When things worked. When there was hope for a better day. She knelt and lifted the image from the wreckage of its captivity. Light from the chamber beamed through the photo paper, revealing markings on the back.

A note.

She looked it over, the musings from the photographer to the man locked in the image. The words of a friend. Another connection to her teacher from a lifetime long since lost. His choice. She made the same, a sacrifice for the task.

One still slipping away.

Sirens cut through her musings, the fluctuating shadows of the Bypass overwhelmed by the onslaught of noise above. The cracked ceiling, another gift from the Night of the Lights, offered her a tighter connection to Portents. One she was grateful for at the moment. Any chance to escape her own self exile. The sound grew, more sirens with increasing urgency sweeping into the mix.

Trouble.

The stone sat at her hip, the ribbons of Kali wrapped along her left arm. She stared at the floating orb in the room's center. Her choice. Her task.

Soriya raced for the stairs and the city above.

CHAPTER FOUR

Flashing lights met Detective Greg Loren as he passed through the police cordon stretched out along the intersection housing Saint Sebastian's Church. Pedestrians lined the block, trying to catch a glimpse inside the closed doors of the church while the media pushed through, bright lights and cameras running non-stop for soundbites.

I should have worn a tie. Loren patted his chest, wishing he had come better prepared. A suit jacket and some black pants. Or at least a T-shirt worth a damn instead of the faded image of a rocket blasting off from an exploding green planet with the catch-phrase *One Way Ticket to Earth* underneath.

His night off came to a crashing end with a single phone call from Ruiz. His captain, his friend, whispered little in the way of details. Only a request for his help. It was enough to pull him away from his couch and his empty apartment. Nights off meant little to him since his return to Portents. When he wasn't trying to figure out what style of furniture suited him best, he was lost in a binge marathon of old television shows. No plans. No company of any kind.

Ruiz needed him. That was enough.

Waving his badge at any questioning officers, which turned out to be more than he cared to admit considering his return months earlier, Loren shuffled through the chaos. He should have been there sooner, surprised at the late hour showing on his Superman wristwatch. Outside the church's front door he stopped and took a breath. There was already panic on the streets, traffic stalled for blocks from the growing crowds gathering. Not the best way to start a case.

Before he could enter, the door opened, forcing Loren aside. A tall suited man slipped from the scene within, towering over the approaching detective.

Rufus Mathers fixed his glasses to his round face and threw a glare at the new arrival. Loren offered a grin but little else, letting the day shift captain race away without a word for the waiting news crews at the cordon line.

They had never seen eye to eye and what little Loren offered with his smile would most likely come back to bite him in the ass. The last three months proved as much with Mathers pulling every arrest report submitted to second-guess and audit his work. Anything to help in his fight to remove Loren from the department, permanently this time. Maybe it had to do with Loren putting his friend, Standish, in the hospital. Or the fact that said friend was in the pocket of half the bookies within the city limits. Mathers saw only the former—that Loren was the problem.

Not that the detective cared. As long as he could continue the real work offered by the department and Ruiz. The cases hidden from Mathers. The reason Loren had his badge back and his office at Central. The true city of Portents and the chaos that came with its existence.

Like tonight.

The atmosphere within the church was subdued. Mutters slipped between waiting patrons, a row of officers trying to gather statements. They kept their distance, corralling everyone present for the crime to the far side of the church, away from the confessional and the rectory beyond.

Police tape marked the scene, forensics working in silence around the crouched frame of Ruiz. He stayed close to the covered body, a friend Loren knew of in passing but had never met personally.

Loren let the captain work, scanning the church until finding Ruiz's wife and two daughters near the front. He stepped over to them, his worn sneakers squeaking along the floor.

"Hey," he called to Michelle. Her hair covered her face, her eyes low. Angela and Teresa sat across the row, the older holding tight to her younger sister.

Michelle turned at his voice, tired eyes brightening for a moment. "Greg."

He pulled her close, hugging the lanky black woman who had stood at his wedding six years earlier. Old friends. Old soldiers. Especially when dealing with work.

And Alejo Ruiz.

Loren refused to drop his smile. "You look great."

Michelle scoffed, pushing away from him. She dabbed at her swollen eyes. "You say that just to get to him. He call you in?"

Loren nodded, peering across the church. "How is he?"

"You talk to him more than I do. I just married him."

"I think I drew the short straw."

Michelle's arms wrapped tight across her chest. "It doesn't feel that way."

Loren understood. He had seen the divide firsthand. The split between work and family—it was something he never had to deal with when it came to his time with Beth. They never had the chance for the argument.

"The kids?"

Michelle wiped her eye, turning across the room. "Teresa is fine. Angela, though… She saw him. Edgar. My God. Edgar."

"Kids are tough," Loren said, hoping his words didn't sound hollow. "You made them strong, Michelle."

"Not for something like this."

His hand grazed her arm. "If you need anything—"

"You haven't been by the house," Michelle said. "Is everything all right?"

Loren hesitated, looking toward his friend. He didn't know the loving woman was offering invites. Something told him he wasn't meant to know about them. "Work. I'll be by soon, though. Promise."

Michelle nodded, waving him on. "Go. He needs you."

"He needs you too."

"Not in this," Michelle said, eyes heavy with tears. "Never in this. Greg…"

She didn't have to finish the request. *Keep him safe.* He was used to it. From Mentor previously. Now here? Always looking out for someone else. He wondered if anyone was watching *his* back, knowing the answer would only sadden him.

"I will," he said. He pulled her close for another hug and smiled. "You do look great."

She grinned. It carried him over to the confessional and the waiting Ruiz, solemn in his search for answers. Even without the right questions to ask.

"Quit flirting with my wife," he said without looking.

Loren ducked under the police tape, skirting the throng of forensics personnel on hand. At his arrival they scurried into the shadows of the rectory hallway.

"Treat her better and you wouldn't have to feel jealous of our love," Loren replied, catching Ruiz's glare. "Okay. Not the time."

"Or the place." Saint Sebastian's—a church, a safe place. *Was there any such thing left in Portents?*

"He was your friend?" Loren joined him next to the body. Ruiz kept the victim covered, fingers tight to the cloth.

"Edgar Rusch," Ruiz said, eyes on the fallen. "Can't believe it."

"No witnesses?"

"Too many."

Loren peered at the line of testimony being pulled on the far side of the room, the periodic glances from Michelle. "Of the murder itself?"

"Just me," Ruiz stood, heading for the confessional. Gloved hands rested on the door. "And I didn't see a damn thing."

"How is that possible?" Loren asked. Ruiz glared at him. Loren nodded, afraid to fail his friend. Afraid he wouldn't understand or see the truth in the man's death. "Right. Hence the call."

Loren crouched next to the body and lifted the cloth. He turned away from the burned-out sockets where the victim's eyes should have been. He took a long breath, letting it settle him. Then he looked earnestly. The damage to the eyes and face of Edgar Rusch was extensive but not the end of it. The robes along his chest were seared, small threads pulled in long strings like he had been assaulted. But there was no struggle, no cries for help in a room full of support.

Loren let it sit, dropping the cloth and heading for the confessional. He looked inside as his gloves tapped along the frame. "I'll need forensics to check this over top to bottom."

"Greg—"

The detective ignored his colleague, trying to track all trains of thought and pin them down for later discussion. "I assume we're asking everyone for a statement? No exceptions?"

"We are, but—"

"I noticed some fibers on his chest. In his clothes. Has Hady had a chance to identify them? They almost look like hair, and if anyone knows scraggly hair, it's that woman."

"Greg."

"What?" Loren asked, irritated. Ruiz pulled him away from the scene to the empty hallway.

"You saw Mathers?"

Loren threw him a curious glance then followed. "Yeah. We shared our usual glare with a side of disdain. Mine was wrapped in a smile so I think I took the high road. What does that have to do with—? Wait. No."

Ruiz nodded sadly. "Yes."

"Mathers is heading the investigation?"

"It happened on his watch."

A bullshit excuse. Mathers didn't care about jurisdiction, not when it came to the work. The cameras outside won him over to the case long before facts came into play.

"He assign a lead?"

"Not yet."

"So you could—?"

Ruiz shook his head. "He wants me as far from this as possible."

Loren sighed. "Makes sense."

"Same as you."

"And we're back to crazy talk," Loren said, throwing up his hands. "Mathers isn't equipped for this."

"We aren't either." Ruiz gripped his right arm, pulling it closer. The recent scars refused to heal, no matter what either of them tried.

"When do the cameras roll?"

"Conference is in ten," Ruiz said.

"Bastard and his glory."

"Hard to hide something like this."

Loren trailed Ruiz's stare down the hall. "What don't I know?"

Ruiz led him deeper into the shadows, stopping short of the rectory's business office door. "When Edgar…when he fell, I thought it was the worst that could happen. I was wrong."

Ruiz opened the door and stepped away, giving Loren a full view. The detective nearly tumbled back from the scene.

Inside the room, bodies lined the floor, some splayed out over their desks while more were crumpled in a small heap in the corner. Men and women of all ages and races, all sharing the same distinction as the dead man left out in the open.

The burned-out eyes.

"How?" Loren choked. He took a breath, refusing to enter the room. "How many?"

"Fourteen."

His heart skipped. "Fourteen…"

Forensics worked diligently, recording everything. Photos of the victims. Markers of where the bodies fell and possibly the order. So many, yet none escaped the carnage? None screamed or cried out? Just like Rusch.

Rusch.

How did he tie into it? Why him out of everyone in the church if this room was the target—and how? Forensics gathered at the left wall, the plaster worn in a large circle, torn and cracked compared to the rest. Aged in an instant. The wall that connected to the confessional on the other side. Two feet to the left and it would have been Ruiz's side. Loren wondered if that was the thought running through his friend's mind when they closed the door to let their colleagues work.

Ruiz stopped across the hall, resting against the wall. "This is Mathers' show for now but—"

Loren stopped him. "I get it. I'm on it, Ruiz."

"Thank you."

"Does Hady…?" Loren closed his eyes, picturing the dead. The blackened sockets. The fear in their faces. "Is there any idea what the cause of death is here?"

Ruiz shook his head. "Discoloration of the skin along the chest indicates massive internal injuries. Like everything just shut down on them."

"Close."

Both turned at the sound of a new voice in the hall. From the entrance to the rectory, locked in the shadows of the approaching night, Soriya Greystone stood. Thin pink ribbons whipped around her left side, caught in an unseen whirlwind, gliding behind her every step into the church's light.

"You know what this is?" Anger crept into Ruiz's voice.

Soriya crouched over the fallen priest in the grand hall. Her eyes were sullen, her face older than Loren had seen before. Soriya lifted the cloth covering the body of Edgar Rusch.

"Their souls were taken."

CHAPTER FIVE

This wasn't how it was supposed to be. Henry sat uncomfortably in the front pew, looking back at the crime scene unfolding, wondering what brought him here. He never meant to stop at the church. The name on the list served as a priest or a pastor or a deacon. Religious titles meant as little to him as the religion itself.

The stop came on a whim. He wanted to see the next name on the list, to hear his voice, if only for a minute. Henry never raised a fist in his life, not even in troubled times during his youth, bounced from foster home to foster home. Violence served no one.

Yet it served him now. Just as the coin did in his pocket.

He met the man, *Rusch*, and shook his hand. A man much like him, yet so completely different. The holy man spoke with grace; he held people with his charismatic smile. He was one with the people around him, something Henry never claimed and never could.

Edgar Rusch held the world in his hands, while everything conspired to take it away from Henry. The disease-riddled soul left their meeting pained and upset—so similar yet so different, the world backing one while shunning the other.

Henry lost it, his anger and fear releasing the creature from the cage of the coin once more. The lights overhead turned off at the arrival of his monster.

He stood in the darkness, listening to the muttered moans of the dying. How was he to know the priest would not be there? He had been only moments earlier, hadn't he?

The church members didn't realize yet. They saw the fallen priest across the room, covered with a thin cloth, and cried. Fourteen others fell not twenty feet away from the pastor but no one knew.

Except Henry.

And the police. Henry watched them closely, the captain—or so he was denoted by the others that arrived later—at the center of it. He passed him when entering the church. Him and his family. They were friends of the priest, the beloved Edgar Rusch. The officer crouched close to his fallen friend and silently grieved between barked orders.

Others joined him. A detective, though Henry might have been mistaken about that given the shabby T-shirt and jeans the man wore. And one other. A woman, young and powerful in her stance. A pink ribbon wrapped down her left arm, tucked under a thin shirt. She was no cop. No—she was something else, someone that recognized more about the scene than the others. Henry kept his head low and away, afraid when the woman's eyes scanned the crowd. Afraid she would figure out the truth.

Not yet. Not with two more names on the list. Only two more.

Huddled close, Henry waited for his interview and the approval to leave the church. Sweat caked to his skin, clammy and pale. The sickness burrowed deep within him, his hands clasped tight in front of him. Most would look at this and believe he was praying. Never an option for Henry. No, he was trying to avoid the coin in his pocket, wanting to feel the pain as long as possible.

"Sir?"

A hand fell on his shoulder. The captain's wife stood behind him, holding out a tissue.

"What?" Henry asked, confused.

"Your nose," she said. "It's your nose."

His hand fell above his lips and he pulled it away. Blood. Lots of blood. He fought to smile. He took the tissue and nodded.

"Right," he muttered. "Thank you."

He wiped it clean and pulled away. The woman pressed closer. "Are you sure you're okay?"

Henry dabbed harder, his left hand shuffling into his pocket. The coin wrapped between his fingers and sweet relief filled his lungs. Life returned.

"I'm fine," he said, a new man. "Happens all the time."

She hesitated then went back to her daughters. He nodded a silent word of thanks once more, then shifted to the end of the pew. He clutched tight to the coin, agony dissipating under its care.

The pain would return. Stronger and sooner.

But not for much longer.
Only two more.
Two small deaths. A small sacrifice.
It was the cost of living forever.

CHAPTER SIX

Under the bright lights of the church, in view of dozens of people in the expansive room, Soriya Greystone felt out of place. The shadows were her home.

In spite of her desires, she maintained a distance. She kept to the darkness to better protect them from the threats unseen by the people of Portents: supernatural elements, creatures of myth and legend. Since the lightning strike, that distance served another function.

It kept the city safe from her.

Officers continued their interviews, oblivious to her arrival. Even forensics failed to notice Soriya slip into the business office to witness the damage wrought. Fourteen deaths—vicious, brutal, efficient. Yet the beast behind the assault remained hidden.

Catching Loren and Ruiz alone was a stroke of luck, her first in some time. If ever there was a need for some level of comfort when dealing with the unique situations that plagued Portents, this was one. Drawing them back to the body of Edgar Rusch, the dear friend of Ruiz, Soriya peered closer at the damage inflicted by the murderer.

Clothing shredded along the chest. Skin exposed but without wound. Only the discoloration offered a clue to the internal injuries beneath—at least until an autopsy was completed. Soriya didn't require the extra measure. She didn't need to see the damage beneath the surface to realize what had been inflicted. And her company certainly didn't need to hear about it, though they pressed for more information.

"Say that again?" Loren asked. Ruiz paced in the distance, the real reason the question needed to be asked.

"Call it what you want. Souls, chi, life-force. I assumed given the venue, 'soul' would be acceptable." Soriya's eyes tracked Ruiz, then lifted the cover off the dead body between them. "The eyes are the major indicator but this level of degradation on the chest, right where the heart is? Their souls are gone. Ripped free and burned out."

Ruiz turned away, unable to form a sentence, though his eyes carried an old rage she hoped to avoid. She didn't come here to press an agenda. She didn't want to be in the mix at all, not with the Greystone's loss of control. Any action taken, any force required, may put innocents in jeopardy and she refused to let that happen again. Figuring out the stone, understanding how the power shifted, how the balance had tipped away from her, was her top priority.

The dead deserved answers as well, however.

Loren threw up his hands. "Okay. Don't say that again. I need to stop asking questions."

Soriya smiled. Evans Tower was in the rearview, the case solved and the threat eliminated, yet Loren stayed. With Portents. With her.

"It's good to see you too, Loren."

Ruiz continued to pace, hands tight to his hips. "What did this?"

Soriya scanned the body again. Ash lined the deep caverns where the man's eyes once lay. Charred flesh. Intense heat. The transference had been quick and powerful enough to keep the victim subdued for the process. Something dangerous, but what exactly?

"I don't know," she said. False hope did no one any good. She needed answers as much as any of them. The sheet covered the body of the fallen priest and she headed for the confessional. The door lay ajar and she stopped before opening it, her hand extended for Loren. "May I?"

Loren handed her a pair of gloves from a box near the tape line and she pulled them on. Ruiz shot a look, batted down by the detective.

"She did ask."

"Don't touch—"

"I won't."

She crept in, the darkness palpable in the confessional. The floor creaked with each depression but remained sturdy under her feet. The walls on either side of her felt the same—solid and unbending. But the back wall, that which connected with the business office of the rectory down the hall, was rotted through. Crumbling splinters broke off under delicate pressure between her fingers. And something else...

"The odor," she muttered. "There's something about it."

Loren shook his head. "I can't smell anything except Hady's damn hand sanitizer."

"*Greg*," Ruiz said.

"All I'm saying is maybe invest in a spa day for her. Everyone at the precinct can chip in."

"Enough," Ruiz snapped. "She lost a friend today. We both did."

Soriya exited the confessional, the odor trailing behind her. She took a short whiff from the splinters. Loren was right. Hady's signature scent was in the mix but something else lingered as well. Like sulfur.

"It used the shadows," Soriya said. "Whatever it was, it somehow used the shadows."

"That's why the wall of the office looks decayed?"

Soriya nodded. "Same as the wood inside."

Loren bagged the splinters and her gloves. Soriya could tell he wanted to press for more information. Not only about the case. About everything since Evan's Tower. Since the hospital and her miraculous recovery. Of course he had questions. Where had she been? Where would they go from here? How could they move forward?

"This shouldn't happen," Ruiz whispered. Hady's people entered from the rear of the church, away from the press, to collect the bodies. The gray-haired captain offered a silent prayer to his fallen friend. "Not here. Not like this."

"We'll figure this out, Ruiz," Loren promised.

Ruiz nodded. "If Mathers finds out—"

"He won't."

Politics. Bureaucracy. Unnecessary obstacles to the work. Soriya never understood them, never cared for them. Rules belonged to Ruiz and the police. Rules that trapped them all.

Ruiz stopped, looking toward his family. His wife was striking, even with the puffy cheeks and reddened eyes from hours of held-back tears. His children were strong, using each other to stay that way no matter what. No, Ruiz was the one who appeared beaten and broken.

And dangerous.

He turned to Soriya, the dead priest's body between them. "I know how this works. I know that my hands are tied in this. That Mathers will run this case into the ground and come up empty."

"Ruiz?" Loren asked, suddenly concerned.

"This thing, whatever the hell it is, killed my friend," Ruiz continued. "In *my* church. Not ten feet away from my child. It doesn't get a pass, no matter what it is. You find whatever is behind this and you end it."

"You can't—"

"Find this bastard," Ruiz said, eyes filled with grief. "Fast."

CHAPTER SEVEN

Hundreds filled the streets, waiting for news from within the church. Officers worked in teams at each cordon line, holding back curious onlookers. The press gathered in the parking lot outside the rectory, spotlights beaming on a small podium. Mathers stood at the center of the crowd, a false image of confidence and stability exuded with each vague answer given.

The patrons from within the church were escorted out the back. Some shuffled away, filtering into the crowd, hoping to forget the night. A man clung to a bloodied tissue, keeping it close to his face. A woman with her three children created a chain, dragging them to their car across the street. Others made a beeline for the press, knowing their story had to be told no matter the warnings issued from the police.

The noise rushed through the intersection like a great wave, filling the void of all rational thought. People, while scared, weren't scared enough to leave for the night. Even with darkness creeping deeper into the city, they remained, hoping for answers that would never be given.

Answers that *couldn't* be given.

Loren understood that better than most. Out of the crowds, the rush of coordination between precincts to contain the scene and forensics cataloguing evidence, Loren stood silent on the church's stoop. The world clamored around him, shouting at the top of its lungs. All the shabbily dressed detective heard was silence.

All he felt was alone.

He wasn't the only one, though. Ruiz followed his family closely to their minivan down the block. He helped Angela into the back seat and hugged Teresa. Michelle waited for a long moment, neither one saying a word before she slipped into the driver's seat and started the engine. Ruiz wavered, his hand on the door, then he let it drop away. The van settled into traffic, carrying his family away.

Loren wanted nothing more than to kick his friend in the ass and send him home, but there was no pressing the issue. Ruiz saw this as an affront to his family's safety, to the delicate balance he had tried to navigate for so many years. Nothing would stop him from trying to make things right, from finding the thing that killed his friend.

The thing that took his soul.

The very thought unsettled him almost as much as watching Mathers schmooze with the reporters. Loren spent so many years fighting against the city—the true city—but now he had started to embrace it. His fresh start.

Some things were still hard to consider.

"This is a nightmare," he muttered. "And Ruiz is stuck right in the middle."

Soriya Greystone shuffled beside him on the stoop, overlooking the throng of people gathered. She shifted anxiously, trying to find a deeper shadow to slip into. She was exposed.

"He didn't believe me," she said, her voice quiet against the crowd.

Loren shook his head. "I think he did. That's the problem. Facing what you're talking about, something that threatens his beliefs so completely? He lost a friend in there, Soriya. I can't imagine what he's going through."

He lied. He knew exactly what his friend was enduring. It was the same pain Loren suffered for so long after Beth. Only Ruiz pushed back harder, fighting against grief with everything he had. *You find whatever is behind this and you end it.* Those were not the words of a man dedicated to justice for his city. They were the words of a desperate man, lost in anger. Loren couldn't let that happen. He needed to stop this without crossing the line.

"You're quiet," Loren said, turning back to his lone companion.

"Listening," Soriya corrected.

"Another rarity."

Soriya nodded, fidgeting with her hands. "I'm not used to the crowds."

"I forget sometimes," Loren said. "You and Mentor and your cave."

"Mentor…"

Loren ran his hand through his hair. "Right. Sorry."

Loss was the one thing they all shared, Soriya more than most of late. Mentor was one of Nathaniel Evans' victims. Along with two close companions, losing her teacher almost took her over the edge. Loren almost lost her that night at Evans Tower. The Night of the Lights. To see her again, the same as so many times over the years yet different, unnerved him.

"It's fine," she said, staring out at the crowd.

"It isn't. Here I am babbling about Ruiz but it hasn't been that long since—"

"Evans." Her hand fell at her hip, to the pouch where she kept the Greystone. The stone changed that night, merging with her teacher's. When he brought it to the hospital, somehow the stone woke her from her coma. It saved her. He needed it to save them all again.

"Where have you been?" Loren pressed. "The city—"

"Has been fine," she grinned, throwing him a knowing look. "I've been around, Loren."

Loren smiled. He thought as much, always looking into the shadows as he rushed to solve the growing number of cases that cropped up since his return. The ghost hunting general of the underworld, Wei Tin, or that damn Will-o'-the-Wisp, and more. No one said the job would be boring, for sure. Still, there were times when a little backup would have been appreciated. Knowing she was there in spirit helped.

"Not like before. What's changed?"

"Nothing," Soriya said. Her hand rested over the pouch on her hip. Her shoulders slumped, carrying an unease he was unaccustomed to seeing. She focused on the growing crowd near the press conference wrapping up in the distance.

Loren stood, dusting off his hands along his jeans. "Don't let Mathers' bluster bother you. He talks a good game but even with all the spin in the world he'll need our help on this one. Especially with what you're saying about souls in the mix. You did come to help, didn't you?"

He turned, happy to ignore Mathers as much as possible. The man gave new meaning to speaking in circles without actually saying anything. How that made him popular with his superiors and the city at large remained a mystery to Loren. Of course, Loren had problems in the opposite direction, always pushing too hard both physically and verbally. Always rubbing his colleagues the wrong way, rather than putting them above the job itself.

No answer came from Soriya. When he looked, hoping to get a jump on the case, to come up with a starting point to investigate, the woman in the ripped jeans and tight bodice was gone. In her place a note sat pinned under the eaves of an overgrown bush off the side of the church's front steps.

Loren sighed, unsure why surprise was always his first reaction. Ending a conversation was not Soriya's strong suit, though it would have gone a long way in helping Loren not to feel quite so alone in the city. In everything.

He lifted the note, clutching it tight from the increasing wind. How she always managed them without being seen was as big a mystery as her disappearing acts. The torn sheet of paper read in small black scribbles:

THE ROOF. MIDNIGHT.

Loren nodded to no one. It looked like he had his starting point after all.

CHAPTER EIGHT

Loren was worried.

He damn well should have been, from what Soriya Greystone saw inside the church. The massacre within the business office, unseen and unheard by the dozens of patrons less than twenty feet away. The speed and precision of the slaughter. The power behind the assault. There was no way to define the situation, to bring it into perspective. To find a lead through the blood and smoking refuse of the fifteen dead.

Was there more than one killer involved? What could have ripped the souls from their bodies so efficiently? How could no one hear it occurring? How did Ruiz not see the killer in front of him while his friend was being murdered? All were lost in a haze of confusion and guilt over the tragedy.

They were the wrong questions to ask as well. The main one slipped from sight, hidden by the noise of the press, the cries of the innocent, and the anger of a police captain mired in grief. Soriya knew the question well.

Why?

It opened the door to every logical extension. Why Saint Sebastian's? Why now? Why these people? Tracking down solutions amid the chaos was impossible.

Loren's worry, though, was not about the case—not completely. The growing concern with each stolen glance her way, with each uncomfortable moment of silence between his musings and her curt responses, centered around her and only her.

The secrets she held back from him.

The Greystone pulsed by her side. There was something within the church, some answer hidden from view. The stone may have uncovered it for her, but her reticence to use the tool, the uncontrollable weapon growing more powerful with each use, let the answer fade into the shadows.

Loren needed to know about her limitations, the truth about her absence from his life, though she did her best to stay connected. To watch from the shadows. Loren stayed. After everything, his need for change, he staked his future on Portents. On the job.

On her.

She couldn't fail him now. But the stone was not an option. *You rely on the stone too heavily.* Mentor's old concerns. Always cycling through her memory. Mentor's lessons, his lectures never leaving her.

Damn him for always being right.

Both observed Mathers playing for the press. He was the statesman among soldiers. His words invoked more fear than confidence in the matter, spreading like wildfire through the city. Mathers played a hero in a drama he failed to comprehend.

Still, the crowd hung on every word. They followed the lights, listening to every rehearsed and coordinated syllable from a canned release used dozens of times over the years. They watched, hearing the fear but seeing a man stand up to it in their time of need. It was nothing more than an act, a dramatic play, for all to see.

Except one.

Lost in the throng of people, he stood. He wore a three-piece suit and a dapper hat. A bowler, Soriya thought, having seen them in dozens of photos throughout Mentor's extensive library in the Bypass chamber. The small rimmed cap was enough to cover his features, his head low. While all eyes remained on the press conference, his focus was clearly on another object of interest.

Her.

Locking eyes for a brief moment, the man turned and departed the scene. He sifted through the crowd like a wraith, and people on all sides backed off as if pushed by some invisible force. Loren blathered on about Mathers, his concern unspoken behind the distraction of the day shift captain and their longstanding hatred of each other.

The note slipped from her hand, the instructions scribbled by the marker she always carried. If Loren had his way, their time together would never end, the conversation turning as meaningless as Mathers' words to the public. There was work to be done. She took off without a word to her partner.

Some things were faster without help. Soriya raced into the crowd, trying to thread a path through the mass of humanity with nothing better to do with their Sunday evening despite the football season in full swing. She immediately met resistance, pushing and needling into the mix while keeping an eye on the departing man in the suit.

"Excuse me," Soriya yelled over the mutterings of dozens. "Please. I need to—"

"Hey, lady," one man shouted. His eyes flared at her pushing.

"Watch it," another lady commented, but Soriya was already through.

The man in the suit, though casual in his gait, managed to cover a full block during her travel through the crowd. Eyes ever forward, she was surprised at his quickened step the moment she passed through the mass of people to the relative quiet of the Knoll.

"He's fast," she muttered, running after him. She stopped a block into her pursuit, the distance growing instead of shrinking. "Let's see…"

Soriya grinned. A series of hotels made up the next several blocks, each one more decorative than the last, including the use of lattices and cornerstones to accentuate the exquisite craftsmanship of each building. Balconies lined the second to fourth floors, allowing visitors the chance to be part of the Knoll's nightlife without leaving the comfort of their overpriced rooms. Soriya raced down the street. Behind her, the man's stride carried him farther and farther.

"Okay then. Be faster."

At the edge of the first hotel Soriya leaped into the air. Hands extended, she caught the lower lattice along the corner of the structure and pulled hard to launch her lithe body forward. Catching a fair breeze under her body, Soriya felt the ribbons of Kali down her left side loosen and launch. Spreading like a web across multiple balconies, the ribbons pulled taut, shooting her ahead like a bullet. She soared, leaving behind the first then the second hotel, the ribbons snapping out and propelling her ever forward down the long stretch of balconies.

During her descent she found the balcony railing of the hotel three blocks from her launch. She used the cool metal to arc back to the street below. The ribbons retracted, slithering up her arm like a snake returning to its master by some unheard command. Her sneakers slammed against the pavement, the impact forcing her into a crouch. Her smile never left her during the journey, gleaming at the man who halted in surprise at her arrival.

"You look like someone with a story to tell, pal," Soriya Greystone said, standing tall before the shadowed figure. "I happen to be an excellent listener."

Blue crystalline eyes sparked from under the shadow of the bowler hat. The man attempted to push through for the open road ahead. "I'm not one for conversation, actually."

"It wasn't a request." Soriya grabbed at his arm, catching nothing but air. "You're quick. I'll give you that."

"And you are quite slow," the man murmured at the mouth of an adjacent alley. "For a Greystone."

Soriya stopped at the mouth of the alley. "How did you—?"

The man smiled, obscured by the shadows. "What I know, child, could fill volumes. Including your fear. Your growing doubt. Traits that will end this the only way it *can* end."

His words boomed, his voice deep, growing from a chasm within his chest. He did not blink. He did not flinch at her approach. He spoke plainly, aware she knew nothing.

It made her angry. His words, his demeanor, the facts of it all. And the sound of his voice. There was something in it—something she heard long ago.

"Stop it," she snapped. She launched into the alley, her fist flying. Whoever he was, whatever he was, held some connection to the church. That made him dangerous.

She could handle dangerous.

Her fist connected with air. The man sidled away from the blow and its follow up with ease.

"Hit a nerve," the man goaded. "Poor child. This is not some game you find yourself caught in."

"Murder never is," she said.

"Murder? Is that what this is?" A laugh escaped him. "You think so small. So human. Yet you aren't one of them. You never have been, Soriya."

Her name. How did he know her name? "Who the hell are you?"

She lashed out, fists flying. The man in the suit dodged them, batting away her blows like they moved in slow motion. Soriya screamed in frustration, spinning around with a kick that arced over the ducking mystery man. Stopping in mid blow, she reversed direction and sliced the air at him while he attempted to stand. The blow caught him in the cheek, knocking him deeper into the alley. His hat fell to the ground, rolling to the side before coming to a halt amid the city's growing refuse.

"I believe you know the answer to your question, child." He grinned, his teeth yellow down to the root. His skin was pale like that of an albino. Deep grooves lined his cheeks and forehead in ever-spinning circles. Unlike simple wrinkles on the aged, they appeared carved into his flesh like those found in a tree to count the years of its life.

A great many circles.

Soriya stepped away at the sight of him, recognition in her face. "It can't be," she whispered. "Not you."

"You never did ask the right question, did you, Soriya?"

He retreated deeper into the alley. Anger flared, the ignorance of youth, and she leaped at him out of instinct. She regretted the act instantly. The man in the suit stood stock still, waiting for her arrival. He deftly caught her assault, his hand clasping her wrist and lifting her up.

The world turned dark like a blindfold dropped over her eyes. Then the feeling grew, rushing down her arm and through the rest of her body. Cold, unforgiving cold, froze her to her core.

"Stay out of this, Greystone bearer," he cautioned. "Your doubt and your fear will not serve you well in this. Let it play out as it is meant to. For all our sakes. This will be your only warning."

"I won't." It was meant to be a shout of defiance, yet came out as little more than a whimper, her lips trembling.

"You will," he replied. "Or death will be your reward."

He dropped her and light returned to the world. She collapsed to her knees as he slipped into the alley's growing shadows. Darkness enveloped him like a blanket and in an instant he was gone.

She wanted to fight. She wanted to race after him, but her body failed to listen, rooting her to the spot. Out of all the questions, out of all the possibilities she had conjured since seeing the fallen at the church, none could have prepared her for this.

For *him*.

"It can't be him. Not now. Not here."

CHAPTER NINE

He waited until she left. Minutes passed after his initial departure, minutes spent watching her from a distance. Her quiet rage at their confrontation. Her confused desperation at the questions left to her. When she stood, the movement was slow and disconcerting.

He returned, not out of a desire to continue his work but to retrieve that which was lost during the conflagration: his hat. Lifting it up, the Suited Man dusted the grime from its surface and slipped the bowler back into place upon his head. A necessary act? The heat trapped within the city seemed to answer the question for him. Still, he returned for the item.

He simply liked the hat.

The black bowler, the style and selection a gift as much as the suit he wore, remained with him for decades. Possibly longer. Time, an elusive trap meant for mortals and something he lost sight of long ago. Another life, another existence—one always creeping into the periphery no matter how much he tried to forget.

Like Portents. He came back to the city time and time again. Inevitable, like his own life: fated and out of his control.

Or was it?

Her presence saw to his trepidation. *Soriya.* He smiled at the name—it was one the man in the suit remembered quite clearly. So much stronger now, yet weaker in some regards than the girl he recalled. Here she was, in Portents, fighting against the great tidal wave of fate. He did not expect her fire, her defiance at the dangerous situation.

Challenging inevitability.

There were rules in place, systems that could never be changed, no matter the pressure applied. No matter the act committed, the outcome never changed. He understood this better than most. Just as he knew it was meant to play out without his interference.

His end had arrived.

The Suited Man ran his fingers along the thin brim then stepped out onto the street. The end had begun, the story reaching the conclusion of its natural cycle. His natural end after so much time, that elusive instrument, measured by the second to the minute to the hour. As inevitable now as in the beginning.

Yet there was Soriya Greystone.

The man in the suit paused and smiled, staring at the fading light over the city. Rules were meant to be changed, to be broken. To rewrite the ending before the fates had their final say.

Maybe it was time to find a different path out of the dark.

CHAPTER TEN

An unspoken edict whispered through the halls of the Central Precinct. It started from the top, barreling down from superior to disgruntled aide and back to the work force. The edict came in glares, in terrible fits of rage over little things like paper jams on the copy machine ten years out of its service contract. It came from the detective bureau's large whiteboard. Fifteen new lines of red all linked together by a single incident with one three-word edict rushing through their heads.

Move your ass.

Anyone standing around, sifting through paperwork too slowly, or making personal calls felt the pressure to button up all the crap that infiltrated their average day and get back to work. This was more than protocol, more than orders from the top. It was their mission, their one focused task that drew them all together into the well-oiled machine known as the Central Precinct.

Except in one office. Instead of the dull hum buzzing through the station and the squeaking steps of racing officers helping keep the flow of information constant, only anger escaped the office of Captain Alejo Ruiz.

And plenty of screaming.

"Who the hell do you think you are?!" Ruiz could hardly think through his yelling. The long night kept getting longer, stretching toward midnight with no sign of letting up. Upon arriving at the station from the disaster of a crime scene—mostly thanks to Mathers' blathering with the press—Ruiz attended his first of three meetings with the commissioner, the mayor with his deputy and entourage in tow, and the aforementioned bane of his professional existence. Praises were showered upon the bespectacled day shift captain, the typical ass kissing for promises that could never be kept, while belittling showered over Ruiz for being unable to save his friend.

Condolences were offered but they fell hollow and the conversation shifted away. Every request by Mathers was approved, the manpower and resources of the entire city at his disposal. When he named his team, however, the room paused. Including his choice for lead on the case. Loren's name came up as a possible alternative, but was immediately shot down by Mathers. His choice ended up with the reins though it didn't keep her from multi-tasking.

She stood across from Ruiz now, hands digging into the upholstery on the chair in front of her. Short black hair to match her stature. Five foot nothing, though her ego filled the room. Ever since her arrival, there had been tension. Questions asked that should never come from someone on their last chance in the department, *any* department. Especially Central and especially only two months in.

Detective Samantha Myers didn't seem to give a crap, though. "I don't have to stand here and—"

"So don't," Ruiz shouted, pointing to the open door. "Get the hell out!"

"I saved a—"

"You countermanded an order from your superior," Ruiz snapped. He stomped to the door, drawing glares from the dozens racing through the hall. Shocked and pained looks. They knew what the case meant to him, how powerless he was to act as his friend was murdered and then to not be involved? Seeing Ruiz blow up was not a stretch of the imagination. Still, he refused to drag the department into his business, slamming the door. It failed to stick, bouncing back. He pushed it away once more.

"I had to—"

"You displayed nothing but contempt for me and this department."

The petite woman, her voice deep and strong, replied, "I saved a man's life tonight."

Ruiz stopped. Her green eyes pored over him. Strong willed. Abrasive. Only caring for the job at hand, not only her own but everyone else's at the same time. And sure as shit never wrong. Never.

The implication was clear. *I saved a man's life tonight.* He didn't. He couldn't. Less than five feet away and all Ruiz could do was watch his oldest friend pass from the world. Ruiz's own world spun wildly, lost in freefall. The pain along his right arm was the only thing that grounded him.

"You want to be captain so badly, take it up with the commissioner, Myers."

Myers shook her head, leaning harder on the chair. "Just admit it."

"I put my team in the field. Where I will. Where I see fit. Not you." He knew her story. Her transfer from New York. A lot of people didn't want to see the young woman in law enforcement again. Zero recommendations from her colleagues from the Big Apple, not after her error in judgment, some of which carried through to now. Her need to be involved in every aspect of the department, unable to follow the chain of command without questioning everything.

Given the chance, Ruiz might have welcomed her to Central. He enjoyed a little defiance when it came to the job. No one should sit back and blindly follow orders. But today? Myers was Mathers' problem; one he seemed perfectly fine in handling. Ruiz wanted her that way again and out of his damn sight.

"Yeah," Myers drawled, tilting her head. "Stellar job on that. I'm sure Alvaro's wife and kids would have been happy with the excuse when he came home in a body bag."

"The situation was handled."

"By me."

Ruiz slammed his left hand against the desk. "Against orders."

"You would have sent him, Alvaro, a man as Hispanic as it gets he may as well be garbed in the Mexican flag, right into a goddamn maw, Captain." The title dragged out to the point of insult. To him, it *was* an insult. "A predominantly black neighborhood during a damn turf war you've been unable to curb. All for a parole violation."

"Alvaro is a smart cop. He would have handled it."

"He would have been killed," she pressed. Ruiz turned away, fists clenched to his side. "Look. You can throw the book at me, but you sure as hell can't look me in the face and not see the colossal fuck-up averted by my timely intervention. A thank you wouldn't be out of line."

Ruiz's jaw clenched. Screaming wasn't the answer. Hell, with Myers, all reason went out the window. He kept his voice low, fighting for control. "Everything about you is out of line, Myers. Now get the hell out."

Myers pushed off the chair. "They might love you here, sir, but you're getting sloppy."

Ruiz smirked. "You're wrong, Myers. They don't love me. They simply hate you."

"We'll see," she said, backing up to the now open door. Both turned, surprised at the unseen and unheard arrival of Greg Loren.

Loren peered around the office, trying not to focus on either of them. "Am I interrupting something?"

Two sets of eyes widened, their voices mingling to one united "No."

Myers smirked at Loren, looking him over while heading for the door. Ruiz felt his rushed dinner start to come up.

"I'm sorry about your friend, Captain." Even soft spoken, the woman's voice carried a blade between each word. "We can finish the interview later."

Ruiz nodded. "Much later."

"Right."

As she passed, Loren held out his hand. "Loren."

She cocked her head to the side, hands firmly in her pockets. "I know."

Loren followed her steps into the hall, mouth agape at the exchange, or lack thereof. Ruiz rolled his eyes, then cleared his throat. Loren shook his head, stepping into the office. He closed the door.

"Friendly."

"Right up until you realize you're just the meal." Ruiz leaned over the personnel reports on the corner of his desk—reports he was behind on, including assignments for the next week. He swatted them aside, sending them crashing to the floor. "Goddamn Myers."

Ruiz collapsed on his chair, feeling exhaustion catch up to him. He ran his left hand over his brow, fingers pinching tight to the bridge of his nose. His phone blared, the ID flashing in red. Ruiz didn't care to look, ignoring the call and letting his voicemail take it along with the dozen messages from his superiors. More work, more responsibilities, threatening to bury him.

Loren waited patiently, surprise plastered on his stubble-covered face.

"What?" Ruiz asked.

"Myers?"

"Yes?"

Loren sat down then stood again. "Wait. Sam Myers?"

"Yeah…"

"Sam. You told me Sam."

"That's her name."

"She looks less like a Sam and more like a…well, a she."

Ruiz stared at his friend in disbelief. "Are you kidding right now? She's been here for two months."

"She has?"

"There were meetings."

"Was I there?"

"I…" Ruiz stopped, waving him back to the couch. "I can't do shtick with you, Greg."

"Hey, I heard the name and assumed—"

"Well, you're an idiot then," Ruiz said. "And a pretty shitty detective."

"Bite your tongue." Loren chuckled. "What did she do?"

Ruiz sighed, looking back at the assignment reports. "Corrected a mistake. One of many lately."

Myers had been right. That was the worst part of the whole thing. In Ruiz's haste, in his distracted mind, he forgot to switch Alvaro's assignment. He screwed up. More and more came down to that fact. With work. With his family. With Edgar. Myers saw it clearly after only two months. Who else did?

"You should go home," Loren said, catching his thought. "See Michelle and the kids."

"I will," Ruiz said, eyes still on the floor. Too much paperwork piled up. His statement was needed. Calls were coming in from the community, all looking to help with the investigation in the worst way possible, offering nothing in the way of concrete tips. Only hearsay and innuendo, all of which needed to be addressed and analyzed. "Soon."

Loren understood completely, sitting back and whistling. "Sam Myers."

"The lead on the Saint Sebastian's case."

Loren shot up in surprise. "Get out. How did she manage that? Mathers?"

"Mathers."

Loren shook his head. Ruiz wondered what his friend thought about the situation, about the woman in particular, not wanting to lead him down the wrong path.

"He gave me my marching orders. Missing person's reports."

"You? Why?"

"A reason was not required. Only my compliance," Loren said robotically. "Like the damn Borg."

"Sounds like him."

Loren stood, tucking the files under his arm once more. "Do I call her Sam? Samantha? Sammy?"

"Are we really talking about this?"

Loren smiled. "It's a legitimate question."

"Not from you," Ruiz said. "Not on this. She might be lead, but I need you. And that partner of yours."

"Double duty." Loren played with his workload. "Better clear my calendar."

Ruiz saw it in his eyes—the emptiness in Loren. He was three months back but still not connected to the world around them. "Greg—"

Loren stopped him. "I've got it, Ruiz. Go home. Your family needs you and you sure as hell need them. Now more than ever. Trust me."

Ruiz nodded and Loren moved for the door. Ruiz watched the lonely detective shift through the crowd of racing officers. Then the captain settled against his desk. He lifted the pile of assignment reports back to their position in the mess that was his organizational system. Opening the first one, Ruiz paused.

The phone flashed red, the new message waiting for a response like so many others over the last few hours. Ruiz pushed it aside and lifted the receiver. He made it through the first five digits of his home number when he realized the late hour. It was almost midnight.

Too late.

Ruiz held the receiver to his ear, his finger hovering, unable to complete the sequence. He put the phone back into the cradle, reopened the first file on the stack, and started to work.

CHAPTER ELEVEN

Loren pulled a report from the printer. Scanning swiftly, he tucked it into the middle of his files secure under his arm. Initial reports continued to come in from Hady's office. Fifteen victims and a cause of death ruled as unknown until more extensive tests came back. There were also the autopsies to perform. Time no one had with the circus the case had already attracted in the media.

Televisions blared from the break room, booming into the hall with each entry and departure. Loren kept his head low, slipping further away from the growing mass of colleagues. He had his work, missing person's cases to keep him out of Mathers' sight. Some dated back months if not longer. Loren never realized there were so many. There was something else going on, something no one else could see.

Portents was changing.

No media attention and no priority set by the department made it even stranger. Over a dozen people vanished from the streets, only counting the ones reported by concerned neighbors or employers. Never a loved one. Never a friend. Loners in a crowded world and they simply disappeared without a trace.

Without anyone giving a damn.

Loren shuffled forward, but was immediately knocked back by the desk sergeant. The middle-aged man looked back with apologetic eyes and a wave, both of which faded at the sight of Loren. With a slight grunt he continued down the hall, leaving Loren to readjust the files tucked under his arm.

It had been that way since his return: the glares, the anger. His star had fallen long before his departure thanks to the assault on a fellow officer. A corrupt officer, but an officer nonetheless. The stalwart friends of Standish, Mathers included, made sure to make

Loren feel welcome, spreading the tales of the detective's fall from grace. Turning everyone against him.

Almost everyone, anyway.

Officer John Pratchett stepped out of the break room, his coffee cup shaking in his hand. He tried to hike up his oversized pants, catch a split second more of the case's news coverage — more like the bottom line running through the day's baseball scores—and balance his coffee. The stains along his forearm summed up the complex maneuver.

"How many does that make, Pratchett?" Loren asked.

Pratchett dabbed the growing stains along his cuff then surrendered. "Detective?"

Loren grinned. "The coffee?"

"Four."

"Ah. One of those days then." The two men headed down the hall toward Loren's office. Pratchett sipped at his coffee, slurping to drain the overfilled mug.

"All hands on deck," Pratchett said. "You too?"

Loren patted his busy work. "The voice of reason saw fit to saddle me with other things."

"Reason?" Pratchett laughed, glancing through the hall before lowering his voice. "More like panic. Even my uncle is calling about this church thing."

It was funny to think of Pratchett as having a family. The bulwark of the department, always present, always working although at a much slower pace than the rest of his colleagues, Pratchett never seemed like the family type. Of having much of a life outside the department. He was always there, doing the work, without complaint. Without the pressure to be more, to do more. Loren envied the man.

"He was a cop, right? Harvey or something?" Loren asked, recalling Pratchett's uncle coming up in conversations with Ruiz.

"Julian Harvey. But don't call him Julian. Way before your time," Pratchett answered, finishing his coffee. "Different world then. Strange stuff."

Loren grinned. "I can imagine."

They rounded the corner, stepping aside for a group of four officers and two detectives, running through reports. The group threw smiles and nods of interest to the towering officer, all of which faded for Loren. Both men watched them continue on, thin looks flitted back at the returned detective before the group disappeared into the bullpen and their next briefing.

Loren understood it. He didn't want to but after months of feeling the shunning head on, little could be done. Accepting it was the smartest move, rather than dwell on every interaction. This was his fresh start.

"They'll forget, Detective."

"They shouldn't," Loren replied. He smiled at the man, patting him on the back. "But thanks. Ease up on the rocket fuel before you vibrate through your car."

Pratchett laughed, lifting his cup. "No promises."

Loren stepped across the hall to his waiting office. He offered a nod to two more colleagues, though both ignored the attempt. He sighed and slipped inside, shutting the door behind him.

He plopped the files on his desk, tossed his jacket on the hook next to twin filing cabinets, and reached for his chair. Pushing it aside, Loren leaned on the desk, stretching his back. A long night lay ahead. Each file needed to be reviewed, without the help of the initial officers involved. They were busy patrolling the city or in a never ending series of briefings over the Saint Sebastian's affair.

Where he should have been. If anyone deserved the case it was Loren. Considering his involvement in the Evans affair, and his successful resolution of the situation, the department owed him. At the very least he should have been helping Myers organize and investigate.

Myers. The name brought a smile to his lips. Her hard edge in spite of being "vertically challenged," as his mother always said. He recalled the confidence in her eyes. Green. Dark like a forest.

Welcome to the party, lady.

Loren shook his head. The case belonged to her and there was no convincing Mathers otherwise. Being stubborn was an art form for the man.

Instead, Loren left the files on his desk for the rolling corkboard tucked next to the door. He started every shift the same. A remembrance of sorts of the one case forever unsolved in his eyes.

Beth's case.

Photos of the scene covered the board, and witness statements and reports from officers on the scene filled out the rest. His own notes ran along the edges, etchings and musings, trying to nail down an explanation. Trying to figure out what happened. And why.

Even four years later, he jotted things down. Lost fragments from her death swimming along the periphery of his dreams, something always missing. The open window of their apartment, the curtains blowing in and out on the windy autumn day. And more. Something in the window.

Shadows.

Clear as day in his mind, yet never explained. He clung to those shadows, knowing they played a part in something bigger. That they meant more. A way into the case. The answers he always needed, the ones he missed despite his obsession over the case. He pushed everyone and everything to figure out what happened to his wife and lost it all in the process.

He refused to let it happen again.

Loren sighed, realizing the long day had barely begun. The files needed his attention now, the echoes of rushing footsteps fading behind his closed door. He checked his watch for the time and found it missing.

The detective rushed to his desk, throwing open drawers. Nothing. No sign of it. He was wearing it earlier. When, though? Work the previous night? At the church? Loren shook his head, unsure, hoping the cherished gift sat on the mantel of his apartment and was not lost after so many years.

The answer to his query came before he could sit down to start the massive amount of work piled upon his desk. A tapping sound clattered against the window to his office. Loren peered into the dark and opened the casement. The cool night breeze whipped into the office, and the top three files fell to the floor. Loren reached out at the source of the sound.

The Superman watch chimed, tied to the end of a long, pink ribbon. Loren carefully released his timepiece and, once free, the ribbon retracted. Loren closed the window before more files joined the wreckage on the floor.

The alarm blared on the watch, the light of the "S" symbol shining bright. Loren turned off the alarm, midnight flashing on its digital face. He turned the piece over and found a note attached to the back.

You should wear this once in awhile. It might help.

"Soriya."

His meeting. Loren slipped the watch back into place, wondering when his partner became so adept at petty theft, curious to know what else he was missing and how closely he should guard his spare change going forward. He picked up the fallen files, promises of investigating them all escaping his lips, before he moved for the door and his waiting appointment.

CHAPTER TWELVE

"You're running away?"

Soriya Greystone sat on the rooftop ledge, her feet dangling over the side. The pink ribbons down her left side returned, her message delivered just as another was delivered to her.

"Not running," Kok'-Kol, the black raven and first of the Miwok, cawed. The immense winged creature pecked at the apple on the ledge, its golden sheen beaming into the night. "Our hand has been forced, child. It is not safe here."

"For anyone," Soriya muttered, unable to watch the raven eat its gift. She thought summoning him to the city would help, that having someone to talk to about everything, about the man in the suit, would clear her mind. That Kok'-Kol could solve everything.

"Attention falls on the darkness," Kok'-Kol continued, his green eyes burning across the sky. "There will be no hiding."

"So don't," Soriya pleaded. Her arms tucked close, the wind rushing through her. "Help me."

The bird snatched at the remaining specks of apple. "That is not our role in this. It is yours. It has always been yours."

Another lecture. Even without Mentor they remained—the lessons, the teaching, everyone knowing better than her. And nothing she did proved them wrong.

The stone threw off her balance. Not just her own, but also everything around her. With the Greystone out of play, her power sidelined, what course of action remained?

Soriya closed her eyes. They were waiting for her—two specks of crystal blue beaming at her. Proving how little she was prepared for the task at hand. Proving how much she truly feared him and what he represented.

"What if—?"

"A distraction," Kok'-Kol said, his beak snapping the air. "Your doubt."

"The stone," she whispered. "You know."

The raven circled her, green eyes intense. "I do. You will find answers."

"How? There's no one left to answer them." She had begged Mentor time and again for some insight into the myriad questions surrounding her past, surrounding the stone and the task laid before them. Protect the Bypass, but from what? What great evil waited for her and why did she get the sense it already resided in Portents?

Because *he* was in the city.

No answers ever came. No insight. Nothing but riddles bouncing over analogies and ceaseless lectures. All preparing her for a task she had yet to handle. Alone, without her teacher and now without the help of one of her trusted allies. One of the few still living.

Kok'-Kol hovered at the edge, his wings spread wide. "A past connection will guide you, but not the one you think. One will help. One will hurt."

More riddles. She stood in frustration, kicking at the pebbles covering the rooftop. Would it always be like this? Fighting to understand the world she thought she always knew? Was this how the rest of them felt? Loren? Ruiz?

"And if I'm not strong enough?"

"The city will fall. It cannot be controlled. Not in the end."

"I can't do this, Kok'-Kol," Soriya said. "Mentor was right. I'm not ready. I'll never be what he wanted me to be."

"He was human," the raven replied, hovering before her. "Fallible. Even in protecting you."

Soriya wished that were true. Prayed that she might have the strength to handle things with the same wisdom her teacher had so many times before. Her eyes, weary from the day, stayed low to the ground.

"I wish you would stay."

"So do I, but there is more going on in the shadows than you know."

"What do you mean? I thought—"

"See through your doubts and your fears. There are answers on the other side." The raven soared above her.

"I don't know how to fix this," she yelled into the night.

Green eyes beamed down upon her. Kok'-Kol stopped, the bird's voice carried along the wind. "You will."

"Enough with the cryptic responses, Kok'-Kol. Lives are at stake."

"They always will be."

"Help me," she said.

"Follow the blood, child," Kok'-Kol hissed. "It will start you on your path. Good luck."

The raven took off, lost in the night. Soriya watched him for a long moment, arms wrapped tight around her midsection. She fought for comfort, for some level of security, although it never came. All that came was loneliness and with it more doubt. This was her task and hers alone now. Soriya stepped to the ledge, the wind threatening to topple her from the six-story structure. Her hand lifted, waving to the raven long gone.

"You mean goodbye."

CHAPTER THIRTEEN

With each step, with each twist along the winding stairwell, rising floor by floor toward the roof, the tension in Greg Loren's chest increased. Closing his eyes failed to alleviate any symptoms. He daydreamed of his couch and a night in front of the television, most likely cartoons since nothing else of interest was ever on. No distraction could penetrate his psyche deep enough. Nothing could deter the growing angst crawling along his skin, breaking out of his pores in the form of thickening beads of sweat. He hated heights, a reminder sent through his thick skull with each step up, passing by each floor until at last coming to rest at the apex.

Loren stood before the rooftop access door, hand tight to his side. He dug out a slice of gum—triple berry—and popped it in place. *Filthy habit.* It was his third slice during the ascent.

Refusing to head back down after so much work, Loren reached for the handle and pushed the door open. Wind rushed over his face, the force pushing so hard he almost stumbled into the oblivion that was the vacant stairwell. He caught the railing, waiting for his hand to slip from the coating of sweat on his palm. It held—barely.

Loren stared out into the night. The rooftop sprawled out before him in all directions. He held to the doorframe, a deep breath slipping from his lungs.

"Damn you, Soriya."

His first step propelled him out on the roof, stone shifting beneath his sneakers. The second came easier, but only due to a heavy adherence to staring at his feet during the journey. In the distance he heard talking. Looking up, then down, and up again, Loren caught sight of the black raven departing from the rooftop for the shadows.

Soriya stood on the ledge, waving into the darkness. For so long she was the strength of their partnership, her confidence and sheer power behind their success. Now there was nothing but doubt rooted in her brown eyes.

Watching her, he realized the same thing he had earlier with Ruiz and a possible rationale to their partnership for so long: They shared loneliness. They buried themselves in their work, using it as a crutch, a distraction, to get through everyday life. They could never find a way out of that hole of solitude, despite others' extended hands offering friendship. Soriya and Loren walked parallel journeys of loneliness, refusing to lean on each other or anyone else.

Loren walked further out on the roof, extending his hand for a friend. "That looked pleasant."

Soriya turned at the ledge. Loren chewed harder on the gum, sucking the last remnants of flavor from the mashed-up mass. He couldn't see the dark-skinned woman for a moment. All he saw was the other woman in his life, even after all these years, still as much a part of his everyday as anyone else.

Beth.

How she fell. Why she fell. Her unexplained death. Swallowed up by the shadows.

Loren's heart pounded in his ears. His dreams had been getting worse. Much worse.

"Loren," Soriya called, snapping him back.

He stopped, an awkward smile working its way to his lips. "This is as far as I go."

"I know." She jumped from the ledge and moved for him.

"Yet here we are," Loren said, eyes to the ground. He pointed out to the dark. "He give us any help?"

Soriya turned back, tracking her departed friend. Then she shook her head. "No. I don't think so this time."

"What is it, Soriya?"

She circled him, slow and deliberate. Her shoulders slumped before she stopped, her voice little more than a whisper against the howling wind. "I want you to drop the case."

Loren flinched back in surprise. "Not a chance. Next impossible request?"

"I'm not kidding, Loren."

"Am I laughing?" he said. She huffed away, heading back toward the edge. His anger carried him after her, his fear keeping his steps cautious. "What do you expect me to do, Soriya? Ignore what's going on? Ruiz lost a friend."

"I don't want him to lose another one."

"A touching sentiment. Now back it up with some answers. What did Big Bird say?"

Soriya glared at him. "Raven."

"I'm aware," Loren snapped.

"Sorry," Soriya said. She rubbed her brow, then spread her arms wide. "About the venue anyway."

"No, you're not." Her game was clear, controlling the conversation. It was what always led to her disappearing act. "Come on, Soriya. It's been months. I didn't push. Didn't pry. Didn't bang on the door of that lovely cave you call a home. Give me something. Why is this different? What the hell has you so damn scared?"

Soriya turned away, stepping up to the ledge. The city stretched before her, before both of them, but she always saw it more clearly than him. Knew it better than he did. This was her city.

When she looked at him, when she brought the news burdening her all evening, he realized the burden of her task, too great for someone so young. The weight too heavy to bear alone, no matter the reluctance to share. He saw more, though. But everything centered on one thing.

"It's Death, Loren." Fear sat in her eyes. A longstanding fear that chilled him worse than the wind swirling around him like a coming storm. "Death has come to Portents."

CHAPTER FOURTEEN
Eighteen Years Ago

She couldn't sleep. It had been that way since her arrival at Saint Helena's Orphanage. The packed room, four beds on either side, left her little in the way of privacy. Less so with the children's constant need to ridicule the girl of four.

Soriya hated the orphanage. Though it was the only place she knew, her previous life lost to a car crash that took the lives of her parents, she disliked every aspect of Saint Helena's. Especially those around her. Mean-spirited young ladies looking to lift themselves up by demeaning others and a staff that kept their heads down to avoid any uncomfortable situations.

Whispers continued about their new arrival. The story of the burned wreck that took her memory and her past spread. It labeled her.

It left her alone.

Four months into her stay she had said nothing to the staff. Most believed it related to her trauma. The girls who shared her room thought her "retarded" from the accident—their word for it and a foul one at that. Few reached out, and those who made the attempt did so only on a dare from the other children. To actually care about Soriya was too much to ask and none bothered trying.

Sleepless nights were routine for her. Most of the time she remained still, fighting for rest that seemed increasingly distant. This night, with winter in full swing and darkness deeper than ever, Soriya decided a walk might do her some good.

Slipping from her bed on naked feet, the young girl inched through the room. The door creaked in her hand, forcing her to slow her escape. The hall was vacant.

She wasn't alone in her travels, however. Resting in her pocket, as it had been since the first day of her second life, sat the stone of grey. She kept it on her person at all times, sometimes spending hours running her fingers over its warm surface. Sometimes when she closed her eyes with the stone in her hand, she felt heat pouring through her.

And a light glowing from its surface.

She had managed that feat twice and each time dropped the stone upon realizing its presence. If anyone caught sight of her, they would turn her in to the staff and she might lose the stone. Soriya refused to let that happen. The stone was all she had left from her former life, her last link to a past forever vanished from memory.

Since her arrival she had set upon creating new memories—a tough job for a four-year-old but she pushed herself harder to be self-reliant. She researched heavily, spending hours in the library buried in books. Her ability to read, while limited thanks to her age, grew each day. Eventually she found a book of names, something she hadn't considered since her arrival.

A name.

When she settled upon Soriya, a smile grew on her face. A rarity in the orphanage, among the naysayers and the bitter angst of those around her. The name filled her with a light brighter than any emanating from the stone. Like it was always meant to be.

Soriya stopped at the top of the stairs, surprised her musings had carried her so far without thinking. She was more surprised no one had spotted her with her thoughts so distracted. The fourth floor stretched before her, empty.

The fourth floor was off limits to all children. That rule alone garnered the restricted wing more attention. Another mystery to be solved by those trapped within the walls of Saint Helena's. They called it by many names, the most popular being the Isolation Wing, the wing for "special" children. Kids never seen again. Everyone knew the truth.

The fourth floor was where little girls went to die.

Late one afternoon, while walking in the courtyard between the school and the orphanage, Soriya noticed a girl standing in front of a window on the infamous floor. She looked pale in the dim light of the winter sun. Soriya raised her hand and waved. The girl returned the greeting with a sad smile, the only time the greeting was reciprocated during her stay at Saint Helena's.

Standing at the fourth floor landing, silence filling the orphanage halls, Soriya decided to visit the little girl. It was a choice to break the rules, a choice to make someone's life a little better. She crept to the few rooms occupied down the hall. The door lay ajar.

The young girl rested on her bed sleeping, or at least struggling for rest, her eyes wincing and her breath labored. Soriya pushed the door open more, but stopped in the doorway at the sight of another presence in the room.

A man sat at the edge of the bed, his hand resting softly on the girl's. He wore all black, a finely pressed suit jacket over matching pants. A hat sat beside him, his pale skin glistening in the moonlight—white, with deep grooves carved into the surface in the shape of concentric circles.

The man stirred from his thoughts, twin specks of crystal blue turning to the newly arrived Soriya.

"Shhh," he whispered, a finger to his lips.

From the bed, the girl fought to breathe. Each gasp was louder than the last, wheezing harder for less air in return. The color faded from her skin, almost draining out of her body.

What was happening to her? Where was she going?

The man in the suit offered a sad sort of smile. "There is a time and place for questions, Soriya. Make it the right question."

The young girl's eyes widened. "How did you know my name? I haven't told anyone."

"No one? Not even the wind? Not even in false prayers to calm the fears of those around you?" He stopped, his hand hovering over the girl in the bed. "That was not the question you wanted to ask."

Before she could speak again, light grew in the room. The thin and brightening strands rose from the girl in various colors. Reds and blues and purples spread over her wheezing body, coming together in a large orb of light. It danced in front of Soriya, the man in the suit watching the orb carefully. The wheezing stopped and with her silence the light began to fade. The Suited Man touched the orb and the room once more fell into darkness.

Then he stood, placing his oddly shaped hat over his matted hair. Behind him, no more movement came from the bed. No more sound from the young girl.

"Take your time with it." His blue eyes sparkled at Soriya. "We will see each other again."

The man stepped around her and started down the hall. She watched him for a moment then called out, her voice loud in the silence.

"We will?"

He stopped, turning back with a sad look. "Everyone does, child. In the end, everyone does."

He started back down the hall and the light returned, this time beside him and not as an orb or color. This time, the light was the girl. She peered over her shoulder and waved.

The man took the girl's hand and they faded into the shadows at the end of the hall. Soriya stood, rooted to the corridor for a long time after, staring into the darkness, alone with the body in the bed.

Wondering when she would see those eyes again.

CHAPTER FIFTEEN

Loren stopped in front of the shop. The sign above the storefront sagged on the left-hand side, the letters worn from weather.
It read *Cobbler's Den* in speckled black lettering except for the "ler"
of *Cobbler*, which had been bleached white over time.

After hearing Soriya's childhood tale, her first encounter with
the man hidden in the shadows of Portents, Loren thought they
needed more than information—they needed help.

Soriya had other plans, as usual.

She kept them to herself, and although the train ride left plenty
of time for questions to be answered, silence ruled over them. Her
past remained a mystery to him as much as it was to herself. The
accident that turned her into an orphan defined her as much as the
loss of his wife. Their pasts could never be closed until they understood these vital mysteries. Yet the present owned them, driving
them ever forward.

The shop inside was small and cramped. Displays amounted to
little more than piles of shoes of various styles and colors, surrounded by a single bench for customers. A display case ran along
the back wall, with a cash register on top. The shoes in sight were
handcrafted. Nothing commercial. Nothing imported from over-
seas.

"Soriya…"

The young woman kept her distance, scanning the store. A
couple sat patiently on the other side of the confined space. Soriya
raised her hand to him. "Not yet, Loren."

A young man with a wide smile and a tight green vest emerged
from the back. He held two pairs of loafers, proudly showcasing
them for the waiting couple. His hazel eyes beamed at the new-
comers. "Be with you in a moment."

Loren shook his head. "We're not—"

"Thank you," Soriya interrupted, pulling Loren over to the counter.

"We're here for shoes?"

Soriya put a finger to her lips, letting the young man work with his customers. Then she pointed at the worn flaps that were once his sneakers. "You could use some new ones."

"These have character."

"They're called holes."

Loren tapped on the glass. "Soriya, I think I've been pretty restrained in the questions department. Especially considering what you told me about your wacky childhood experiences."

She nodded. "You have. I appreciate it. But…"

Loren took the cue. "Why are we here? We should be at the Courtyard. With their help we might—"

"It's empty." A breath escaped her and her shoulders slumped. "The Courtyard. They left."

"All of them? Because of—"

"Yes," she said, drawing out the word. She stared out the back window at the night sky. "I think."

Loren rubbed his eyes. "That's what the damn bird—"

"Raven."

"*Soriya.* You should have told me."

"I am. Right now." Brown eyes fell to the glass, her distorted reflection staring back at them. "It's just us, Loren."

"Against Death."

Soriya shook her head, her voice little more than a whisper. "A piece of Death. An avatar."

Loren's brow furrowed. "Semantics."

"No," Soriya snapped. "Fact. He was once a man. Same as all things."

The couple moved for the register, the young cobbler circling the counter to process their payment. Loren and Soriya shifted away to a nearby display.

"I don't understand."

"I know," Soriya said through gritted teeth. She reached for him, her hand crooked in his elbow. "That's why you should walk away, Loren. The forces involved—"

"I'm not leaving. It's not happening. So tell me—"

"How can I help you?" The young man's hazel eyes glowed under the shop lights. The nametag adorning his vest read *Jon*. The couple, content with their new footwear, exited the store. A chime escaped from the bell atop the door before it closed, and the sounds of the marketplace were silenced once more.

"We're just—" Loren started before Soriya jumped in front of him.

"I was hoping to speak to Johannes."

The name shook the young man. "I don't...I'm the only one here."

Soriya grinned, leaning close. "Could you check the back for me?"

"I..." The young man stopped and shook his head. He blinked hard at the request then his eyes went blank and his voice fell low and distant. "One moment."

Loren waited for the young man to slip into the back before moving beside his partner. "Okay..."

Soriya sighed. "They are among us. Constants. The forces of life and death. In the world around us."

"Like Death?"

She nodded. "For every religious belief, for every fictional account or true sighting, there is an avatar in the world. Regular people who choose to play a larger role either consciously or subconsciously. Like a mask, their new function controls them."

Hidden among them. Like the myths and legends before them. The city held wonders and terrors around every corner. *Portents was changing.* Loren was only beginning to see the extent of it. The bartender at McDuffie's, his new friend, for one. There were others tucked in the periphery. Now another layer. Would he ever know the truth? Would Soriya *let* him know the whole truth?

"You're talking about your new playmate?" Loren asked, referring to the pale-skinned man in the suit she encountered at the church.

"He's one of them, yes," Soriya replied. "I don't think he's the only one but he's been doing it for a long time."

"None of that explains why we are here."

"A question I would like answered as well."

An old man stood at the back entrance. Long, knotty strands of gray hair ran ragged from atop his head. His wrinkled skin was covered with liver spots. He shambled over to the counter, breathing hard at their presence.

"I thought…" Loren fell silent as the man stood before them. He wore a green vest and khakis, the same as the young man. Then Loren caught the same hazel eyes as deep and vibrant as before. "Jon?"

"A name I much prefer these days." The old man's accent was thick, German. He glared at them then turned to Soriya. "Greystone."

She smiled. "I need your help."

Loren coughed. "We need it. I think."

"You most definitely do, Detective," Johannes said, peering down at the man's broken sneakers. "Still wearing those dreadful shoes?"

"Who…?"

He shot down the question with a wave. "I knew your wife. Lovely woman. Used to come looking for the right pair for you. Not that you ever wore them."

Loren's eyes flared. "You knew Beth?"

"We used to talk quite a bit."

"She knew. About you, I mean." It was a secret she took with her to the grave. The true city. It wasn't until after her passing that Loren first learned about Portents. From Soriya. The information came in fragments, parceled out over years of working together. Yet the secrets remained. A new one every day.

"I was sorry to hear about her passing." The hard look of his eyes faded.

"Do you…?"

Soriya's hand fell on his shoulder. "Loren. This isn't…"

The question came anyway. No matter the case. No matter the time passed. "Do you know who might…?"

The old man stopped him, shaking his head. "No. I'm sorry."

Soriya shared a glance with the old man, who turned away. He circled the glass display and began organizing the unsold stock heaped on the floor. The young woman joined him, bending to assist.

"Someone is collecting souls."

"I'm aware." He sighed, offering a pair of boots to the confused detective. Loren shook his head and the man placed them soundly beside the register.

"Why?"

"We've discussed your footwear problems."

"The souls, Johannes," Loren said. "Why?"

"Souls hold power. Not only in ambient energy but also in trade. Currency."

Soriya handed over a pair of Oxfords, which joined the boots on the counter. "To buy what? What would Death need to buy?"

"She wouldn't."

"She?" Loren's question was swallowed up by Soriya, who dropped another pair of shoes on the counter.

"Someone is controlling Death."

"Wait," Loren said. "Why?"

"The only reason mortals ever needed."

Soriya nodded. "To keep death away."

Johannes cursed under his breath. "Schmucks. The endeavor of fools. No one should live forever."

"Immortality?" Loren balked at the notion. Was it possible? It permeated myth for so long, the idea of avoiding death. Of escaping its cold embrace, the only true constant in the world.

Soriya paced the room, lost in thought, but the old man remained. The answer lay in his eyes, in his disgust at the act. He understood exactly how possible it was. And how much it should be avoided.

"Like the Fountain of Youth or the Holy Grail?" Loren asked.

"No."

"Both were lost long ago," Soriya finished. "This is something else. Something…"

"Soriya?"

She took off, racing for the door. The pink ribbon fell down her left side, whipping behind her like a lifeline. "Come on, Loren. I know where we have to go."

Loren hesitated. The old man nodded and pointed for the door. "She might not say it but she's going to need you."

"You know what this is, don't you? You've seen this before?"

"I've seen centuries pass, Detective. I've seen civilizations rise and messiahs fall," the old man said. His hands shook at the words and tears speckled his eyes. "But I have never seen this before. Someone is playing a dangerous game and we will all pay the price if they succeed. Don't let that happen."

CHAPTER SIXTEEN

This was how it always started for Samantha Myers: a question and a lack of trust. Or a lack of trust that led to a question. She never knew the chicken or the egg theory behind her own pathos. That energy was typically diverted in other pursuits.

Twenty-seven and on her last chance. One would think that fact would be enough to keep her on task, to put the questions aside and use the assets available to solve one of the worst acts committed in Portents' shady and dubious history. Instead she found herself concerned about the one asset taken off the board.

The lock to Loren's office clicked under her delicate ministrations and the door creaked open. She palmed the lock pick and stepped inside. No one noticed from the hall, and no one cared to notice. They rushed from one briefing to the next, passing along information as quickly as possible. The involvement of the press in the Saint Sebastian's massacre meant a clock on their work. Answers were needed. Links between events that had just come to light needed explaining. All centered on a single killer in their midst.

Unfortunately, Samantha Myers was asking different questions.

Loren's office was spotless. His desk remained clear except for a table lamp, a phone, and a small pile of reports. Work was organized in two four-drawer filing cabinets along the right-hand wall. Cramped but pristine, unlike the man himself.

Myers dropped her own work on the desk. Files containing the preliminaries sent over from the coroner's office in the last hour. Fifteen victims from Saint Sebastian cataloged for her reading pleasure. A busy killer and an effective one. Fourteen people died in the business office of Saint Sebastian's. How could they not overpower their assailant? How did no one cry out or run away while the monster behind this focused on one of the other victims?

The files remained thin on information. The burned-out eyes tied them all together but could not be listed as the cause of death. Systemic organ failure was noted on each one. The depression of their chests, the discoloration of their skin meant an incredible amount of damage beneath the surface. Autopsies were scheduled but in all likelihood little would be discovered.

Then there were the first three incidents. Recently uncovered through her diligent searching, Myers found seven other victims over the last three weeks—not local, but all carrying the same signature as the Saint Sebastian's case. The bodies were being flown in for analysis, the hope for a lead tenuous at best.

Myers needed the case solved. She needed a damn lead. She demanded the case, pulled string after string to make it happen, and now she felt the weight of it all on her shoulders. Concern spread, those concerns becoming obstructive micro-managing from Mathers.

She tried not to think about it. Her error in judgment, the pressure of her work in New York City, forced her out of the city and almost out of law enforcement completely. Portents was her last chance to make things right.

Some things were harder to stop. She circled Loren's office, the man a curiosity to her. Everyone else read pretty much the same. They did their best and each carried their own weakness. Food, sex, money. The typical pitfalls of the modern day civil servant. Loren was different. He stayed separate from the rest, part intentional and part ostracized from past discretions. Much like her own.

She thumbed through files, picking one up at random before slipping it back into place. Loren's notes were thorough, his work extensive. He had an amazing track record at the department and no one faulted his talent.

The corkboard behind the open door told another story, though. Myers stepped over to it, looking at the well-organized case publicized on the rotating easel. She heard rumors. Anytime Loren came into question, the same story was mentioned, talking of one person who meant more to Loren than anything else in the world despite that she had been gone for over four years.

Photos from the scene, reports, witness statements as well as Loren's notes covered the board. Suspects withdrawn then reposted with new theories behind them. A treasure trove of obsession.

"Yeah," Myers muttered. "This is healthy."

She pulled the image of Bethany Loren off the board. A beautiful woman with deep blue eyes, bold blond hair, and an inviting smile. Not a wrinkle could be seen, not an imperfection anywhere in sight. To lose someone so young and someone so vital to your very existence…it reminded Myers of her father.

There was a shadow at the door. He loomed, as he always did with her, his watchful eyes peering through the round frames of his glasses. Whenever he showed up unexpected it sent chills down her spine. Not in a pleasant way. Not anymore.

"What the hell do you think you're doing?" barked Rufus Mathers, captain of the detective bureau's day shift.

Myers didn't bother to look at him or his flaring nostrils. She placed the image back on the board and returned to the empty desk holding her waiting files. She had seen the man angry enough over the last few weeks. Hell, she had seen entirely too much of the man since her arrival two months ago.

"Working," she said coldly. "I know the lack of cameras might confuse you."

He grimaced, stepping into the office. "I am your captain, Myers."

"Then act like it," she shot back. "Lead."

"I did," Mathers said, towering over her slight frame. "You got your big case despite my reservations."

"Your confidence is inspiring."

"You could thank me, you know," he said. He reached out for her and she pulled away.

"I think we're past that phase, Rufus."

"It didn't have to end, Sam," Mathers continued. She shifted away from him for the door. "You didn't have to end it."

"Says the married man."

"Is that what this is about? Or is there a reason you're in this office?"

Myers grinned at his flushing cheeks. "You mean…Loren?"

Their history was clear from every meeting, every shared briefing between the entire department. Mathers' dislike for the newly returned Loren was infamous, and the feeling was reciprocated by Loren.

"He's not to be involved in this case," Mathers warned.

"So you've said. Multiple times now," Myers said, tapping at the filing cabinet. "Funny thing about that. This seems like the exact kind of case he would handle."

"He's a loose cannon. He can't be trusted."

Myers walked up to her captain. Flustered, he stuck out his chest, looking at the door nervously. She pulled at his tie. "Trust is a fickle thing coming from you, Rufus," she whispered. "I wonder between the two of you who has the largest collection of skeletons?"

Mathers backed off for the door, readjusting his cravat. He tried to calm his reddened face. "There's a killer out there slaughtering people."

"And I intend to catch him by any means at my disposal."

"Except him."

Myers huffed. "Is that an order? Captain?"

"Keep me apprised," Mathers grumbled, inching into the hallway. "Detective."

She waited until his clacking heels dissipated. Then she let out a thin breath. His presence annoyed her to say the least.

It was her fault. Her arrival brought with it an unease. She needed to reclaim some of that comfort she held in New York City. That control that centered her, a lesson repeated ad nauseam by her father. That control empowered her. Mathers was more than willing to help, their affair quick and nasty before she ended it. She never should have let it happen, but it had its advantages. Like her assignment to Central and the case at hand. Like many other things she kept in her back pocket.

Right next to her lock pick. Tools of the trade.

Myers gathered up her belongings and started for the door when she observed the open bottom drawer of Loren's desk. She circled the empty work surface, reaching low to pull the drawer open. More files, all carrying the same heading, the same name.

SORIYA.

Myers pulled out the first in the row, dropping it on the desk. She flipped through it until coming to an image in the back. A dark-skinned young woman, a small hand-woven pouch wrapped around her belt on the right side and a pink ribbon flowing from her left arm. She matched the description by a dozen officers at Saint Sebastian's earlier that night who had been discussing the case with Loren and Ruiz. The curious detective studied the image closely.

"Just who the hell are you, lady?"

CHAPTER SEVENTEEN

Myers closed the drawer to Loren's desk, the file returned to its proper place. She turned to leave the office only to find the door obstructed. Tall and filling, wearing a goofy grin, the mountain of an officer stood nervously, knuckles tapping on the frame.

"Detective?"

Myers sighed. "Everyone seems surprised by that."

"More confused," the officer said. Her eyes flared, silenced by his tilted head at the name by the door. "Not your office."

"Oh."

He extended a hand at her approach. "John Pratchett."

She nodded, the files secure under her arm. "Yes. Pratchett. Of course. I was warned about your…" *Aloofness? Goofy grin? Endless meandering?* "…Height."

He laughed. "I'm the short one in the family."

"Raise 'em big. Raise 'em right. That's a thing, isn't it?"

"I don't think so."

"I'm sure it is somewhere" Myers headed down the hall. Pratchett followed in step. "Come on."

"Where?" He pointed back to the open office. "What were you doing in Loren's office?"

Myers stopped and circled back. She locked the office door and closed it, checking the knob twice before letting it fall out of her grip. Then she turned to Pratchett. "You know him?"

Pratchett glanced down at her. "I guess."

"You guess?"

"How much do we really know anyone?"

Myers rolled her eyes. "Don't get philosophical on me, Pratchett. There's a reason I requested you."

"Meaning no one else wanted the job?"

Goofy but somewhat intelligent. She needed someone to coordinate while she worked. Someone able to follow orders without question. Someone *controllable.* Myers shrugged. "Beside the point. About Loren…"

"Why?"

Myers stopped, leaning on the wall. "No one knows what he works on most of the time."

"So? I don't know what I work on most of the time."

Myers let his words hang in the air for a moment before waving them away. "A separate issue there. But you're right. It's more than that. He left then came back. Right with that whole business at Evans Tower."

"I was there too," Pratchett said, puffing his chest.

"In the thick of it?"

"At the door, actually. The lobby door. Also important."

"Not quite, but good on you," Myers said. "So Loren just shows up and is back to being Ruiz's go-to guy around here."

Pratchett shrugged. "Loren's a good cop."

"Not doubting it. Just trying to understand the man."

The burly officer smirked. "Him or Ruiz?"

Both peered down the hall at the open office door at the end. Myers let out a deep breath. "He doesn't like me."

"I wonder why?"

Myers saw it on his face. The rumor mill was in full swing and she was the front-page story. The best distraction from the murderer in their midst. There was always time for a little distraction. Especially when it came to the new detective on the force going head to head with the decades-old captain. Her insubordination was part of her charm, she believed. She was the only one.

"You've heard."

"Everyone's heard."

"Great." Glances were exchanged with each colleague rushing by. The same knowing glare.

Proving that she had the talent to close the case to herself was one thing, but to prove it to everyone in the department? Maybe she should let Mathers coordinate with another detective, someone with more experience in Portents. Unfortunately, tucking her tail between her legs and walking away was not in her repertoire and she refused to let others influence her decisions.

Myers tried to focus on the case, on the deaths of over twenty people in the last three weeks. All with the same method, the same destructive force behind them. Unexplained yet vicious and efficient. That was the priority.

Down the hall, Ruiz stepped out of his office. Mathers tried to flag him down to no avail; Ruiz blew past his counterpart's office without a glance. Myers handed off her files to Pratchett, the curious officer bobbling the mountain of preliminaries in an attempt to keep them from slipping in the quick exchange.

"I'm down the hall on the right," Myers said without looking. Ruiz tried to circle the bullpen, stopped every few inches for questions about unapproved reports. Myers waved at her new sidekick. "Set up. I want to go through these."

"Tonight?" The files slipped to the floor in a heap. She looked back and he waved her off. "Happy to help. That's what I meant. But Myers?"

"Thanks, Pratchett." Myers raced after Ruiz, catching up before reaching the stairs to the parking garage. "Captain!"

Ruiz's head fell to his chest, short of his exit. "Oh, God…"

"Heading home?"

"It does happen, Myers," Ruiz replied. He moved for the elevator instead. She followed closely, listening to his groans with each movement.

"No, I know," Myers continued. "After what happened I would—"

Ruiz turned, eyes thin. "Analyze me another time, Detective. Right now? Focus on the killer out there."

She was surprised at his anger. "You have a problem with my handling this case, sir?"

Ruiz bit his lip. He leaned close, dropping his voice. "I have a problem with Mathers on most everything but I get him assigning you over his seasoned vets. I understand him better than most, Myers."

Myers' brow furrowed. Ruiz cocked his head back down the hall. She turned to see Mathers watching from his office door. Concern left worried wrinkles along his forehead and thick crow's feet branching from his beady eyes. When she turned back to him, Ruiz gave her a knowing look.

Oh, shit, she thought before clearing her throat. "I don't—"

"Yes, you do," Ruiz interrupted. "And if you want to pull that garbage with me, you're barking up the wrong married man. The rest of the department might look the other way or are too blind to see it but I don't hide my feelings around here. We have that in common. Look where it's got me."

"Captain. Not bad at all in my book."

Ruiz shook his head. "A glass ceiling with no floor beneath my feet. Try to remember that the next time you spout off."

The elevator door slipped open and Ruiz stepped inside. Myers fought to find a way into the conversation much less the man's good graces.

"Sir, about that—"

"Catch your killer, Myers," Ruiz said, pressing the button for the ground level. "Then think about some vacation time. I could use the break."

The doors closed to the elevator and Myers stood in front of them for a long moment. He didn't give her a chance, refused to even try with her. Not from the work or her inability to follow orders without question. No, it was because he knew more about her than she believed. He wouldn't give her a chance. She earned that anger, that disgust. One hundred percent.

"Nice one, sir," she muttered to the closed elevator doors. "Hilarious."

CHAPTER EIGHTEEN

Atticus Hollowell had a dream. Ever since he was a kid he held it tight wherever he went, in whatever he did. He chased that dream, pursued it ceaselessly, using every avenue of study and every resource at his disposal to make that dream a reality.

To own a bowling alley.

It wasn't easy. Nothing truly desired in life can ever be counted as easy; this held true for Atticus Hollowell's grand vision. There were endless hurdles. They began early. His parents' admonishments of his dream, their inability to see beyond the wishful thinking of a child and envision the practicality of owning a business within the heart of downtown Portents, led to years of resentment on both sides. If Atticus heard another word about settling for a degree in accounting he would have torn what little remained of his hair out.

From there the troubles grew in leaps and bounds. Financial nightmares plagued his pursuit of the dream. Loans burdened him, the jobs of his youth barely able to keep up on minimum payments month to month. Each time one was paid Atticus whispered a silent prayer to no one in particular—his parents gave up on God quicker than their own son—thankful for four more weeks to fulfill his dream.

And he did. It took three decades and more bookkeeping magic than he would ever admit to the federal government or any other elected official—though they would surely appreciate the effort and possibly offer him a spot on their staff—but Atlas Bowling opened its doors to an eager public.

That was four years ago. Now the alley stood as one of the few hotspots able to survive the city's lackluster nightlife. Talk of fear and safety never penetrated the ears of Atticus or the walls of his new church. Inside Atlas Bowling there was only the sound of crashing pins and satisfied dreamers.

Night play was limited to three times a week but it helped sustain the leaner months. Most profit came from the league play generated by local retirees during the afternoon. Business was business. It would never be a wealthy dream. But it was Atticus Hollowell's.

Circling the building, noting the substantial number of cars still loitering in the lot, Atticus entered the alley from the maintenance door in back. He took the small stairwell, cursing his widening waistline and his belligerent hatred of exercise.

What he loved, however, was the guts. The operation at work. Churning bowling balls, spinning back to their return. The sound of collapsing pins and winding pistons to replace them. It sounded like heaven.

He wasn't the only one.

"Jacob?"

Jacob Gephart. The dream would not have been possible without Jacob. At a time when Atticus almost gave up on ever being able to open the bowling alley, when he considered returning home to his waiting parents with their "I told you so" lecture, with his financial woes that outpaced what little remained of his savings, Jacob rode in to save the day, a shining knight. In Jacob, Atticus found a new lease on life and a new lease on a recently opened property that could be converted to suit his needs. Jacob's previous enterprise failed spectacularly, leaving him with a twenty thousand-square foot warehouse with nothing but potential.

They became partners. First on the bowling alley of Atticus' dreams, something Jacob became impassioned about listening to late-night tales from the aging dreamer. Then they became partners of another sense, fulfilling a longing neither of them imagined possible until they met each other.

Jacob handled the night shift most of the time. He enjoyed the quiet, roaming the halls to make sure everything operated smoothly. What few employees they had were more than happy to handle customer service, giving Jacob the privacy he enjoyed.

Atticus reached the ramp leading to the pin drops. The broad metal walkway clanged under his every step, overshadowed by the sound of pins falling into place for the next potential strike. When working perfectly, the back of the alley sounded like a concerto piece.

Something was wrong tonight. A small trickle of pins fell out of sync with the rest of the symphony. The pins crumbled along the platform, rolling toward Atticus like a bad omen—one fulfilled moments later at the sight of the fallen man on the platform.

"JAKE!"

Atticus rushed to his side, flipping the switch on the machine and ending the slow stream of pins falling on the man's legs. Atticus crouched low when his burgeoning gut refused to get out of his damn way. The dreamer shook his lover and pulled his body over for a glimpse at his face.

"No, no, no…"

Jacob Gephart's eyes were gone.

Atticus sobbed, tears flowing free down his cheeks. He shook at Jacob's body, attempting to force life back into him. It was far too late; his lover's body was cold and clammy to the touch. He sat and wept, his tears louder than the row of machines surrounding him. Louder than everything it seemed. Atticus took a deep breath and fought for his feet. There were no balls being rolled down the lanes. No cheers at strikes thrown, no jeers at gutter balls. No sound at all despite the crowd of cars out front.

He rushed down the walkway, tripping twice on the loose pins scattered across the path. Atticus pushed through the pain running down his legs and grabbed at the access door to the main floor of the alley. Then stopped at the sight.

"It can't be…"

Dozens of bodies littered the room. Resting in their seats, face down on their lanes. He recognized Tiffany working the counter, now her final resting place. All bore the same mark as Jacob—their eyes gone and the sockets charred black. Every body in the place matched his fallen lover, the man he loved more than anything in the world.

Even his precious bowling alley.

Atticus screamed at the sight of those massacred and wondered if his parents had been right all along.

CHAPTER NINETEEN

Another late night. Henry hated them but it was all work would allow. His job teetered on dismissal more often than not now, his notions and theories ridiculed where once they were praised throughout academia. He was once sought after, and now his phone stayed silent. In spite of his early advances, the bright and prosperous work of his youth, most considered him the joke of the department. Professionally his life was over. To everyone his life ended three years earlier.

Henry dropped the coin to the bottom of his pocket, breath filling his lungs. Life returned as he crossed another one from the list. This time he kept his distance, not wanting to be there at the end. Not wanting to see what occurred. If the sirens were any indicator, it had been the right move. Jacob Gephart remained a stranger, his life serving one, final purpose.

His purpose.

Henry felt alive, the disease abated. One more name and it would be that way forever. Then his colleagues would recant and prostrate at his brilliance. His professional life would return to prominence. Friendships would rekindle. Everything would be perfect.

It shot through him suddenly and without warning. Henry cried out before dropping hard, his hands reaching out and grabbing tight to the edge of the produce display. The basket upended and melons joined him on the grocery store floor. Henry gripped his sides, sickness screaming throughout his body.

"Mommy?" a little boy called. "That man is hurt."

A woman rushed to his side. "Sir? Are you all right? Here, let me—"

"I'm fine," Henry snapped, his eyes wide with rage. The pain blistered and split like lightning in his veins. He wanted to scream and cry, his anger holding the flood back.

Too soon. Much too soon. The latest death was only hours old. When this started, the relief lasted for days. Henry could smell the sweetness of the air. He could taste his food and savor every morsel. Life was his again.

Now it slipped through his fingers like grains of sand, a tease of his desire. What he earned from enduring so much for so long. The pain, the disease, the ridicule. His entire life ripped from him, all control lost.

Henry fought to stand, the woman reaching out for him.

"You're bleeding," she said. "Please, let me—"

He slapped her hand. "Back off!"

The mother scoffed. Hurt and scorned, she returned to her cart with her curious toddler, pushing down the aisle. "I knew I shouldn't have come tonight."

"But Mommy—"

"Let's get out of here," she shouted, hoping Henry would hear. Anything to be noticed—the pride of modern civilization. She pulled the boy out of the cart. "Sickos in this city. I swear it gets worse every day."

Henry shook his head, regretting his reaction only for an instant. He didn't require help and he certainly didn't desire the pity plastered on the woman's face. Others in the store stopped their shopping and stared. Their eyes matched the young mother. More pity. They kept their distance, however, not wanting to incur more anger from the staggered man.

Blood showered his lips. Thin and streaming, it was worse than ever. He felt the liquid down his neck, exiting his ears in small drips. He ran his hand over his mouth, wiping at the river to no avail. Crimson fell down his chin to the floor below, covering the produce surrounding him.

He was running out of time.

The constant pulling of his body, from disease to the eventual cure had reached a breaking point. The strain grew with each pull and would continue until the end.

Standing, his hands wrapped on the grocery cart for support, Henry wiped his bloodied face along his sleeve. Dizzy but on his feet, he reached into his pocket for the coin. It was too soon to act.

Too soon to let the beast out of the cage again. The coin offered momentary relief, a soothing balm that slowed the flow of blood and pushed back against the sickness raging in his body.

Staving off death for a little while longer, at least.

Sickos, the mother had said.

"Not for much longer."

Henry smiled, swiping at the blood with his bony fingers. The crimson liquid dripped from their tips until they came to rest on the honeydew in his cart. He smeared the blood along its pale surface, spreading it into a grin. Then, under the watchful eyes of the other patrons, he walked to the front door, confident and assured.

"One more," he muttered under his breath, the coin wrapped tight to his palm. "Just one more."

CHAPTER TWENTY

I know where we have to go.

Greg Loren had heard it before. A hint, a nudge, at some larger world within the confines of Portents. It typically came with a smile and a sharp jab to his arm to pull him along, racing through the streets. This time, Soriya was slow and deliberate, mulling over the decision rather than running headlong into it.

Their travels took them east, slipping away from the Exchange on Allure and deeper into the shadows. Soriya stayed silent during the journey, from trolley car to bus interchanges that eventually placed them south of the pier.

Loren knew the district well. When he first arrived in Portents, he worked at the Eighth Precinct. They handled the Bowery and the Pier exclusively, feeding into the Third to the north for joint activities when necessary. Loren walked the streets nightly, never really achieving the elusive goal of finding a home.

Portents wasn't his city though he attempted to make it one. Especially here, at the beginning. He recognized the deli at the corner of Kalm and Rogers, the repair shop at Wheeler and Bouchard. He had spent plenty of time in the area, noting the hot spots of activity. For the job. Everything was for the job then.

It still was. Only different.

The shine of the city no longer present, Loren saw Portents in a new light—one that took away the hidden elements, almost like solving the Evans case had peeled back some secret decoder ring to unlock Portents. When he noticed the deli, it wasn't in the usual hustle and bustle of commerce, but rather a safe house for people hiding in plain sight. The repair shop owner, a kindly old man who related tales from his youth about better days, was more than he purported and it was Loren who observed the truth behind the man's façade instead of Soriya this time. Loren waved to the old man sitting outside his closed shop, eyes covered yet seeing the detective clearly. He waved, and Loren could only return the gesture, his own eyes unable to peel away from the strange man that once appeared so normal.

The world opened up for him after his return and he let it in, wholly accepting his new role. No matter the consequences.

"It's this way." Soriya pulled, dragging him south. Each step brought more desolation. The city, while booming at its epicenter and the suburbs north, neglected the southern districts. Once visitors looked away from the grand theaters to the west and the residential palisades of the coves, nothing but grime and waste remained to the south. Lowtown was the new name given to this area, one earned over the decades.

They passed his old apartment and he stopped. He remembered the holes marking the walls, the floors and the ceiling. The beginning for him. Before Beth. Before the true city and Soriya and the insanity that surrounded them like gremlins, old souls and even Death itself.

Suddenly the shitty apartment didn't seem so bad.

"Do you even know where you're going?" Loren called, rushing to keep up with Soriya. She powered on, unable to tire. She stopped short at the end of the block, Loren almost bowling her over from behind.

"Through here," she muttered. She ducked into a wide alley beside an abandoned plaza. Loren followed cautiously, hand to his hip. No one came down here anymore.

"What is?" Loren whispered, eyes on every shadow surrounding them. They moved through the alley before coming out the other side and the warehouses lining Menkin. "There's nothing here."

Soriya smiled. Then she pointed to the warehouse before them. Loren took the lead, unsure. The building, a single floor from the looks of it, looked polished compared to the run down structures surrounding it. Shipping trucks parked in front of docking bays, their metal doors closed.

From across the street there appeared to be nothing special about the building. It matched the status of half the structures within a mile radius. An anonymous business, this one carrying the initials L.U.M. on its edifice, like that explained what was being done on the inside. The parking lot must have been to the rear, no doubt empty at this late hour. To the left of the docking area was an unmoving shadow of a security guard within a doorway.

Soriya nodded, reading his thoughts. She pushed him forward with a wave and he headed across the street. The door carried a scanning system. Access cards granted entry to the employees but this one bore no lights—red, green or otherwise—or a connection to the door in any way. The door itself was real enough and resisted Loren's pulling. The inside, however, offered nothing in terms of a clue. Just the single shadow within, one not even curious about the man at the door.

Loren huffed, jumping down the short stoop. He moved for the trucks and the metal doors. Only they weren't actual doors at all. False fronts. This was no warehouse.

"What the hell? Soriya?"

She stood at the end of the building, pointed down the long lane on its side. "Here."

Loren followed her down the lane. The brick was sullied by a single block of stone every few feet. The stone, each a shade of gray in color and none quite the same, carried a small symbol upon it, one immediately recognized. The thin flame rising from a small torch.

"The same as the Courtyard," Loren said, his hand grazing the cool stone.

Soriya nodded, moving deeper into the alley. "That one won't do anything."

"What is it supposed to do?" Loren asked, pulling away from the wall.

"You'll see," Soriya said. She stopped, pointing to a marking tucked among the brick. One not of simple stone like the others but bronze in color. The symbol matched the others. "You might want to take a step back."

Loren did as instructed, watching closely as Soriya's fingers pressed the bronze square. The symbol depressed into the box, which she then twisted hard to the right, rotating the small torch clockwise until a clicking sound echoed around them.

In an instant, the wall shifted. The bronze marking collapsed within the wall. The brick surrounding them pulled away, depressing piece by piece then retracting out from the center. With each movement, Loren could see beneath the edifice of the faux warehouse. Where brick and stone once sat stood a door, the small torch emblazoned at its center.

Loren said nothing, watching the bizarre transformation in awe. No matter the experience, no matter the time passed between them, he remained surprised at the depth of Portents. The endless secrets collected under the surface waiting to be revealed.

Soriya smiled at his silence. Her movements may have been slow and deliberate, her thoughts troubled by the events occurring around them, but her enthusiasm, her pride at sharing the true city with her friend and partner were clear. She stepped up to the door, her hand resting on the upside-down torch. She pushed on the image and rotated it back to its original position. A second click resounded in the alcove and the door opened.

"Loren," she said, blocking the door. "Stay here."

"What?" he asked, trying to peer into the darkness. She stopped him with a touch. "Soriya?"

"You have no idea—"

"You're right," Loren snapped, refusing to back down. "So educate me."

"This isn't the time for that," Soriya replied. "Or the place."

Loren shook his head. "You're worried, I get that. It scares the hell out of me but I get it. You brought me here. You think this place can help and I followed along. Now we do this together or not at all."

"Fine," she said, backing through the door. Lights activated at her presence, running up the walls and in large rows along the ceiling. Some failed to flare but the majority worked to illuminate the massive structure hidden within the warehouse's false front.

Loren stood in the doorway, unable to speak. The room was sprawling, much larger on the inside than what should have been possible from the exterior, similar to the Courtyard. However, unlike the Courtyard, which housed a microcosm community within its shell, the room appeared to be just that: a single room. Shelving lined the walls, filled with books. Thousands of them.

"Welcome to the Library of the Luminaries."

CHAPTER TWENTY-ONE

"Luminaries?" Loren tried to glimpse everything around him. Books towered over him, both extensive and thin texts. Old, leather bound editions. Some worn and ripped along the binding. Others never opened and in pristine condition.

Soriya nodded. She pointed to images marking every row of books, every column stretching to the ceiling. Everywhere they turned, the thin flame rising from the torch. A name to go with the symbol.

"A small collective. They've worked throughout history in secret to change the world."

"Past tense?"

"They made a mistake." Soriya turned the corner. Shelves of books opened up to a display on the west side of the room. She stepped aside, letting Loren take the lead. "Let's just say the world didn't need their kind of help anymore."

"What kind of mistake could have—" Loren stopped. Images lined the table, all depicting a single event—one that sparked a century of conflict and war. June 28, 1914. The assassination of a seemingly inconsequential archduke by a Serbian national. A single death escalating to the then-largest conflict in history.

"The First World War? Are you kidding me?" Loren asked. "No, of course you aren't."

Soriya ducked back into the stacks of books and Loren left the display, the dark eyes of the Serbian assassin stabbing through him. When he rounded the corner, he was alone. A hand fell on his shoulder and he nearly jumped out of his skin. Finger to her lips, Soriya led him deeper into the room.

"The war splintered the group."

"It has that effect."

Soriya nodded. "Most walked away to live quiet lives. Some came to Portents."

"To become librarians? Super secret librarians?" Loren smirked. He reached for a nearby text, curious what could be so important to hide from the world. Soriya snatched his hand, pulling him away from the book.

"Don't. Touch. Anything."

"But—"

"Unique and cursed books are on the first level." She pointed to the center of the room. A spiral staircase split the floor, the wide stairs leading deeper into the structure. "The other six hold the rest of their collection. A repository of the world's secrets."

Seven levels? All filled like this? "That's a lot of secrets."

Soriya stopped at the stairs. Both peered into the darkness below. "You should wait here, Loren."

He shook his head and she sighed.

"Stay close then."

"I always do."

Her eyes thinned. "Loren."

"Right," he whispered, both remembering his first visit to the Courtyard.

Soriya started down the steps and Loren followed within arm's reach at all times.

"Where are these luminaries now?"

"I don't know," she said. "Ten years ago they closed the doors on this place."

Loren looked out as they passed the second level. Art filled the space, much the same as the books of the first. Never much of a critic of the arts, Loren still recognized the work surrounding him. From Picasso to Monet. The Colossus of Rhodes and an image of Winston Churchill. So many forgotten treasures, tucked out of sight. Hidden from the world.

"You've been here before?" The third level lit up beneath their feet.

"Once," she replied distantly. "Only once. Mentor dealt with them often."

"Not a fan?"

"When was he?"

He chuckled. "True." The third level appeared to be armaments. Hand guns to rifles. Cannons and catapults. Even manmade objects of war. Spears. Arrows. Loren patted his hip and his own weapon for comfort. He followed behind Soriya, already making her way to the fourth level. "So how can this place help?"

"Something Johannes said," Soriya recalled. "Someone is controlling Death. Using Death to commit these murders."

"For immortality." Loren struggled with the word.

"Right."

"You're saying there is something here that can do that?"

"There are many tools kept here, used for many different purposes. I saw something similar before. Right before our dealing with the Church of the Second Coming."

"The less said about that, the better," Loren muttered, drawing a glare from Soriya. "Sorry."

"It was a wooden blade," she continued. "A summoning tool to call upon dark forces. This kid had one and was using it to summon Jenglot—infant vampires. Don't ask. I stopped him with some help."

"Mentor."

"He made the connection to the library." She stopped at the fourth floor landing "He always made the connections."

"How would a kid get a hold of something from this museum?" With the long process of entering the building alone, how would anyone find this place tucked in plain sight in the city? "Did these luminaries seriously leave the keys under the mat?"

"Secrets always find the light, Loren. Always."

Loren leaned on the railing, peering down from the landing. "But no protection? Nothing?"

Soriya grinned. "Oh, there's plenty of protection."

Loren followed her stare, turning around to face the standing display of a knight in full armor. The silver plating on his armor beamed under the spreading light. More displays carrying the same style of armor cropped up every fifty feet or so in all directions. Armed with a large broadsword, the knight stood at attention, guarding the stairwell.

"Yeah, it's doing real well protecting the place," Loren said. He walked up to the display, reaching out with a single finger.

"Don't!"

"What?" Loren flicked the knight in the chest. A small dinging sound reverberated up the armor plating before dropping the room to silence once more. Loren turned, arms outstretched. "It's just a statue, Soriya. What could possibly—?"

A shadow grew over Loren. Clanking feet shuffled behind him. The detective turned to face the approaching knight. The statue raised its sword, and two more of its brethren matched its movements.

Surrounding them on all sides.

"Oh, crap."

CHAPTER TWENTY-TWO

What the hell were you thinking? Soriya cursed her ignorance, watching in horror as the closest security knight lifted his sword over the frozen Loren. This was bound to happen, with Loren's own curiosity matching hers. Only he didn't know any better. Of course something bad was going to happen. It always did when they were together.

"Get back, Loren!"

The detective shuffled away, falling on his back as the sword came down. Soriya charged, screaming at the top of her lungs as she collided with the behemoth. Armor clanged, the knight's balance thrown off by the jolt. The sword crashed into the floor inches from Loren's open legs.

From all sides, more company approached. Slow and steady in stride, the knights held tight to their weapons, empty masks somehow more terrifying than anything else.

"Soriya!" Loren called, fighting to get to his feet.

"Run!" Soriya yelled, ducking under a strike from the weaponless knight. She punched the armor plating, pain shooting up her arm.

"But I can—"

Soriya leaped away from another strike, pushing Loren further from the conflict. "I've got this, Loren. Now run, dammit!"

He nodded, racing deeper into the library. One of the knights broke away from their convergence at the stairs and pursued, the other continuing to assist his weaponless brother.

She should have left him at the Cobbler's Den. Hell, she should have left him at the precinct and never involved him. Was loyalty what kept her from walking away? The sense that no matter what, the explanation was important to keep them together? Or was it fear, more fear than she ever knew she could carry inside? The fear of a child, watching death win out? Without a hope of escaping its grip in the end?

The knights struck in tandem and she fell back, feeling the wisp of air sliced by the sword of one. Pushing off the ground, Soriya shot into the air, narrowly missing the right fist of the first knight, the sword of his brother catching her on the left arm.

She cried out, her legs kicking out in reprisal. They connected soundly, breaking apart the pair of foes. She fell hard between them, the ribbons of Kali covering the cut skin and searing the flesh to cauterize the wound. It hurt like hell and she wanted to pay it back.

The ribbons, finished with their work, snapped to life. Snaking along the ground, they reached the sword at the top of the fourth floor landing. Soriya, surrounded by the two knights with two more inching their way over, jumped into the air and pulled back hard to retract the ribbons. They grew taut along the broadsword's hilt, prying the weapon loose from the hard marble floor. The weapon soared into the sky, pulled by the reeling ribbons. The hard canvas grip slid against her palm and she landed between the curious knights.

She smiled, holding the weapon close.

This is more like it.

Loren held back the urge to scream. It felt unbecoming of a grown man running for his life from a lifeless pile of armor carrying a millennium-old weapon. Not that he was jealous or anything. He was too busy running, after all.

His ribs flared with each stride, the initial knight's blow at the stairs reminding him of his idiocy. *Flick the knight? Great idea.* Loren pulled out his sidearm, struggling to take aim while racing between the displays of shields and armor set up throughout the floor. The knight continued to pursue, unflinching. Of course he wasn't afraid. Loren had brought a gun to a sword fight.

Idiot.

Loren turned sharp, slipping on the tile into a display case. Shields, ornate with large horns adorning them, rattled to the floor. Viking, based on their appearance. He tried to pick one up and was surprised at its weight.

The knight's sword fell hard on the shield and Loren let it rest on the floor. Even without a face in the open mask, the knight appeared to sneer at the fleeing detective. Hoping the grin was only his imagination and knowing it wasn't, Loren picked up the pace, his well-worn sneakers squealing with each step.

Sounds died out in the distance. The violence ended for the moment. *Soriya.* His worry didn't last long, however, as he came to a dead end. Displays blocked each side; the far wall taunted him with its display of helmets encased in thick glass.

"Fantastic," Loren muttered. He turned to backtrack and found his path was barred by the waiting knight. Trapped. Loren pulled the sidearm, his only refuge, and took aim for the unmanned armor's helmet. He fired twice, the bullets cutting through the shining metal.

To no effect.

The knight continued its approach. The gleaming armor raised its sword, prepared for a final strike. The knight inched closer then staggered. Loren watched as the knight's helmet slid from the top of its armor and fell to the ground, sliced clean through. The rest followed suit, dropping in pieces into a crumpled heap on the floor.

Behind the wreckage stood Soriya Greystone, a broadsword resting against her shoulder. She stepped over the fallen clumps of metal, reaching for Loren.

"That sword looks good on you," he said, relieved.

She smiled. "Everything looks good on me."

"No arguments there."

She helped him back down the path, kicking aside the helmet. Loren followed it with his eyes to its final resting place against the wall, a satisfied smirk on his face.

"Thanks."

She stopped, looking him over. "Loren."

He raised his hands. "I know. Don't touch anything."

When they reached the stairs, Soriya rested the sword against a nearby display. Loren stepped carefully, avoiding the wreckage littering the floor. Four knights were collapsed in heaps around them.

"No stone?" he asked.

"Hmm?"

"You didn't think the Greystone was needed here?"

"We were fine," she said without looking. The sword slid from its position and clanged to the ground. Loren's heart stopped. Both he and Soriya were unable to move in the aftermath, the echo spreading like wildfire in all directions. As the clattering dissipated, Soriya sighed and started for the stairs. "Come on."

Loren hesitated, kicking at the air around the fallen knights. "Yeah. Fine. Right."

Soriya took the steps slower, with Loren following close behind, neither wanting to let too much space open up between them. "It should be on the seventh level."

"Of course," Loren replied. "Never by the entrance. What are we looking for again?"

She stopped. Her eyes were distant, lost to memory. "Something I haven't seen since I was a child."

CHAPTER TWENTY-THREE
Thirteen Years Ago

Soriya was nine when she visited the library's grand hall. Relentless curiosity and endless enthusiasm filled her with wonder at the sights. Each level viewed increased those feelings, the need to know everything about every single item here restrained by her teacher.

And business.

"I disagree," Mentor said to the three cloaked individuals on the altar table's opposite side. They met on the seventh level, the lowest in the library. There were no overhead lights, only the flickering of torches throughout the intimate setting.

The three luminaries wore stark white masks over their faces, only their lips exposed. Anonymity was crucial in their belief, a precaution they espoused to their guests. Mentor called it arrogance.

Soriya, seeing the tension between the two parties, kept to a dark corner. She knew better than to be directly involved in whatever conversation had brought them there.

It wasn't her place. Nothing was lately. Since Mentor's injury, the bloody cut that ran from his left eye down his cheek to his ear, she was cut off from the flow of information that once came freely between them. He claimed the change was for her protection.

Fear was closer to the truth.

"You always disagree, Christo—"

"Not in front of the child," Mentor snapped. He glared into the darkness and Soriya tucked away, toward the trinkets lining the shelves of rotted wood.

"Apologies," the luminary in the center said. "Mentor."

"It changes nothing," the figure to the right interjected. "The Bypass is threatened."

"It always will be," Mentor said. He grazed the wound along his cheek. Though not his worst, it remained the most visible from his work.

"The library would accommodate the burden," the individual to the left said. A softer voice. More feminine, one that matched her slighter frame.

"Hidden from all," Mentor sneered. "For how long?"

"Long enough."

"Stubborn fool," the one to the right said. "We offer protection."

"At a cost. Or did we all forget your own ambitions with the orb?"

"Knowledge, especially tucked within the Bypass, should be explored."

"Exploited," Mentor corrected. "The Bypass will reveal its mysteries in time. To those ready to listen."

"The same argument," the luminary to the right hissed, turning away from the conversation.

"Then why continue?" Mentor asked. "Why persist? What is it you fear?"

"There are rumors," the first muttered, his head low.

The woman to the left shifted closer. "A darkness hidden by the light."

"It would threaten all," the third said, his back to them. "Even the Bypass and all your work."

"Then I will be here to stop it." Mentor peered into the darkness behind him and smiled at the young girl watching in silence. The scar did not detract from the glow in his smile. It filled her with hope and confidence, almost as much as his words. "We will be here to stop it."

Soriya turned away from the conversation. Instead, she filled her imagination with the room's secrets. Boxed items lined the shelves, their contents hidden from view. Some remained visible, however, including a wooden blade with ornate carvings decorating the hilt.

She stopped short. Something glowed in the torchlight above her. The small object sat on a pedestal.

A coin.

Long tendrils of hair formed snakes curling from the sneering face on the coin's surface. Wide eyes glared, threatening to devour her. The more Soriya stared into the coin's face, the closer she inched toward it. Small fingers reached out, drawn to the coin. Compelled to touch it. To hold it. To possess it.

"I wouldn't, child," a voice called. Soriya stopped, shaking her head to remove a cloud over her thoughts. The owner of the voice drew closer, a white mask hiding all facial features. "The coin is marked by death."

"I didn't—"

"Soriya?" Mentor rounded the corner. When Soriya looked back to the luminary, they were gone. Mentor's hand fell on her shoulder, tugging her away from the coin. "We should go, little one."

She stopped, the menacing sneer of the coin pulsing under the dim light. "I was just—"

"Come, child," Mentor said again. He leaned close, blocking her vision of the coin. "Some things should stay secret. For all our sakes."

CHAPTER TWENTY-FOUR

"Soriya?"

The young woman shook her head, releasing the memory back into the ether. She stood at the base of the stairs. Below her, the seventh level was wrapped in darkness. She reached out and grabbed the small torch at the bottom of the railing, then handed it to Loren. He took the wooden handle, looking to her.

"Don't pretend you stopped carrying your lighter around, Loren," she said.

"If only," Loren said, pulling the Zippo from his pocket. *Damn, he missed smoking.* A thin flame sparked and he lowered it to the torch.

Soriya lit the other torches, and light entered the room. The far end remained dark. Not that she needed it—she knew exactly where she was going and what she sought in the library's lowest level.

"Soriya? Where are—?"

She didn't stop, heading for the back corner. She slowed as she rounded one of the three square columns supporting the ceiling. The shelves were dotted spaces of emptiness, the collected artifacts of centuries nowhere near as considerable. Items were missing. Too many to remember from her single visit. Soriya sprinted for the back corner.

"It's gone." The small pedestal remained on the shelf. Only empty now.

"What's gone?"

Soriya ran her finger along the shelf, wiping away a decade of dust. "They say it happened thousands of years ago. A story really. About a gorgon named Medusa."

"I've heard that one," Loren said smugly.

"Not the whole story. No one has. She was a beast, a creature, but only turned into one by Athena's jealousy. Thanks to the Goddess of Wisdom, Medusa lashed out at the world."

Loren nodded. "Turning people into stone. What does that—?"

"Loren."

He stepped away. "Right. Sorry. This place creeps me out. Might be the whole knights trying to kill me thing we just went through."

Soriya's grin faded and she returned to the empty shelf. "Before Medusa was killed by Perseus, she claimed a final victim. A woman who had everything the gorgon dreamed of in life: a devoted husband and children. Seven sons.

"From the stone that was once the woman's body, Medusa crafted a coin and forged it in gold. One never replicated, though many have tried over the centuries. It protects the user from death. It *controls* death."

"Yet it didn't save her."

Soriya nodded. "Some believed the coin was bound to the family of the final victim. That their family was forever tied to death, as if it was meant for them and only them. Religions have adapted the story for centuries. The martyrs in the book of Maccabees. The Talmud. All variations pulled from this one event."

"Soriya."

She pulled away. "It's a stupid story but it's real and it's happening now."

Loren pointed to the shelf. "That's what's missing here? The luminaries found it somehow?"

"Only to lose it," she whispered, recalling the blank eyes and sneering face. "Someone took it, Loren, and they're using it. Someone took the Medusa coin."

"Oh, it's much worse than that."

Both turned toward the darkness that enveloped the other half of the room. Torches burst into flames, filling the seventh level with light.

Soriya gasped. "*You.*"

Death stepped forward to the altar in the room's center. His suit was perfectly pressed, his bowler hat resting upon the crowded table. He grinned at their arrival.

"It's about time you two showed up."

CHAPTER TWENTY-FIVE

"Don't move!"

Loren was surprised to hear the words escape his lips and not those of his exuberant partner. Gun in hand, he inched to the center of the room and the pale-skinned man's waiting smirk. Soriya held back, torchlight throwing her shadow along the floor.

"Loren," she called. He refused to turn away from his target, Death itself.

"Detective," the suited man said calmly, his exposed hands outstretched. "I didn't come for a fight."

"Good." Loren cocked the hammer of his sidearm. "That makes this easier."

"What do you believe that toy will do exactly?"

"You'd be surprised."

"So would you." The man in the suit waved his hand at the weapon. The pistol shook in Loren's hands then shattered in a dozen pieces, collapsing on the stone floor.

"How the hell did you do that?" Loren tossed the remaining handle, the last piece of the gun intact, to the ground and raced toward Death.

"Loren, don't!"

Loren leaped at the man in the suit, unafraid. This was their chance at answers, at putting an end to the nightmare gripping the city. Discussion was no longer needed. They had answers within their grasp, within the bright, blue crystalline eyes of Death, and Loren refused to let them slip away.

Loren's fist shot out and caught nothing but air. The man in the suit deftly avoided the strike, tripping Loren's unbalanced body forward. A pale hand fell on the detective's arm and pulled him upright, dangling him in front of his target.

"You should have heeded her warning, Gregory," Death said.

"No," Soriya cried, approaching. "Don't do this."

"Don't do what?" Loren asked.

Then it hit him. Darkness swept over Loren. Breath escaped and refused to return. His lungs begged for a reprieve but none came. All the heat in his body slipped away, cold waves of emptiness infecting him like a virus. His mind shut down, all rational thought gone in an instant, leaving him in nothing but darkness.

"Feel it?" Death asked, his voice a whisper. "The blistering pain? The fear? The complete loss of all control? That is what it feels like at the end. You thought you could face the truth, Gregory? To face the city in all respects and truly understand it?"

"You're killing him," Soriya said, her words so far away.

"This city will kill him," Death said. "Portents will be the end for you, Gregory. And for what? Who will stand with you at the end?"

The hand fell away and Loren collapsed against the stone floor. Feeling returned to his extremities, the stone's coldness almost a comfort from the sensations filling him. His lungs heaved for more air, afraid it would be taken away again.

Loren closed his eyes. "Beth…"

"You fight for the dead," Death whispered in his ear. "We are more alike than you realize."

"You're wrong." A hand pulled Loren away. Warm to the touch, Soriya's fingers interlaced his, sending a chill throughout his frozen form. She lifted him to his feet, supporting him despite his heft. Anger raged in her eyes, burning at the man in the suit. "I only see one willing to fight. The other is content to sit and do nothing."

"Child…"

Soriya helped Loren to the side of the room, propping him against the wall of empty shelves. Her touch, soft against his cheek, was quick before she left him to recover.

"You know what this is. You could stop it. Whatever is happening, it could end with a single act from you. But you won't. You don't fight for anyone. Not death and certainly not life."

Death seethed, slamming his hand against the altar. The book positioned before him shuddered, the thick pages whipping up and down before collapsing into place. "Both hang in the balance here."

"Then how?" Her fear was gone. The pained look of a child dissipated with the man's arrival. All Loren saw in her was the strength he had always known. The true Soriya Greystone returned. "How can you just stand around and watch this happen?"

"There are rules…"

"Bullshit. And you know it."

Death grinned. He reached for his hat on the altar and placed it on his head. "You remind me of him so much. Enkidu. Our time together too short, our arrogance too great. We paid for it in kind. Just as this city will if she gets out of her cage."

"She…" Twice now it had been said like that, the first time from the mysterious cobbler downtown.

"Who?" Soriya asked. "Who else could pull a soul from the living?"

"More than you know, unfortunately, though I like to think I do it with my own unique flair." He circled the altar, letting the ornate table split the room. His hand rested on the book laid open before them, caressing the pages. "In this instance, however, there can only be one player involved."

He stepped back, palms open and inviting. Loren joined Soriya at the table, the waves of nausea abating. The man, Death or otherwise, could have done much worse to him considering the circumstances. There were plenty of opportunities to end this in his favor.

The pages opened. The text was in a different language. The images, however, were clear. Though varied, each depicted the same creature at their heart. Hollowed out eyes, scarred over, covered by a black cloak with thin, black tendrils escaping from underneath. Elongated fingers stretched from overgrown arms, thin and bony without any flesh at all. In some images the beast carried a weapon, a scythe. Others showcased the monster on a boat along a black river.

Soriya's eyes flared. "No."

"What is it? It looks less than pleasant."

"The Charon," Soriya answered. She bit her lower lip and shook her head. "Don't let this happen. You could make a difference."

"I hope I already have," Death replied.

"You could stop this!"

"There is no stopping this." Death fell away from the altar. "The cage will break if you are too late. Like Rome and mighty

Uruz before it, Portents will fall and be lost to history. Forgotten in memory. Dust to dust."

"Uruz…" The word slipped from her tongue.

"Unless you find the coin."

Loren understood that much. "The Medusa coin."

Death nodded. "Destroy the coin. Or all is lost."

He backed up, the shadows growing. Torches extinguished around them, dropping him further into darkness, twin specks of blue crystal piercing the night.

"Don't even—" Loren jumped over the altar, rushing for the man in the suit.

"Loren! No, you—"

Loren flew back, hit by a solid wall of shadow. He soared over the altar, slamming his back into one of the columns. Breath jolted from him, his body screaming, before sliding to the ground. He blinked hard into the darkness.

Death was gone.

"Are you all right?"

"Fine," Loren huffed. *Who will stand with you at the end?* He rested uncomfortably against the altar. The book sprawled across the center, the creature staring through them.

"Good. Now go home."

"What the hell are you talking about?" Loren yelled, holding tight to the table for support. His body screamed with each movement, with each word. "And what the hell happened back there? Why didn't you use the stone on him?"

"The stone," she said with a breath. "I can't."

"Can't?" Loren pressed. "What's going on, Soriya?"

"It's out of control, Loren. I… There was a fire."

"A fire? What are you…?" Loren stopped. He was at McDuffie's, the night of his reinstatement. The sirens during his celebratory water. So many sirens. All responding to a single incident. A fire. The cause never understood, never found. "The apartment complex. That was you?"

"Something is wrong with it." Her hand shifted to her side, to the pouch. The stone stayed with her. Never used. Never trusted. No wonder she felt more comfortable with the sword above.

Loren's fists clenched. "Why haven't you said anything? Why didn't you tell me? I could have—"

"Done what?" Her words were sharp.

"We're partners, dammit. Remember?"

She shook her head, pointing at the book. "Not in this."

"What are you talking about?"

"Death is loose in the city, Loren."

"So what else is new?"

Soriya growled in frustration, throwing her hands in the air. "Everything! Don't you get it, Loren? I can't protect you from this. Not you *and* the city. He could have killed you. This damn place could have killed you because you can never understand it. Not really. I won't watch that happen. I won't watch you die."

"I can take care of myself," Loren said, wishing his chest wasn't on fire. Soriya rested her hand near his heart, her eyes full of sadness.

"Then do that. Stay out of this."

His hand fell on hers. "Soriya, the stone—"

"Is my problem." She pulled away from him. "So is this. I'll fix this. I'll fix everything."

Loren shook his head, eyes falling on the book. "Against this thing? Don't be—"

Soriya was gone.

"—Stupid." He sighed, rubbing his aching ribs. "Or do the opposite. Great."

Loren reached for the book, wondering if the department had someone available to translate the text on the page. Then he recalled the security measures in the library. Not wanting to tackle any more problems, Loren staggered to the winding staircase empty-handed. He stared up into the darkness above, seven flights of stairs ahead of him.

"Couldn't put an elevator in this place, could they?"

CHAPTER TWENTY-SIX

It didn't hit her until the alley outside the library. The knot in her gut, the tightening noose around her neck. Visions of Loren dead at her side, the city fallen into darkness. All thanks to her inability to handle the situation. All because she couldn't do the job the way Mentor wanted.

Soriya fought for breath, thoughts spilling from her like yesterday's lunch all over the alley wall. Her chest heaved until nothing came up, and she took gulps of air to calm her nerves. Definitely nerves, not fear. She refused to let it rise and overtake her. Never fear.

She held back from confronting Death. She listened patiently to his warnings. The Charon. The Medusa coin. She listened, hoping, begging for a solution.

"Dammit," she whispered. The slight echo built, worse than the knot at her heart, until the whisper turned to a scream. "DAMMIT!"

She punched at the brick alley wall. Her fists pounded against the edifice, chipping it away with each blow. Blow for blow, her anger flew forward until she fell to her knees in defeat. No answers came. No great illumination at Death's warnings of what hid in her city, threatening everyone within its borders. And no one to help her solve it.

The way it was always meant to be.

Loren almost died from jumping into the thick of things without a clear understanding. She couldn't let that happen again. This task was for her and her alone. This was her job and she would handle it just as Mentor had asked.

The dark light of the torch sigil on the wall stared back at her. She preferred the golden glow of the symbol upon the outskirts of the Courtyard. It filled her with hope, having something bigger out there in the city. Watching over them all.

Like the Courtyard itself, yet not. Not this time.

The Courtyard was empty, the denizens of a dozen worlds no longer willing to risk a connection to the city. Not with Death in their midst. No help there and she wouldn't ask for it.

Follow the blood.

She had nearly forgotten Kok'-Kol's advice—the blood. She didn't understand it at the time. It was just another vague clue meant as a teachable moment instead of practical learning.

Same as Mentor and just as frustrating.

But now? The coin was the tipping point. Soriya stood, her hands pulling her weary frame up.

Follow the blood.

The story of the seven sons. It made sense. To use the power to its fullest tied it to its origins. The coin came from death, powered by death, to save the bearer. The seven sons paid the price and were paying it again. It connected the victims—some of them, at least—lost in the flood of bodies. A hidden pattern, a story told within those already lost and those still alive.

Footsteps echoed from within the library. *Loren.* She needed to keep him safe, to keep him distant from the situation as long as she could. No one else would suffer because of her.

Soriya raced down the alley for the open streets of Portents. The blood was the key and she knew where to start her search— alone.

CHAPTER TWENTY-SEVEN

They parked three blocks over. Floodlights and foot traffic created a natural roadblock, ending their journey to the bowling alley prematurely. Pratchett parked, two wheels skirting the curb. Myers white-knuckled the entire ride over, her grip threatening to pull the fixtures from the patrol car with each start and stop. How Pratchett survived his day was a bigger mystery than the slaughterhouse that had become the city of Portents.

"What a nightmare," Pratchett yelled over the muttering of a hundred civilians surrounding the front of Atlas Bowling. The crowds pressed against the cordon, phones flashing and pictures instantly available on social media. "Myers?"

She stopped outside the line, looking over the entire block. People were everywhere, with news vans offering their own cordon of sorts a block over on Grange.

"Push them back. Another block. Use the news vans if you have to. I want the line at Grange and Trudeau. Call in whoever you have to."

Pratchett pointed to his chest, looking around for another uniformed officer. He rubbed his head, scratching the thinning surface and nodded. "I'll get started."

"Do that." Myers shuffled through the crowd.

Ducking under the rope line, Myers found two officers standing outside the front doors to the alley. She grumbled a few choice obscenities and took a sharp breath before confronting them.

"Who's in charge here?" She recognized the pair of them—Danvers and Sloane. Traffic cops from Central.

Danvers, the younger of the two, cocked an eyebrow to his partner. He stood tall and confident. "Lady, I—"

Then he saw her badge. "It's Detective."

Sloane laughed at Danvers' screw up, his eyes shooting to his feet at her glare. Danvers wiped at his brow. "Christ. Sorry. Mathers is in charge. That is, Captain Mathers."

"Great." She saw him with the media. The camera crews should have been a clue who was involved. She didn't need him here, no one did. Not with what she heard over the wire. This was serious and he was playing the spokesman again.

Myers turned back to the pair of cohorts at the door, pointing for the cordon. "Pratchett will coordinate out here starting now. You give him whatever he needs."

Sloane started with a stutter. "But the captain—"

"Made me lead on this case." Myers leaned in closer. "Is there going to be a problem?"

"No."

They hesitated before she barked, "Pratchett. Go."

"Right," Danvers uttered, following on the heels of Sloane.

Myers surveyed the area, her comfort level dangerously low. She was the lead on the case and this felt like anything but, the pair of idiots racing after her personal gopher supporting her theory perfectly. They didn't know her. How could they? Since taking on the case she had handled everything she could on her own, refusing to trust her new department with the few details she had.

She walked away from the front doors outside the concluding press conference, watching Mathers at work. His confidence was staggering, even with no clue as to what was actually occurring at any of the crime scenes. His ease in front of the cameras was almost unnatural as if talk show host was his fallback career before he had enrolled in the academy.

It was the confidence that led her to him. Or him to her, anyway. The first week in Portents, they ran into each other at a dive bar down the street from the precinct. He asked how her week had been, and she let him follow up on it that night.

Into the morning.

Now, watching him work filled her with disgust. His ease with reporters, with anyone in a position to benefit his status in the city, made him look empty—and coming from someone like Myers, that meant something. That's why it never would have worked. They were too similar for their own good.

"…Will update you as soon as we know more. Our people are working around the clock. We'll find this monster."

"Captain Mathers," a reporter said as Mathers stepped away from the impromptu podium.

"Captain," another shouted over the first. "A question ab—"

He climbed off the stage, almost running down Myers in the process. She sidestepped him, falling beside him for the bowling alley's front door.

"Your makeup is running," she commented without looking.

"Sam," he grumbled under his breath.

"Detective Myers," she corrected. "You remember me, right? The lead on this case?"

He stopped, argument ready. "Now don't—"

"Why was I not the first call the second the bodies were found?"

Mathers put his hands to his hips, towering over her. "I asked to be kept in the loop. Something you seem incapable of doing. With anyone."

"At the expense of a crime scene." She pointed at the camera crews. "Did they sniff this one out or did you call them here?"

"The public has a right—"

"To go one day without seeing your ugly mug on the television." Looks from reporters shot their way and she held her tongue. "One night, in this case. You're off the clock. Sir."

"What the hell is wrong with you?"

"With me? I'm thinking about the dead people in there right now. You're thinking about the headlines tomorrow. Who has their priorities in the right place?"

He leaned close. "I've reprimanded people for a lot less, Sam."

"Yeah, well, I'd be more afraid but I've seen you naked."

"Dammit, Sam," Mathers looked around nervously. He fell silent at the approach of a sweating John Pratchett.

"Detective?"

"Cordon in place?" Myers asked, ignoring the flushed cheeks of her superior.

"Getting there," Pratchett replied, nodding to Mathers.

"Good."

"Ronne's still inside."

"Even better," Myers said, reaching for the door. "Captain?"

Mathers hesitated, Pratchett standing awkwardly between them. "Go," he said. "We'll talk about this later. Understand?"

"No. We won't." The door opened and she held it for a moment. "*Understand?*"

The door slammed shut behind her, the sound ending their conversation with finality. It had been a long day and looked to be a longer night. With the news about the scene, Myers believed she had prepared herself for what was to come.

She was dead wrong.

Bodies lay scattered along the floor, eyeless victims greeting her from every angle. Forensics scattered throughout the wide arena, taking photos while others dusted for some physical evidence, knowing all efforts were futile.

Nothing could have prepared her for the level of death in the room. Or for the calm, calculated look of the coroner as she sat at the snack bar, oblivious to the corpse hanging off the other end.

"Detective," Hady Ronne said with a slight glance at the approaching Myers. Then she went back to her paperwork. Not ten feet away, the dead woman stared at them with burned-out eyes.

"How many?" Myers struggled to ask.

"Twenty-two," Hady answered. Myers imagined her snacking on one of the aged hot dogs on the reel behind the counter before her arrival. Nothing fazed her; nothing impacted the work, no matter the horror surrounding them.

"All the same?"

"Yes." The woman's eyes remained glued to the paperwork, focused and undeterred. Small beads of sweat pooled along her hairline. "Same as the church."

"And before." Myers bent down, catching Hady in a stare and drawing her away from the reports. "I've been going through everything. I flagged seven other cases for your review. They should have arrived earlier today but I haven't seen any reports. Why?"

Hady's eyes flared then fell flat. "Been busy."

"Right," Myers said, curious. Hady Ronne was infamous for her efficiency and diligence at the job. Her cool, collected behavior had drawn the ire of most of the force, not that she cared. Something else presented on her face and in her slumped-over frame at the bowling alley's snack bar. Pain and concern that gave Myers pause.

"Everything all right?"

"Fine," Hady said. She stood, holding tight to the bar for support.

"I know it's been a rough couple of nights but—"

Hady gathered up her reports and turned for the door, ignoring Myers' concern. She staggered down the carpet.

"Hady?"

"Doctor Ronne," she said in a deep voice, almost like someone else entirely.

"Of course."

"I'll need the bodies."

"I'll be quick."

Hady stopped at the door. "Good."

Myers turned back, trying not to focus on the woman or her behavior any longer. She didn't need the coroner's office against her on top of Ruiz and Mathers. She needed someone on her side through all this. Someone more useful than Pratchett at least.

A few reports sat on the snack bar. Myers spun back to the door. "Had—Doctor Ronne? You dropped—"

Hady was already gone. In her place was Mathers, barreling toward her.

"Sam."

"Not again." Myers suddenly wished for more dead bodies to distract her, but then she regretted the thought with a glance around the room.

"You might not want to talk about us but—"

"You do." Myers focused on the reports left by Hady, trying to keep from looking at her superior. "I got that. Very clearly, in fact. If only we weren't dealing with the worst mass slaughter in the city's history." She slammed the report closed, looking up at him with disdain. "Damn inconvenient, isn't it?"

Mathers huffed. "Now you listen to me, Sam. I—"

"What the hell?" Myers held open the bottom report on Hady's forgotten paperwork, blinking hard at the notes marking what appeared to be preliminaries on some of the bodies shipped in from the first murder scenes and the name of one of the men at the alley.

"What?"

"These five—" The names on the page, their blood samples. Preliminaries Hady Ronne had denied only moments earlier. All noted in black and white on the pages before her. Myers knew enough about the system, about procedure to know the coroner had found a link. Five of the victims were connected.

By blood.

"What about them?" Mathers asked.

Myers ignored him, tucking the reports close and starting for the door.

"Detective?"

"You have mustard on your tie," Myers said. "I'm sure the cameras appreciated the color."

"What?" Mathers glanced down to investigate.

Myers shook her head and reached for the door.

"Wait!"

"I'll be sure to keep you in the loop," she said. "Promise."

CHAPTER TWENTY-EIGHT

"Greg…"

The darkness sifted around him like a giant cloud. It surrounded his senses, drowning him in black. The voice reached through the barrier between them, calling to him through his dreams.

"Greg…"

The black faded, light penetrated, yet the scene remained a haze. The smell of lilacs surrounded him. Her lilacs. The same as every night. Greg Loren knew where he was. Even in sleep, he recognized where he would end up. It was the same place he always traveled. Against his will, against all odds.

The rooftop's cool concrete rushed up his naked feet, and he shivered from the sensation. Despite the lack of footwear, he was fully clothed. More than that, he wore a suit—the only one he ever owned. The one he wore on every significant occasion of his life: his graduation, his first day at the Central Precinct, the day he met his wife, his wedding day. So many memories wrapped into a single outfit, one long since hidden away in his closet.

Those memories were overwhelming, much like the scenery surrounding him. The rooftop. *Their* rooftop. The multiple air conditioning units, the beach chairs from the tenants in the apartment above them, and more. All the way they used to be. Except not at all—each and every item was covered in lilacs. Blue, white, lavender, all distinct, covering everything in sight.

Except for her.

"Greg."

He blinked and she appeared, the same as always. Beth. Her red sundress with the yellow lilies dotting the trim hugged her hips. Her blond hair settled along her shoulders, not a single strand out of place.

Behind her, the sun raged. It grew not only in size but intensity, threatening to blind the dreaming detective. The sun rose next to their apartment building.

Beth stepped back to the ledge, inching toward the light. Her smile gave him hope but her eyes shattered it, the sadness centered in each blue ocean grounding him.

"No more sunrises, Greg."

He knew what came next, where the dream ended. How Beth slipped away, the same way he imagined her falling so many years earlier. No matter what he did, it would be this way—the same way each dream ended, every single time. He was powerless against the rushing tide of inevitability.

It didn't stop him from trying.

"Wait!" he cried out, the word catching him off guard. The dream controlled his actions or lack thereof, never giving him a chance for more. More explanation. More interaction. Only the fall.

Until now.

He reached out, his hand fighting against the dream. "Please wait."

Beth turned toward the light, her toes inching over the ledge. "They're calling to me."

"Who?" Loren asked. He fought to reach her, each step bringing him closer yet endlessly distant from the ledge. "Who is calling, Beth?"

She turned back, hands pressed tight against her sides. "The shadows. They form a circle."

A circle?

"Is that why there are no more sunrises? Please, Beth." His voice pleaded. He reached for her, never close enough to touch.

Her smile cut through the glare, sad and cold despite the intensity of the light. "I wish I could help you choose. You'll try. I know you too well. You'll always try but—"

A tear streamed down her cheek. She caught it on her fingertips, watching it run over the edge into the darkness below. She stared into the abyss, tracking its descent.

"Beth?"

Her arms were outstretched, her balance precarious on the shrinking ledge. When she turned, there was no more doubt. No more sadness. Only what came next.

What always came next.

"You can't save them both, Greg," Beth said, shuffling away. "One has to die."

She let go, falling into the darkness. Loren rushed to the side, faster now, but never fast enough.

"BETH!"

Her words echoed and the sun above them blinked out like a light bulb, shrouding everything in darkness.

Beth's hand reached out while she fell, begging for help. Begging for her life. Too late. Loren watched her disappear, swallowed by the shadows.

The last glimpse of her smile carried him out of his dream, back to his empty life.

CHAPTER TWENTY-NINE

You can't save them both. One has to die.

The dream continued to replay for Greg Loren despite his wishes. He wasn't likely to get back to sleep after watching his wife fall. It never came easy to begin with, but once the dream took hold, rest was impossible.

Work was an option. The missing person's cases consuming his coffee table begged for answers. So did his time with Soriya at the Library of the Luminaries. The Charon? Soriya's fear over the possibility frightened him. He tried to call her, to no avail. Her fears over his safety won out over their partnership, their shared responsibility. He was on his own.

Alone.

Which is probably why, when it came down to where he would spend the night, he found himself back at McDuffie's. Since his return to the city and his reinstatement, Loren had made the sparsely populated bar a frequent stop. Not for the atmosphere and certainly not for the alcohol, though on nights like this a beer or three sounded heavenly.

Dominic brought him back. Call him a kindred spirit, call him an oddity—his gills attested to that—but Loren appreciated the man's candor and the level of friendship afforded between bartender and patron. Loren needed the distraction and some humorous banter.

The dream had that effect on him. Beth's fall. Now it brought more, more than in the past. When they started, the dreams were sporadic, short glimpses of the rooftop, the sun and her descent into the shadows. When she spoke the first time, his heart stopped. And now? Now it brought more information.

You can't save them both. One has to die.

What did she mean? Why were the dreams growing, *evolving* over time? Did it have to do with his encounter with Death? His hold on him lingered, the waves of cold only dissipating hours after their meeting. Then there was the frequency of the dreams to consider. He used to go weeks between visitations and now they were almost nightly. The dream was growing…but for what reason? What did Beth's message mean?

And how much time did he have to figure it out?

Loren entered the pub, head low, making a beeline for his usual spot. He put the missing person's reports in front of him, happy for a distraction during his sleepless night.

"What can I get you?" a man asked, delivering a pint glass of dark lager to a patron. Loren didn't answer immediately, surprised at the man's presence. He was middle aged and wore an apron stained with what looked like hot sauce or ketchup. A cook pulling double duty. No Dominic in sight.

"Water," Loren said.

"Really?"

Loren sighed, dropping a fiver on the bar. "I'll even let you put a lemon slice in it to earn the tip."

The stand-in bartender returned without the lemon. The glass stopped short of the five dollar bill, which was swiftly pocketed.

"Hang on a second," Loren called after the man before he could return to the kitchen.

"I'm pretty busy, pal."

Loren held out another fiver. "Where's the usual guy? Dominic?"

The man stopped, shuffling back to the bar. The fiver joined its brethren in his front pocket. "Wish I knew."

"What do you mean?"

"Listen—"

"I plan to," Loren interrupted. His badge slipped free from his breast pocket and he placed it upon the bar between them. "When you answer my question."

"Whoa," the man uttered, his hands up on instinct. "I didn't know. Is Dom in some kind of trouble?"

"Kinda what I'm asking you about, slick. When was the last time you spoke to him?"

The nervous man leaned close, lowering his voice. His elbows rested on the polished counter, trying to hide the badge from others' view. Loren took the hint and tucked it away.

"Been a week now. No word. I called, texted, social media, everything. If he didn't want the job, he could have said so."

Loren's brow furrowed. "Did he ever say anything to make you think that?"

"Never," the man answered. He pulled back from the bar, arms crossing his chest. "Thought he loved it. Acted like he did, anyway. I can get you his info if you think—"

"Yeah. I do," Loren said. "Thanks."

The man nodded then slipped into the back. Loren didn't notice when he returned with the address, letting the note rest on the bar next to his unopened files. The growing number of missing people in Portents. Another concern added to the pile, one that worried Detective Greg Loren greatly.

He only wished he knew why. And what it all meant.

CHAPTER THIRTY

Sam Myers winced at the confusion on the lab assistant's face as Liam Schultz looked over the notes once more. His cheeks swelled up like a blowfish. Not an attractive pose for the overweight technician with the candy wrapper stash overflowing from his open desk drawer. He needed all the help he could get in that department.

"Is this a joke?" Liam asked for the third time.

"Do I look like I'm joking?" she said through gritted teeth. She towered over the seated kid in the lab coat, her hands on her hips.

"A little," Pratchett muttered from behind them.

"Pratchett." Myers caught the giant of a man's discomfort at being at the coroner's office. She understood the feeling. The dead, still being trucked in from the bowling alley scene, lined both sides of the long hallway. The few staffers on hand moved rapidly to process the new arrivals, all coordinated by Hady Ronne.

Any thought of the woman brought a shiver to Pratchett's body. Whenever Myers brought her up in passing, sweat formed on the man's brow. His wariness landed him at the door to the lab, monitoring the hall for her presence, something they both needed to keep an eye out for considering the situation at hand.

"Maybe I should wait in the car," Pratchett said.

"Good idea," she said, shooing him to the hall before closing the door in his face, a rebuttal already slipping from his lips as silence returned to the lab.

Myers let the blinds fall over the half window. Then she clicked the lock. Liam Schultz gulped audibly when she returned to his desk.

"Is this going to take long?" His voice cracked at the question.

"Busy night?"

"Another joke?" Liam pointed to the closed door. "I have seven bodies shipped in at top priority followed by this bowling alley nightmare. It's going to take all night just to process the bodies let alone run preliminaries for the morning briefing."

Myers pulled the reports away from Liam. "I'm only interested in five."

Liam shook his head. "Cold."

She agreed. Twenty-two people were dead at the bowling alley. Fifteen at the church. Seven before that from other cities. The bodies were piling up and the answers elusive—except for one thread, the possible link between five of the men. One hidden by the coroner herself.

"Priority," Myers snapped, not in the mood to feel slighted by the tech. "I need the samples run for these five first."

She dropped the reports back on his desk, the list of names written separately on a note clipped to the top page. Liam stared at her through his thick-framed lenses, then lifted the papers back for a fourth review.

"I've only seen this Rusch guy. I handle all the preliminaries here," he said. He flipped through them, pointing to the names at the top of each report. "Wait a minute. Who processed these?"

"You handle all the preliminaries here. You tell me." She leaned close. "They came from this office, didn't they? Looks like someone is trying to hide something."

"What? What are you talking about?"

Myers shook her head, snatching the reports from him. "Obviously not your job, Liam. At least not for much longer."

She started for the door, her steps slow and deliberate. His agitation was palpable.

"Wait," he called when she reached for the door. "Just wait, okay?"

She stopped, tapping on the reports resting on her chest. Liam fixed his glasses to his face, cheeks flushed a shade of dark red. He held out his hand.

"May I?"

"Please." Myers grinned. She passed them back to him. Slower this time, Liam paged through the pile, growing concerned with each glance.

"These…these samples never came through my station," Liam stuttered. He rolled the desk chair to his terminal. The computer came to life with the shift of his mouse. He pounded on the keyboard, his password rejected twice from his sausage fingers. Successful on the third pass, he clicked through until he came to the reported findings on the five men. "Where did these come from?"

"Is it there? Does it show any link?"

"None. No genetic markers. No ties at all for any of them."

"Who put these in the system?" Myers double-checked each report. He was right. No matches at all.

Liam scrolled over the document, landing on the signature at the bottom. "Doctor Ronne."

"Is that abnormal?"

"It's not unheard of," Liam said. His voice was quiet, his eyes shifting for the door. Both waited for it to open at any moment, not that Myers minded the interruption. She hoped to see Hady next, once the evidence was in hand. If Hady Ronne was involved, it stood to reason she knew the truth behind the deaths. And, possibly, the identity of the killer among them.

Time was not on Myers' side, however, and neither was the information necessary to confront the coroner. She needed proof. Rushing into events, basing decisions on instinct instead of fact destroyed her professionally before her arrival to Portents. She needed to be better, to prove herself capable. To herself and everyone else at Central.

"Could she have switched out her actual findings with other victims?" she asked. "Previous cases unrelated to these?"

"I suppose," Liam said softly, his confidence building. "I mean, yeah. There are any number of cases she could have pulled from here." Liam coughed. "Can I—?"

"Take new samples from these five to confirm the genetic link listed in these reports? Why, thank you, Liam. That is truly a generous offer."

His mouth fell open, his glasses slipping down his sweaty nose. "That will take hours."

"I know." She reached into her pocket and pulled out a dollar bill, dropping it on his desk. "Here. Next round's on me."

"Coffee machine's broken."

Myers' jaw clenched. "Buy a candy bar."

"I'm dieting."

"Really?" Myers asked, recovering. "I mean...it's working for you. Good for you."

Liam smiled, sitting up straighter in the chair. "What about the bodies out there?"

She patted his back hard. "You'll get to them in a few hours. After you call me when my five are set."

Myers started for the door, phone in her hand. There was too much to do, too much to consider. The tech called out to her as her hand collapsed along the door handle.

"Where are you going?"

To talk to your boss. That was what she wanted to say. It was how she preferred to handle situations, head on and solo. Without complications. But everything about this case screamed complications. This was her last shot, her chance to prove she had complete control over her career and its fate. Hady Ronne needed a softer approach—from someone she trusted.

"I need to make a call."

CHAPTER THIRTY-ONE

Follow the blood.

Soriya Greystone carefully opened the ceiling vent to the lab and slipped inside. She crept down the hall. The young intruder stuck to the shadows, in case someone was curious to step inside.

It was a simple enough extrapolation that even Soriya realized it soon after leaving Loren behind at the Library of the Luminaries. If a connection existed between the victims, if the story of the seven sons was being re-enacted on some level with the Medusa coin, it stood to reason that Kok'-Kol's hint of the blood could be attained at the coroner's office.

Sneaking inside was another matter, and not one she sought to repeat anytime soon. Walking through the front door was not an option, not since her multiple visits only months earlier when she lost so much of the joy in her life. It had been three months since she heard Mentor's voice or seen Vlad's smile.

Being among the dead was the last thing she wanted.

The ventilation system therefore provided the only ingress available for her. The pipes snaked throughout the complex, giving her total access. She moved slowly, not wanting to draw attention—not that many would have noticed any unusual noises, with the amount of work flooding the halls.

When she found the lab in question, she stopped and listened. A young woman gave orders to an overwhelmed kid with thick glasses. She carried a badge like Loren's. The detective had somehow learned about the possible connection between the victims.

Soriya needed to move faster. She hated working against the police but if one detective figured out the truth, others would as well. Loren would learn. Then he would be in danger again. They all would be.

Mentor had been right to go it alone. To take the burden of the job, solo and uncompromising. It was the only way to ensure everyone else's safety, the only way to make things better in the city. Her reliance on others had become much like that of the stone and she knew where that had landed her. Powerless. A lack of control.

This was the right move.

With the room now empty, Soriya rushed to the computer terminal. Files were present on the monitor, and their physical copies rested on the desk. She flipped through them, scanning the names on each label. Edgar Rusch she recognized immediately; the others were a surprise but not when she read their backgrounds and physical characteristics. Late forties, male, dark hair and green eyes—when they still had eyes anyway. The preliminary photos attested to their similarities as well. How no one else observed the connection was a surprise but with the massive influx of victims and the first three spread out over the state, it made sense.

And gave Soriya the time she needed to find answers before the rest.

The refrigerator unit in the back of the lab hissed. Soriya ducked behind the terminal, listening to the bespectacled tech's off-key singing. He hit a high note and she worried the tubes of blood clutched in his grasp might shatter. When he turned to close the unit, she slipped from her hiding place and rushed to intercept him.

He nearly fell backward at her presence. "Who… Where did you…?"

"I'm sorry about this," Soriya said.

Her fist shot out, smashing into his nose. The tech reeled from the blow, the tubes of blood soaring into the air from the shock. The young man fell to the floor. Soriya caught the blood samples, then crouched beside him to check his vitals. *Still breathing.*

She looked over the samples, matching the names to the files procured from the tech's station. *This was the right move,* she thought again, looking back at the unconscious man.

"I really am sorry about this."

CHAPTER THIRTY-TWO

The lock snapped and the door creaked open. Loren dashed inside the apartment to avoid being seen. He didn't need any witnesses to his movements. Enough doubts floated through his thoughts.

This was not a distraction he needed. With Death in Portents, his promises to Ruiz, and now his struggle to try and find some common ground with Soriya, Loren's dance card was full enough. But then there were the missing person's reports he had been saddled with by Mathers. A way to sideline him from the spotlight, something Loren never sought. A stack of files rested on his coffee table, their names and details ingrained in the detective's mind.

Now, with dawn only hours away, a new name found its way to the list.

Dominic.

Loren barely knew the man. He was a bartender and a friendly face. Nothing in their time together screamed anything more, yet Loren took comfort in the man's presence and felt concern at his sudden absence. Plenty of other possible explanations justified the man's actions. Maybe he truly did hate his job. He could have taken a sudden vacation or simply been a flake about informing his boss about using his sick days. Loren had no basis to judge, no real connection with the man to assume anything about his behavior.

Yet Loren decided to break into his apartment.

Ruiz called it obsession. With the same attention to detail that kept Beth's case plastered on his corkboard, the growing number of missing people had become his new fixation. It was important work, though, just like the current case plaguing the rest of the department. He needed to keep a hand in both.

If dedication meant a little breaking and entering, so be it.

Dominic lived in a small one-bedroom apartment. Loren noted the frigid temperatures, the air conditioning blasting. Loren peeked inside the full bath and noticed the almost overflowing bathtub, thankfully unoccupied.

"That would have been an awkward conversation starter," he whispered. He pulled out his flashlight and continued deeper into the place. His free hand rested next to his backup sidearm, just as a precaution.

He went through the place methodically. He had more stops to make, but something in the way the owner of McDuffie's spoke about his wayward employee worried Loren. Hell, everything worried Loren, but this was something he could actually handle now that Soriya had shut him out. Her action wouldn't stand, not with so much to do, but for the moment, Loren focused on the missing rather than the deceased.

The living room, the kitchen, and the bedroom were in pristine condition. Not a sock out of its drawer. No laundry piled up in the corner. Not a single dirty dish in the sink. Every book in its place, every Blu-ray filed. Too clean.

Suitcases remained in the man's closet, his drawers full of clothes. Even his toothbrush sat in its holder in the medicine cabinet. Dominic hadn't gone anywhere, yet remained nowhere to be seen. Something happened to him.

Loren stopped at the living room threshold on his second pass. Time was not on his side. No report existed on the missing bartender, no file opened by the authorities. Only Loren's instinct that there was more, some connection between those missing. What that might be remained obscured, lost in shadows.

Like the image tucked in the living room corner.

"What is that?"

A marking on the wall, scrawled in black. He inched closer, stopping at the sound of a phone ringing. It took him two rings to realize it was the phone at his hip. Looking at the display, not recognizing the number, Loren hesitated, then answered.

"Loren."

"Good. I was hoping this number still worked for you," a woman said. "Never know how often HR updates the personnel files."

Loren didn't recognize the voice. "Can I help you with something?"

"I pulled an 'it's me' without realizing it, didn't I?"

Loren turned up the speaker on the phone, trying to catch every word.

"It's Myers."

"Myers?"

"Yeah. Myers."

"Right. No. I know." Loren took a breath. *Do I call her Sam? Sammy?* And Ruiz thought that was a ridiculous question. "What's up?"

There was a long pause on the line. Loren looked over the sign on the wall. A warning. Another mystery, like the woman on the phone.

"I need your help, Loren."

CHAPTER THIRTY-THREE

The line went dead. Samantha Myers looked to the screen then sighed, tucking the phone away. "Right. You're welcome."

Not how she expected the call to go, but considering how she reacted at their first meeting, there was little surprise at the abrupt ending. Hady's possible involvement threatened to destroy any hope the detective had at making inroads with her colleagues. This was her chance to prove herself worthy, and turning the entire department against each other was not how she foresaw the investigation going.

Myers rounded the corner, the playground swings creaking eerily in step with her movements. The city had done its best to remove the playground from the grounds of the newly refurbished coroner's office, but the community rallied to keep it in place. Myers wondered if they had second thoughts considering the activity surrounding the building of late.

The parking lot was small, tucked behind the building. It made for a long trek that could have been avoided with the maintenance access and loading docks used for incoming transfers, but protocol made it impossible. Staffers were the only ones able to enter through any of the doors; visitors and officers were forced to walk around the brick building for the security doors at the front.

Pratchett sat in the cruiser, tapping steadily on the steering wheel. Myers paused at the edge of the lot, reconsidering their next move. A full shift with Pratchett felt like ten, with his driving and constant need to converse off-putting. Unfortunately, he was her only backup on the case by choice, but one she hoped to rectify with her phone call.

She wanted to call back, to secure a bond that didn't exist. Staring at her phone, she remembered the pudgy lab tech inside and cursed. Pratchett stared at her and stepped out of the cruiser.

"Myers?"

Myers started back to the front. "Hang on a second, big guy. Didn't give him my number."

"Who?" Pratchett asked.

Myers smiled at his jealous tone. "Don't worry about it!"

She rounded the corner and slid her access card through the reader. The light turned green, the door clicked open, and she ducked inside.

The door to the lab sat open and Myers jumped inside, afraid of Hady's presence down the hall. "Kid, I completely forgot to give you—"

Liam Schultz lay on the floor, wheezing from his nose. Unconscious. Looming over him was a dark-skinned young woman, brown eyes flaring at Myers' unexpected arrival.

"Hold it," Myers called out. Her gun slipped from the hip holster, settling in her grip.

"No, thanks." The woman dashed deeper into the room, Myers drawing on her.

"Don't even—"

The woman leaped into the air, kicking off the wall and catching the bottom of the hanging ceiling grate with one hand. With ease, she launched upward. Her legs looped into the vent, her body flowing in one graceful movement.

"—think about it," Myers finished.

She listened for movement in the vent, not surprised to hear it distantly and then not at all. The woman was fast. Much faster than she was prepared for, if one could prepare for something like that. For *someone* like that.

Soriya Greystone.

What the hell was she doing here? Myers crouched beside the fallen tech. The fridge in the back was opened and the reports she had left were missing.

"Dammit," Myers muttered. No samples and no files. A suspicious head coroner and a downed lab tech. Not to mention the mountain of bodies accumulating throughout the city. Part of Myers wondered if her need for control outweighed her common sense, if there was a better way to live.

She patted Liam's cheek, then struck him with heavier slaps to wake him up. The young man kicked his legs out as he sucked in a large breath, announcing his return with as much drama as possible. He grinned at her, his hands reaching to keep her close. She pushed away and the kid's head slammed to the ground.

"Ow," Liam said, rubbing the back of his head.

"Here." Myers tossed a nearby roll of paper towels over to him. He looked at her and she pointed to her nose and lips. "You're bleeding."

"Right. Another ow." He dabbed at the blood, wincing with each touch.

"It doesn't look broken at least."

"Lucky me," Liam said, fighting to stand. Myers kept her distance, pacing the room. "I need to go home and change."

Myers shook her head. "Or you could get those samples tested for me like we agreed."

"That lunatic took the samples," Liam snapped.

"We'll need new ones." It wasn't ideal. None of it was, but she needed the evidence.

"Let me get this straight," Liam started, staggering to the open lab door. He peered down the hall. "You want me to go to the autopsy theater, pull the bodies in question and run the preliminaries?"

"Exactly."

"Right next to the office of the woman that might be hiding a mass murderer? Can you see the problem I might have with that?"

Myers took a slow breath. She smiled at him, running her hand through her hair. "I can. I also don't give a damn. I need those samples, kid."

Liam Schultz sighed then nodded.

"Good," Myers said. She handed him a business card, her number in bold on the front. "Call me when it's done."

"You're leaving again?" His voice cracked as he spoke.

"No choice," Myers answered. She slipped by him for the hall. The lights flickered above, dimming then brightening. Late night personnel rushed up and down the hall, weary eyes falling on the line of bodies surrounding them. So many dead yet all centered on the five men in question. Five men connected by blood. Myers needed to learn more about that connection—and fast.

"Someone has to look up the rest of the family tree."

CHAPTER THIRTY-FOUR

What the hell are you doing?

The thought followed her from the coroner's office until she stopped running three blocks over. Away from the world atop a rooftop overlooking downtown Portents, Soriya took a moment to breathe.

And realized the mess she had made of everything.

She cradled the samples in her arms, looking them over one by one before tucking them in a pouch off her belt opposite the Greystone. *Follow the blood.* The damn raven's words came back to haunt her. She found the blood in question, cross-referencing the names on each tube with the files procured. She could have worked with the young man, learned the story behind the samples and the ramifications. She could have brought Loren with her.

Soriya Greystone did neither and in the process made a new enemy—a cop.

"What a damn mess," Soriya mumbled, kicking loose pebbles from the rooftop. Taking the samples and the files from the police gave her an exclusive on the information. At least, for the moment. It kept them safe. It kept Loren safe.

But what did it mean? Having the samples and the records were a start, but where to turn now? Despite her many talents, science was not her forte. Hell, anything grounded in reality seemed to be out of her reach of late, meaning science on any level was an impossibility. Mentor would know. Even with his edicts, his general rules of living in solitude, he would know where to turn.

Soriya sighed, resting against the wall of the adjacent building. Her body ached. Thirty-six hours without sleep caught up with her the instant she stopped to take that first breath. She needed to rest; she needed a moment's respite without having to think about the constant threat of Death, the Charon, the coin, and now her new cop friend chasing her down for her actions.

She needed Mentor.

Sliding to the ground, careful for the tubes resting along her side, Soriya reached into her pocket. She pulled out the image of Mentor, Christopher Eckhart, in his life before the one they shared. His smile brought her a joy she had not felt in longer than she cared to admit. His confidence beamed through the image, so clear in his convictions. Before he became her teacher and family.

Things were simpler with him. He kept her balanced, pushing her yet always there as a safety net. Now she had none, her only alternative pushed away to keep him out of harm's way.

Soriya groaned, the frustration behind her decisions becoming an irritant. She slammed the photo against her knees, Mentor's smiling face continuing to beam at her. She flipped it over, unwilling to lose another second in nostalgia. Then her eyes widened.

The note on the back. She had forgotten all about it.

Scrawled in black ink, worn by age, it took her a moment to read through it. The second time went quicker. The third was a race, her heart thrumming faster and faster. A note from the photographer but more.

A past connection will guide you back.

Kok'-Kol knew. More than just the significance of the blood and the possible connection linking some victims. He knew about the note on the image.

Christopher,
Thank you for opening my eyes to the truth. We will change the world.
Your friend,
"Professor" Erikson

Soriya stood, holding the image so tight the corners crumpled under her fingers. Mentor trusted him, this past connection. He considered him a friend and a confidant.

To Soriya, he was a place to start. Exactly what she needed.

CHAPTER THIRTY-FIVE

His coffee was cold. Alejo Ruiz sat at the kitchen table, hands clasped to the cup. On the side was a photo of his three kids smiling, the words *Number One Dad* printed beside the image. His favorite mug.

Better days. Much better days than those of late.

Even home, Ruiz was alone. Sleep continued to be a struggle, no matter the exhaustion tucked under his eyes. No matter the length of time awake, rest remained out of reach.

His family followed suit. The girls were off from school. Michelle booked a substitute for her classroom for the whole week. No use pretending things were going to turn around for the girls, Angela in particular. She screamed through the night, ever since she had seen the dead body of her pastor. Teresa did her best to comfort her sister, sleeping on the pullout bed beside her.

Both parents stalked the halls at night, protectors against the dark world closing in around them. Separately, though—never together. Few words passed between them. They were unable to find the right way into a conversation, the perfect words to reaffirm the bond they once shared. Blame rested in his wife's eyes, resentment at the growing silence over the years. He had no argument against her feelings.

He felt the same damn thing.

He spent the better part of the last two decades fighting against the city's secret nature. The true city, Soriya Greystone called it. He hated the moniker, struggling to keep it away from his life, working tirelessly to distance his family from the strange things that went bump in the night. Until the true city came crashing down on them.

It was his one job in this world—a silent vow when he learned the truth about Portents. When his wife gave birth to the first of three beautiful daughters, he made the decision to protect them from the truth. He would keep them all safe and let them have the normal life he still believed possible even with all he experienced in his work over the years. Nothing would stop his kids from living and loving life, right here in the city of his birth. Their city. Only, it wasn't their city at all. No matter what he did, the distance grew between them.

He should have been at work. Deep down he understood his role at home as a necessity. His family needed him, now more than ever. His absences, however, cemented his separation from the rest of his loved ones. The unspoken anger in Michelle's eyes, frustration and sadness built up from the great divide he created almost right from the beginning. The constant questions from his daughters, wanting to be there for him and no longer knowing how, thanks to his time away.

Work, though, was where he could do something, *anything*, to end this nightmare. The disconnect was one thing. To not know what was occurring at work was another. His thoughts, his worries and mounting concerns, circled around in his mind.

And now his coffee was cold.

A knock at the door made everything irrelevant. His doubts, his nightmares, the circling thoughts of failure and disconnect. Even the coffee cradled in his hands. Everything faded at the sound of the man knocking at his back door.

Ruiz stood, wiping the exhaustion from his eyes.

"How bad is it?" Ruiz asked the waiting Greg Loren.

The detective said nothing at first, wiping his feet before entering the Ruiz home. Ruiz closed the door and circled back to his coffee. He made a silent offer to his companion who turned it down.

Loren told him everything: the walking Death among them, the trip to a hidden library containing the secrets of the city, including the arrival of another member of the Death family, this time that of a mythical Charon, the creature that killed Edgar.

Loren told him about the bowling alley and the mountain of bodies found there. The connection found at the scene, the hidden link of some of the victims uncovered by Myers came next. Then the final known piece.

That Hady Ronne might be involved in the whole affair.

It was enough to make a man crumble, to tuck into a ball and cower in the corner waiting for the world to right itself, yet knowing it never would, knowing that sometimes the world changes and you either change with it or leave it—permanently.

Ruiz wanted to question it all—the information from Myers, the circumstances with Hady. With that last bit of information he realized what brought Loren to his door. *Because* of the questions that had to be asked.

His breakfast fell into the garbage can, his cold coffee dumped down the sink. Ruiz reached for his coat. Loren offered a sad smile before departing for the driveway. Ruiz grabbed the keys to the van and moved for the door.

Turning back, he saw Michelle. She stood outside their bedroom, alone. Her eyes screamed for him, pulled at him to stay—to make things right, and to be the husband and father he promised to be so long ago.

He wanted to explain, run to her and hug her close, tell her the truth about Portents and the nightmares in the dark. Everything. But it would never help, not really.

The only way to help was by being out there. Where he was needed. Ruiz's eyes fell away. *After Hady. After this case*, he would be there, part of his family's life again. It was the same promise he always made, the promise he never kept, allowing their divide to widen further with each passing moment.

She only needed a word from him, a minute of his time to show her he was still with her and would be forever. But it would never be enough. Not to wipe away the secrets and the lies from so many years.

Not anymore.

Without a word, Alejo Ruiz listened to the door slam shut behind him.

CHAPTER THIRTY-SIX

Liam Schultz was not a happy man. In a sea of discontent, Liam found nothing satisfying with his current employment prospects, present or forthcoming. Instead, a stream of unending corpses filled his vision, more by the hour. And his reprieve from the night? Not an early shift, letting him see the daylight for the first time all week. Not a night off to enjoy some Dungeons and Dragons with friends he hadn't seen in over a month despite living with most of them.

No, his reward involved sneaking behind his boss' back.

Edgar Rusch's body sat on the slab before him. Liam finished pulling another vial of blood for testing, adding it to the other samples taken from the fallen pastor. Above, the lights hummed, the constant noise making his eyes grow heavy.

The detective had been right, though. If these samples led to a connection between the five victims hidden in the mass of bodies lining the halls, then it might help find the killer. That was supposed to be his job, wasn't it?

If Hady Ronne, or Doctor Death as she was called, conspired to hide evidence, this was the last place he wanted to be found. This was her domain.

To Liam it made little sense. If his boss wanted to steer the investigation away from these victims, there were easier ways to do it. Why hide them? Why take the chance of discovery when you could destroy them and the accompanying paperwork instead of letting them fall into police hands?

And why the hell did he have to be involved in it at all?

Liam sighed. Enough needed to be done without a wild goose chase, though it appeared more like a witch hunt centered on his boss. Still, Liam was little more than a grunt in the coroner's office.

He had barely earned his lab coat. Now, with college debt crippling any chance of living alone this decade, Liam took his job into his hands by working against his boss…who might be harboring a murderer.

Damn that good-looking detective.

But if Doctor Death *was* involved? If she was ousted and say, a strapping young lad found the connection and brought it to light? A promotion would be nice. One that afforded him more time at home and away from the Hershey bars in the vending machine down the hall.

Liam grinned at the thought. Coroner Liam Schultz. A hope tucked under the autopsy room's flickering lights. His gloves snapped and another tube of blood joined the rest on the metal table beside the slab. *Only a few more to go.*

He stopped at the sound of the doors opening behind him. Liam covered the samples with his discarded gloves, keeping his focus on the body as much as possible.

"Doctor Ronne?" he called, without looking. "I was just finishing up some tests on—"

The lights dimmed, the humming becoming more erratic. Liam jumped as a light popped on the far side of the room.

"We should really get that looked at," he joked, his voice cracking. "I'll be done and out of the way in one—"

When he turned, he expected the plump woman he had called boss for the last two years. He expected to be reprimanded for his presence, for skirting procedure and not filing the correct paperwork before performing his work. He expected to cower and take his punishment, hoping and praying she didn't see the samples, that she didn't fire him on the spot.

However, he was not met by Hady Ronne at all. In the last moment, before the lights flickered then faded to darkness, he did more than hope and pray at the massive presence lumbering toward him.

Liam Schultz screamed.

CHAPTER THIRTY-SEVEN

"What do you mean they aren't in the system?"

Myers tapped her foot in a steady beat against the leg of the metal chair. She clenched her jaw, feeling her teeth grind against each other. It was all she could do to stop from screaming at the young woman across from her, happy and oblivious to her mounting rage.

Frankie Gibson, her name as bubbly as the gum snapping between her lips, slammed on the keyboard. Her hair screamed in hot pink highlights and tattoos adorned her lower neck, poking out from her shirt. She turned the monitor to Myers, the search results blaring on the screen as loudly as the detective's thoughts.

Frankie cocked her head to the side and blew an enormous bubble. "Well, I could rephrase it but—"

"Where the hell are they?" Myers said through gritted teeth.

Frankie pulled a pencil from behind her ear and twirled it between her fingers. Another annoying habit. They were stacking up and Myers had only been seated across from the woman at the Child Services Center of Downtown Portents for fifteen minutes.

With Loren in play to question Hady directly and the lab samples lost to a vigilante thief with replacements hours away, Myers was left with one option.

The family tree.

The five in question came from some genetic link, the results listed clearly in Hady's hidden findings. Same age, same gender, same ethnicity, all lined up with one solution.

Adoption.

Dozens of agencies operated throughout the city. All kept their records centralized at the CSC hub, a cubicle nightmare if ever Myers saw one. Requisition forms made up the first hour of her visit, Pratchett humming a tune the entire time.

After the paperwork nightmare came the waiting game. Frankie Gibson was the resident system's expert and came in to assist when the initial inquiries brought back a total of bupkus. Now the so-called expert joined in with the same lack of results.

"If they aren't here?" Frankie clicked her tongue. Myers watched the wad of gum flow back and forth behind the woman's teeth. She tapped her foot faster.

"Yes."

"The cloud? Digital paradise?" Frankie shook her head, leaning close. "The only ones who have access are government employees. The clearance required is, well, it isn't handed out lightly. I only know a few with—"

She stopped, looking behind Myers. The scowling detective turned to join her stare. At the end of the cubicle, a tall man chuckled.

"What's so funny this time, Pratchett?"

Pratchett held his side, fighting to hold his laughter. "Sorry. Just… Digital paradise." They stared at him in confusion. He motioned with his fingers, his eyes watering. "Little files sitting on a beach of ones and zeroes, drinking…" He stopped, his face suddenly dead serious. "What do you think they would be drinking?"

Frankie Gibson snorted. Myers refused to look at her.

"Do. I. Care?"

"Maybe?" Pratchett said with a shrug. "Sorry. I'll wait over here."

He headed for the lobby. Frankie followed him with her eyes, twirling her pencil faster and faster between her fingers. Myers snapped her back with a slap to the desk.

"Now listen, I.T. lady from hell—"

"Frankie," the woman corrected without looking.

Myers groaned. "I need the records on these four gentlemen. According to his file, Edgar Rusch was adopted from the Evans Halfway Home. It stands to reason the others were as well and I need them—"

"Evans?"

Myers stopped. "Is there an echo?"

Frankie opened the drawer to her desk and pulled out a sheet of paper. "There might be a way to get the records."

"Do I have to guess?"

"Huh?" Frankie asked, confused. Myers pointed to the blank sheet. "Oh. No." She scribbled then tore the piece in half. "Here."

Myers looked at the paper. It held a name and an address, the latter she recognized. "This is Evans Halfway Home."

"Yup."

"I came here for the information. Why the hell would it be—?"

"Herman can help you. But you might regret asking the question."

She did. She regretted more than the question. Samantha Myers regretted every choice in her life that led to this moment. From her mistake in New York City to her time with Mathers, the assignment at Central and the case in general. *Regret* wasn't the right word anymore. What Myers felt was lodged between mania and blistering rage.

Herman Kampe, the main contact at the Evans Halfway Home, had worked at the residence for the better part of forty years. Most of the work done at the home had been taken over by other branches and agencies in the city, the orphaned numbering less and less thanks to community efforts.

Herman was a relic, shuffling through the dungeon-style basement of the home, his office. Seventy years old going on 200, Myers and Pratchett could only stand in awe at the man's boundless enthusiasm and complete lack of speed.

"Nope." Herman slammed another filing cabinet shut. The third one of the afternoon, time rapidly slipping away from the frustrated detective and her slapstick comedian of a sidekick. "Not this one either."

"Can we help?" Three might have been knocked off the list but according to the great mind of Herman Kampe, a man long since the appropriate point of retirement, 157 more units occupied the room.

"Please?" Pratchett begged. He jingled the keys to his patrol car, cocking his head to his partner. Myers shook her head. No way in hell was she sitting through this one alone.

Herman shrugged their impatience off, shuffling for the next unit. He tapped his head. "No fancy computers when I started down here. Just the ol' noggin."

Getting older by the second. Or the hour at this pace.

Myers pointed to the station in the corner of the room. The desktop computer appeared to be a decade out of date, the old style monitor hogging half of the workspace. "What about that?"

"Never turned it on. City couldn't be bothered to teach and I didn't care to learn. Don't trust them."

"Skynet," Pratchett muttered.

Myers sighed, hands on her hips. "Pratchett, we talked about this."

"Right. Sorry."

Another unit closed with a loud creak. "Doesn't look like this one did much good either, Detective. Now, if you wanted to find out about the Burroughs boy who grew up to become a congressman in the nineties, this would be the file for you. That boy was something else, I tell you. A real terror." He cackled, slapping at the metal cabinet. "Even worse in Washington from what I heard, not that I hear much of that stuff but if you were to ask me I wouldn't be surprised about that kind of thing."

"Don't care."

Herman stopped. He cupped his ear. "What's that?"

"I. DON'T—"

Pratchett coughed. "We're looking for five names. Not just Edgar Rusch."

"Five brothers." Myers nodded a silent thanks to Pratchett then turned back to Herman. They started with Edgar, believing the search would be simple. Herman had proved easy was in the eye of the beholder.

"Five brothers?" Herman rubbed his chin. He raised a finger, readying another tale from yesteryear.

"YES," Myers yelled over him. "Five brothers! And no, I don't want to hear how you once knew five brothers that performed in the circus that came through town every October and how you used to assist them with their trapeze act and sometimes they let you wear the tights and it made you feel oh, so pretty and one day you actually stole them and sometimes you wear them under your clothes when you come to work and DON'T DO YOUR JOB!"

Dumbfounded stares followed her as Myers rushed from the room, slamming the door behind her. The booming sound echoed in the long basement hallway of the orphanage. Myers sucked in a deep breath and held it, trying to slow her pulse. Behind her, the door opened and Pratchett stepped out. He grimaced, fighting to find the right words.

"Wow."

"Not a word, Pratchett," she said.

"Not a circus fan, I take it?"

"What did I say?" Myers groaned, running her hands deep into her thick black locks, pulling them back hard. "What the hell is wrong with everyone in this city?"

"You sure it's everyone else?"

Myers shot him a thin glare. "Subtle."

Pratchett smiled. "Not my strong suit."

"I'm aware. I've seen you drive, remember?"

Pratchett cocked his head, hands to his hips as he paced the hallway. "What is it? I mean, you can keep ripping everyone's face off—Mathers, Ruiz, the good looking woman at the CSC—"

"Good looking woman?" Myers asked, catching his grin at the mention of Frankie Gibson. "She gave you her number, didn't she?"

"Yes," Pratchett answered, then shook his head. "Don't deflect. You've pushed everyone away on this. The entire department has a vested interest in finding this son of a bitch but you've put it squarely on your back. Why?"

Myers let out a long breath, gnawing on her bottom lip. "I screwed up. In New York. The city, not upstate. I know that's a thing with people. Never mind.

"My father taught me one thing in this world, Pratchett. Control yourself—your body, your intentions, everything in full view—and you control your world. He did it his way and paid the price. I learned enough from him to be better. Not only control for me but control over others. Reading people. Manipulating people. I was the youngest detective in my department. I was the top profiler in my district. Recruiters from the FBI were calling me for interviews. Turned out I was just as wrong as my old man was."

"What happened, Myers?"

"Hostage situation. Everyone was working on the case, running leads to track down where the bastard was hiding. I found him first."

"And went at it alone."

Myers nodded. "Absolutely. I knew enough about the guy. Divorced, unemployed. He was more scared than violent. I didn't take into account his desperation. When I went in, I figured I could talk him down.

"He had a gun. I didn't see it until it was too late. He killed all the hostages because I walked in there to talk. I never even made it in the room before it was over. Four women lost their lives."

"And the guy?"

"Killed himself," Myers said. "He wasn't supposed to have a gun, Pratchett. Not in a million years should he have had a gun."

"That's why you're here? In Portents?"

"I was censured immediately. No more calls for advancement. No more cases without strict oversight, until it was clear they would never trust me ever again. Just like I never trusted them."

Pratchett sighed. "Looks like you didn't learn a damn thing then."

She turned to him. "Excuse me?"

"You're doing it again, aren't you?"

She paused. He was right. Of course he was. It was clear from the moment the case came in. From her manipulation of Mathers in making her lead on the case, to her inability to work with the resources at her disposal. Even pushing Pratchett at every turn.

"You're not alone in this, Myers," Pratchett continued. "You have to trust in that, at least."

"I don't," Myers said. "I keep trying, keep thinking I can, but I don't."

"Maybe it's up to us to prove it to you." He reached for the door back into the records room. "Shall we?"

Myers grinned, heading inside. She stopped next to the towering officer. "She really gave you her number?"

"Why is that so hard to believe?" Myers turned to reply and he stopped her. "Don't answer that."

Myers laughed and patted his chest. "She's going to eat you alive."

Herman Kampe stood before an open cabinet on the far side of the room. He reached into the waiting drawer and pulled out a large file.

"Sorry about that, Herman. I shouldn't have—"

"Seven," Herman said, dropping the file in front of them.

"Seven?"

Herman nodded. "Never had any cases of five brothers here at Evans. Not in the seventy-five years it's been around. But around fifty years ago, before my time, there was a story of seven brothers here. Seven sons. They were called that at any rate."

"Seven sons," Myers whispered.

"You say there were five brothers?"

"Murdered," Myers said. "Yes."

Herman held out the file. "Sounds like there are two more out there."

CHAPTER THIRTY-EIGHT

Jeremy Bennett dreamed.

In the dream, which ran every time he closed his weary eyes, there was always a woman. Young and beautiful. Stark black hair that ran down her back. Her hazel eyes shone against the blue dress she wore. She danced before him, smiling and beaming to an audience of one.

All for him, always for him, like he had known her his whole life. The truth, however, was that she was a stranger. Not some famous actress from television. Not the woman at the convenience store down the street. No one from his waking life, yet in his dreams she was more real than the world he occupied.

Always dancing for him.

Then the dream shifted. The dance ended the same as it always did—from laughter echoing in his ears to screams. The blue dress replaced with an apron. No, a hospital gown.

Positioned on a bed in the center of the room, the young woman with the shining black hair and the perfect smile shouted to the world, announcing her pain. But there was no comfort offered. No words of support. No hands from the shadows surrounding her. Nothing to help.

In the dream there was nothing but her eyes filling the great screen behind Jeremy Bennett's sleeping lids. Within the deep hazel orbs of light a child reflected back, crying over her own screams. She held him tight, the newborn flailing in her grip.

More cries, a chorus of sounds, filled the room. And the eyes, green as emeralds when the light hit them just right, opened wide and never blinked again. The first infant clutched tight to the woman's hand, and then others joined him, swarming over the unmoving form on the hospital bed. More children.

Seven of them.

"Dad."

Jeremy Bennett woke with a start. The rocking chair nearly tipped from the sudden movement, his hands falling hard against his knees to steady himself. He panted, the aches and pains of the world returning as quickly as the dream faded from memory.

Another mid-morning nap. The newspaper sat unopened beside his chair, the only one on his home's front porch. He had every intention of catching up on the news before working in the yard. The weeds were taking over the garden again. The car needed washing as well, but adding to the list amounted to disappointment by the end of the day.

When he sat on the chair, though, his eyes grew heavy. The exhaustion returned, the same as it had for the last few weeks. Multiple naps during the day, followed by a staggered but extensive night of sleep. All showing the same dream behind his eyes.

"Dad!"

It faded from view, escaping with the sound of his daughter's cries. Who was the woman haunting his dreams? It wasn't his wife, who had been dead these past eight years. His wife, who filled him with such joy and hope in his heart.

Jeremy fought to stand. His knees popped.

"Coming," he said, rubbing the pain away while shuffling for the front door. "I'm coming."

The wood under his feet creaked with each step, the house feeling its age just the same as its owner. *Too soon*, he thought. Not even fifty and already Jeremy Bennett saw it in his slower gait, his slumping posture. The wheels of time. Yet, there was still too much to do. Too many people that needed him.

Natalie peered through the screen door, hands to her hips. Twenty-six years old yet with the responsibility of a woman twice her age, she glowered at him and his weary eyes.

"You were sleeping again," she said—a statement, not a question. "You feeling all right?"

He stretched his back. It popped louder than his knees. "Resting my eyes. Big difference."

"To you maybe," she said. She stepped out on the porch and the screen slammed into place behind her. Her apron was crooked and her hair threatened to escape the hastily constructed bun at the back of her head. "Jack is—"

"Not resting," Jeremy chided. He knew his seven-year-old grandson, having cared for him his entire life. Being home sick was an excuse to steal time for video games and comic books. "More likely playing in his room rather than trying to feel better. And you're working. Go. Work."

"Are you sure you're—?"

He smiled wider, fighting back the dream and the exhaustion. "Work."

She sighed, thumbing open her purse while racing down the stairs toward her well worn sedan. "I'm going."

"Nat." Jeremy opened the screen, reaching in for the hook on the wall.

"Right," she said, hopping back up the stairs, still trying to thumb through the pile of receipts and wrappers in her purse. She stopped and hugged him close, delivering a small peck to his cheek. "Love you, Dad."

"Damn right you do," he said. "But I was talking about these."

He held out the car keys for her. The overburdened single mother slapped her forehead then snatched the keys.

"Thank you," she said. "Leftovers are in the fridge for lunch. Homework when he's up and then television."

"I always mix those up. Food's not in the television?"

She leaned against the car. "Funny man. Give him a kiss for me. Like he cares."

"He does," Jeremy replied. "We do."

She smiled, needing to hear it from someone. She worked too hard, pushed too hard to make things perfect for her son and for him. He should have been the one, but after his long-term disability dried up, he could do little to contribute to the mounting pressures that came with raising a family and keeping a home. Helping with Jack was the next best thing, and the only thing that shouldered some of the responsibility weighing down his daughter.

The car sped out of the driveway, almost clipping the delivery van stopped across the street. Natalie waved, speeding down Loyola for work. *Always late.*

Jeremy waited a long breath, wondering what else might have been forgotten. When the car turned for the expressway he counted to five before turning around, heading for the door.

Jack waited inside and the old man smiled at his grandson through the screen. Seven years old and skinny as a rail, Jack wore a baseball cap with Spider-Man on the rim to match his Marvel pajamas.

"Mom going to work?" he asked, his eyes glowing.

"For a few hours, yes," Jeremy answered, stepping inside. "I thought you were resting."

"I was."

"Uh-huh," Jeremy laughed. He reached for the object hiding behind Jack's back. His grandson handed over the remote control, and both shared a grin. "Cartoons?"

Jack nodded. Jeremy patted his back, prodding him to the waiting couch. The dream disappeared and with it the pain and aches of age.

"Cartoons it is."

CHAPTER THIRTY-NINE

The car roared to life, the muffler weeks away from the scrapyard with little chance of a replacement in the aging vehicle's future—what future remained.

The young brunette behind the wheel shifted the sedan into reverse and slammed on the accelerator. Then her brakes blared as she approached the end of the driveway and the delivery truck stopped across the way. Her eyes raced over to the passenger seat, finding her phone in her jacket's breast pocket. A woman frustrated, mostly with her own second-guessing, she cursed under her breath before resuming her journey.

The sedan sped down the one-lane thoroughfare for downtown. The woman kept her eyes focused though her lips joined the catchy pop song on the radio, the same one that would be on every local station within the hour.

Her mind, so focused on the day ahead—and the chorus of the future one-hit wonder—Natalie Bennett never noticed the man sitting on the bench at the corner of her block. Neither had her father, who fell asleep despite the early hour. Neither glimpsed the man watching them.

That was how Death saw them, his bowler hat blocking all view of the deep lines circling his cheeks and his eyes of liquid blue diamond. Small lives, yet now more important to him than any in the city.

The man in the three-piece suit stood, circling the bench. The single floor domicile across the street, home to the Bennett family for over twenty years wore the badge of honor in the form of bent gutters and cracked siding. The home honored the members living within its brick structure with its orange spotlight hanging from the garage and the icicle lights long since out of season.

A small place for small lives, not the great streets of Uruz or the Cedar Mountain. The places that forged him, that tempered him, yet still failed to save him. No, these were smaller places yet more a home than he ever knew in life. Or desired. Not during his years in the world. His ambitions were greater, his dreams wider in scope. Yet he stood in this place, admiring the view of a small home—the Bennett home.

And Jeremy Bennett.

He recognized it the moment he caught his first glimpse of the man. Noticed it in his tired eyes and found the spark in the dream running behind his closed lids. Jeremy Bennett was a marked man. The same as the others.

Except different to the man in the suit. Why?

How can you just stand around and watch this happen? The Greystone's question rocked him, shattering the journey and its eventual conclusion. The conclusion was all he wanted. The ending he sought for so long—longer than time allowed him to consider.

Did it matter how the end came as long as it did? Soriya's question told a different story. As did his reaction.

"Such a small home," he muttered, securing his hat to his head. The delivery truck skirted down the road, blocking the home from view. Death saw enough. He knew enough about what was about to occur. Of the ending to come for Jeremy Bennett.

The final target.

CHAPTER FORTY

The hall was devoid of life. The clicking of the lock, the loud boom of the door opening into the coroner's office that had once been an elementary school, echoed throughout the building. Loren winced, his card slipping into the breast pocket of his jacket now resting on his arm. Ruiz followed close, weary from the events taking their toll on his languishing sleep schedule.

Their drive over from Venture Cove was plagued with awkward silence. Loren didn't push the conversation, letting the man coast along the inner city streets without the distraction. Numerous minivan jokes were prepared but he put them away, allowing his mind to drift to the local scenery. There would be plenty of time for chatting after the fact. Once questions were settled with Hady Ronne over the mixed-up results found by Detective Myers, they could all laugh about the whole situation and get back to the business of catching a murderer.

The Charon, Loren thought. *Not a murderer. A monster.*

The door shunted to a close, the scrapping metal grinding in their ears. Both men turned back, waiting for silence to return. Ruiz insisted on the upgraded system, keycard access to enter and depart the facility. Hady never considered security a necessity even with the number of kids playing in the field less than fifty yards away, yet Ruiz pushed for the system. A failsafe with the department separated from the inclusive nature of the Rath Building.

"I could wait in the car," Loren whispered as the pair started down the hall. Both men peered down the L-shaped structure. Only one door was opened, that being the service closet at the end of the hall. Everything else was closed off, no sound escaping the series of labs and viewing rooms down both branches of the building. There was no personnel present. Odd, considering the bodies lining the walls, each on a separate gurney awaiting testing.

"You dragged me here," Ruiz said, his thoughts matching Loren's.

"You want me to ask Hady some questions?" The answer was obvious, though Ruiz's glare confirmed the sentiment. "That's what I thought."

"Leave the snark outside."

"Me?" Loren asked, hand to his heart. "I'm a professional."

"Professional ass."

Loren slipped a stick of gum between his lips, then pocketed the wrapper. He snapped the watermelon flavored crutch at Ruiz with a smile. *Filthy habit.* Ruiz turned away in disgust, his point made. The detective settled down, his steps slow along the tile in the long hallway.

"I hate this place. I spend too much time here."

"We all have lately," Ruiz said, looking down at the covered corpses.

"Sorry, Ruiz, I shouldn't have asked—"

"You were right to get me. If there is a connection and Hady knew about it… I can't even imagine what the hell that means, to tell you the truth."

"You could have told Michelle."

"Told her what?" Ruiz pulled at Loren's arm. "Seriously, Greg, what the hell should I be telling my wife?"

Loren could see the hurt in his friend's eyes, the exhaustion from the job and now the tragedy of losing someone so close. Having Hady involved on some level, any level, was enough to break the bank that was Ruiz's steely reserve. He didn't need Loren adding to the problem list. Still, the grumbling detective pushed.

"She lost a friend too."

"Later," Ruiz said, moving for the office at the end of the hall. He stopped outside, hand poised to knock along the glass on the top half. Loren stood behind him, chewing on his gum. Ruiz sighed then tapped the glass twice. His hand turned the knob, the door pausing at the sight of a shadow in the distance. "Hady?"

"Go away," a voice called out of the darkness. Her shadow leaned on the desk, hands outstretched to fully support her weight.

Loren opened his mouth and Ruiz stopped him with a single finger. He shoved Loren aside and took a deep breath. They didn't need Hady upset right from the start. That would come later when the questioning began.

"It's Alejo. I just want to talk."

"I…" A groan escaped her lips. "I need to finish something."

"I can wait."

"No," she croaked, shaking her head.

"It's important, Hady. I wouldn't be here if it wasn't."

Hady, hunched over in shadow, let out a low grunt and nodded.

Loren nudged Ruiz toward the autopsy room, the captain concerned for one of his oldest friends. Hady Ronne earned the respect of the department a dozen times over for her diligence at the job, but definitely not for her social skills.

The pair slipped into the lab, the double doors swinging behind them. No personnel again, but plenty of bodies on display. Loren took the lead, dropping his coat on a nearby tray, then immediately lifted it up, wondering if the instruments below had been cleaned.

He turned back to the door and the worried eyes of Ruiz. "She's charming as always."

"Snark?" Ruiz asked. He rubbed his eyes and took off his jacket.

Loren threw up his hands. "Packing it away. Sorry."

Ruiz peered around, lifting up the cover on the body closest to the door before letting the sheet fall back. "I figured this place would be swarming with personnel."

"I've been thinking the same thing," Loren said, shuffling deeper into the room. Bodies lay on various gurneys in the center. One was Jacob Gephart, a name recognized from his call with Myers. "Maybe they're retrieving bodies still? There were a lot, I heard."

"From Myers."

Loren stopped. "Yeah. Why?"

Ruiz shrugged. "Nothing."

"Then what's with the look?"

"I don't trust her."

"I don't need protection, dad," Loren replied with a smirk. "She called about Hady and let it slip."

"Against Mathers' orders."

"Another reason to give her a chance. At least someone is keeping me in the loop."

"Soriya?"

Loren shook his head, letting out a long breath. An entire day had passed since their time at the Library of the Luminaries. Plenty of time for her to regroup and reconsider their strategy on taking down a seemingly out-of-control avatar of Death with another hiding in the shadows.

It wasn't like her to dismiss him completely. On some level they both recognized each half of their unique dynamic as necessary for the whole. He legitimized her approach, while she provided him with new avenues of thought to better solve the crimes investigated. It worked for them.

"Not a peep." Loren looked over Gephart's cooling body, the man's charred eyes burning into his memory. "Soriya's scared. This scares her."

"Which scares you."

"Exactly."

Ruiz hesitated. "Something else?"

"Not sure," Loren sighed. He turned away from the body only to face another and then another. Bodies everywhere and no answers in sight. "After Evans, I thought everything would be easier. With everyone."

He regretted saying the words the second he finished. It was selfish and stupid, yet always in the back of his mind. Ruiz had enough going on to think about Loren's solitude.

"Takes time, Greg," he said. "But everything is change. Not always good change."

He was thinking about Edgar Rusch. Loren thought about Beth, always Beth. Death was running unleashed around the city, set free by some unseen hand carrying a centuries-old coin. Death hung over them all. There was no guarantee they would walk away from this one. Loren never thought about it that way before. Beth's case was always in front of him, the answers just out of reach. It was impossible to think of anything else. And now? The cold embrace of Death hung over him from his earlier library visit, the chill up his spine and the darkness that had infected his entire being. His time might be up.

But not without a fight.

"We'll find out who did this." A silent prayer for the dead ran through his heavy thoughts.

Ruiz nodded. "The Charon, you said?"

"So I've been told."

Both smirked. The idea that they could casually talk about a mythological figure struck them as dismally amusing. Loren moved for another gurney. He didn't remove the cover, noting Edgar Rusch's name on the tag. "So much death. And for what?"

"Hopefully Hady has some answers."

"Ruiz," Loren started then paused before asking, his earlier promise making him rethink his phrasing. "Do you really think Hady—?"

"We'll ask the question," Ruiz interrupted. "Same as why she left those reports for Myers to find."

The door swung open and a shuffling of feet entered the room.

"You should have left," Hady Ronne grumbled under her breath, her voice deep and distant.

Loren kept his mouth shut, fighting back his patented sarcasm, though he had a few choice one-liners on his tongue. He kept inching to the next slab. Myers mentioned a tech being involved but he was nowhere to be found.

The sole of Loren's sneaker caught something on the floor. Loren bent to see what it was under the dimming lights of the room. *A business card.* He looked over the lettering adorning the front and the name at the top.

Samantha Myers.

"What the hell?"

"We couldn't, Hady," Ruiz said, inching for the door, eyes still on the victims in the room. "We had some questions."

"Ruiz," Loren called from the far side of the room. He stood, noticing the body on the gurney before him. Thick fingers and a burgeoning gut. Nothing like the other five bodies. Loren's heart pounded in his ears. He lifted the sheet off the body and immediately went for his gun. A young man, half the age of the other five, lay on the metal bed. The same scorched eyes and discoloration of the chest but neither distracted from the white lab coat or the ID card hanging from his breast pocket.

LIAM SCHULTZ. MEDICAL EXAMINER TECHNICIAN.

"Get away from her, Ruiz!" Loren cried.

Ruiz spun back to the door, his heels squealing. "Hady?"

The black tendrils of hair were Hady's, but they ran longer, covering her face—though not enough to hide the scabbed-over empty eye sockets. Her cheeks, once plump, sunk in like she were sucking on a lemon. Her fingers stretched out like claws from extended arms, almost like an ape rather than a woman. Her swollen bosom hung low, tucked under the lab coat and ID of Hady Ronne.

Hady, however, was no longer present.

Only *the Charon* remained.

CHAPTER FORTY-ONE

The damn raven knew. All his talk of past connections and following the blood, all signs of where she should have been looking. Instead, Soriya Greystone failed to listen—as usual. Her head was lost in the players, the background drama threatening to overtake her at every turn.

Death, the Medusa coin, the Greystone itself—all swirling around in her mind. How did they all relate? What was happening in the city of Portents?

She made a mistake with Loren, believing things could be the way they were. Taking him through the library was the epitome of reckless, the encounter with Death solidifying her feelings. Loren almost died. He could have tripped any number of security measures throughout the library. And then to rush headfirst toward Death? Damn Loren, always charging through places like a bull in a nuclear power plant. Waiting for the explosion to occur, always surprised when it did.

Nothing would happen to him, of course. She refused to let it—not after his long road back into the world and not after giving her so much over the years.

She was alone now, the way Mentor wanted it. Why she doubted his words after so many years remained a question she would never be able to answer. Too much danger infested the city, too much happening too rapidly, and putting others in the line of fire was no longer an option. This was her task and she would do it no matter the cost.

Which appeared to be adding up. Her time with Death gave her a clue to the connection between some of the victims involved. *Follow the blood.* Kok'-Kol's warning returned. Her stop at the coroner's office was a necessity. Her actions, however, brought new concerns.

Desperation marked her course. Stealing the samples from the tech, almost coming to blows with that detective? Putting the police at odds with her work was not a good position from which to work, but she did everything in her power to achieve such a dynamic. How long before Loren would be forced to choose between her and the department? How long before any hope of allies faded and she was truly alone in the city?

She paused, thinking. Did any of it matter as long as the job came first? As long as a killer ended up caught before they acted again? As long as Portents was secured and the Medusa coin destroyed? There was Soriya's answer, and then there was the right answer. She hoped they would line up someday. Soon.

"How much longer?" she asked, wringing her hands. The blood samples rested in a small bag beside her folding chair. The hallway was empty except for a young man working on a laptop at a small desk along the right wall. A series of classrooms lined both sides of the hall, stretching down the long corridor.

The note on the back of the photo brought her to Portents University, where Mentor once worked before walking away from the world. Professor Erikson was a genius, working as a consultant with the police on a number of occasions over the years. He was a renowned hematologist—he studied blood.

A past connection will guide you.

"Shouldn't be long now," Derek Carruthers said. He eyed her eagerly, drawing out his words to keep from heading back to his work. She noticed his long stares that ignored the cuts and bruises along her hands and cheeks, running up her long legs and tight shirt instead.

Derek introduced himself as Erikson's aide. It sounded professional enough, but he said it with a side of disdain and impunity. Soriya didn't understand the dynamic between aide and professor but something told her it did not typically work this way.

"Shouldn't you be in there?" She kept her voice soft, her smile present. Anything to throw off her discomfort.

"Me?" He shook his head. "It's just a conference and I'm basically a paper pusher for the man. Don't get me wrong, I can keep up with the guy on theory but it's not my major, you know?"

"No." Majors and minors and everything in between—none fit in Soriya's world. Of course, nothing seemed to lately.

"Where are you from again?" Derek asked, turning away from his computer. His leering eyes grew ravenous. She tried to look away, peering down the hall. "Definitely not a student."

"Prospective student," she lied.

"For Erikson? No surprise there."

"Why do you say that?"

"Let's just say the doc's reputation has been on the decline for awhile now. Ever since he got sick. I mean, have you read his last few papers?"

She had. Her research had been quick but thorough. Erikson had left the mainstream after a bout with a serious illness. Before that, his research stood at the forefront of modern medicine. Cancer research, hard science, bloodborne diseases. He was a pioneer of a number of new tests and theories all now commonly practiced.

Things changed, however. More pseudo-science than practical application took root. A skewed view of the universe. Studies on stem cells, organ harvesting, even cloning. Others that bordered on myths and legends long since forgotten. Most debunked his theories as outlandish claims that crossed the ethical line more than once, discrediting him at all turns. He was closer to the truth than most would ever know, his theories hinting at the real Portents, the world just beneath the surface, and the mysteries within.

"I can't believe they even published that crap." Derek laughed. He stopped when it wasn't reciprocated. "Look, all I'm saying is the man's visitor list has been a little *freaky* of late."

A door opened. A young woman skirted down the hall, joy held on her upturned lips. Then she saw Derek Carruthers at his desk. The smile faded and her eyes fell to the ground. She rushed from the building with a glance in Soriya's direction. Panic and fear, Soriya recognized. Derek's thin glare trailed the young student out the door.

Soriya stood. She sauntered to the desk, hips swaying rhythmically. Leaning over the desk, Soriya caught Derek's attention immediately.

"Is that what you see here?" she cooed. "Someone freaky?"

"I like freaky. I can work with freaky." He grabbed her arm and pulled her closer. Hunger raged in his eyes.

"I'll bet," Soriya said, no longer resisting his pull. She settled close to him, her fingers running along his arm.

"What are you doing?"

She smiled, her fingers trailing along his skin, up his arm. They danced around his own, wrapping tight around two of them. She pulled them back hard until they snapped under her caresses.

Derek screamed, falling from his chair to the floor below. He cradled his broken fingers, Soriya looming over him.

"Work with that, pretty boy," she said. She leaned close to the flailing man-child. "Don't ever look at a woman like a meal again. Now which room was it again?"

"You crazy—"

She jumped at him and he slammed his head against the floor hard.

"End of the hall," he shouted. "On the left!"

Derek Carruthers' moaning pain echoing behind her carried her down the length of the hall. Her bag hung from her hand, the clinking of the samples adding to the sweet melody.

A small lecture hall spread before her at the end of the hall and she stepped inside. Six rows of desks on a slight incline to better view the lab set up at the front of the classroom. A washroom and a small office were tucked behind the half wall where the chalkboard sat. More equipment piled on worktables, five of them positioned for more hands-on lessons.

In the center of the lectern stood a slight man, tall but thin, almost gaunt. The writhing aide in the hall had mentioned illness but not the extent to which it appeared to have ravaged the man over the years. Bones were visible, his flesh stretched and pale. For a man approaching the mid-century mark he appeared older—much older.

"Office hours are over, miss," Professor Erikson called from below.

"I'm not a student." Soriya stepped deeper into the room. He looked up at her, the blood samples in her hand. "I need your help."

CHAPTER FORTY-TWO

"Hady?"

Ruiz inched closer to the staggering monster. *The Charon.* She matched the description from Loren perfectly. An avatar of Death, he had said. How had he not seen it before?

"Not Hady anymore, Ruiz," Loren called from the back of the room. Ruiz turned and fled from the growing shadows. The lights flickered and faded above, in tune with each breath of the beast blocking the doors.

"What the hell are you talking about, Greg? It's still—"

Loren pointed to the body beside him, gun level with Hady's monstrous form. Ruiz's eyes widened. A lab tech.

"Dammit, Hady," Ruiz said. He spread his arms and turned to the silent creature. "This doesn't have to—"

The creature screamed, its arms lashing out. Slabs along with the bodies upon them soared to the sides of the room. They crashed in heaps, the metal beds clattering against the walls. The Charon rushed toward him, empty eyes swallowing the frozen captain.

"Ruiz!" Loren yelled. Ruiz couldn't move. He was frozen, waiting for the Charon, the incredible beast pulling its arms back in preparation.

I'm so sorry, Michelle.

All he wanted to do was close his eyes and wait for the end. The dark chasms that functioned as the creature's eyes filled his view and then light grew. *Where was the light coming from?*

A searing pain spread from his heart and out, flowing like lightning in his veins—the way it had been moments before Edgar's death.

"Dammit, get down!" Loren slammed into his side, breaking the connection. Ruiz felt the cold tile and suddenly everything refreshed. His body was his own again, the light gone.

The Charon screeched in anger, swinging wildly. Loren ducked under, fighting to reach his fallen friend.

"Greg!"

"The door, Ruiz, get to the—"

The claws of the beast connected and Loren flew away, whipped back across the room. He slammed hard against the closed metal bays, collapsing atop the heap of corpses on the floor.

Ruiz moved to help, immediately cut off by the craven creature. The Charon's malformed lips spread wide. His body stiffened, the light draining from the room once more.

A shot rang out. It hit the beast in the back and the creature screamed out. The Charon turned away from Ruiz, who saw Loren in the corner on bended knee, taking aim.

"The door, Ruiz!" Loren screamed, firing two more shots. The creature bellowed, reaching for the trapped detective.

"But—"

"*Now*, dammit!"

Ruiz raced for the unguarded door, pushing the left side open before skidding to a halt. Loren unleashed another pair of shots at the Charon. No effect. Bullets were wasted on something like her, a being of pure death.

Hady. How did this happen?

"Come on, Greg!"

"I'm trying," Loren snapped. "Dammit, Hady. I know we haven't been the best of pals over the years but do you really want me to be the one to tell you how you've let yourself go?"

The Charon lifted Loren, pulling him close. His body went limp, his eyes unable to peel away from the withered and distended flesh of the monster. A whisper passed between them.

"GREG!"

Loren's body flew away from the beast, skidding across the floor toward the door. He stopped face down, and Ruiz raced to his side. He pulled him up, eyes still affixed to the lumbering creature.

The pair sped into the hallway and Ruiz quickly propped Loren up against the closest wall. Then he flew back to the door, pulling a nearby gurney in front of the swinging doors. The Charon charged forward and Ruiz held firm to the back of the metal bed, the doors straining back to a close.

"That can't be her," he muttered, grabbing at two chairs and throwing them on top of the gurney and the corpse sitting atop. Silent apologies slipped between breaths, before finding more loose furniture along the hall to cram on top of the growing barricade. "How could I not know?"

Ruiz stopped to listen to the screams of the raging Charon. She slashed at the door, the barrier shifting. It held and Ruiz backed off, afraid to look away, afraid to blink.

"There were signs," he continued, flitting glances to Loren, who fought to sit up straight behind him. "Of course there were. But who in their right mind reaches *that* as their conclusion?

"I'll call it in. She's trapped there. For the moment anyway." He took a deep breath, hands on his knees. Ruiz tried to focus, stars on the periphery of his vision. "Hady is the damn killer. I can't believe it. It's just—"

"You're rambling."

Loren's voice was choked, straining to get the words out, and they snapped Ruiz back to the hallway. Back to reality. He turned to his sitting friend and stared, new fear gripping him. The door continued to push out, the cries of the beast filling the background. All lost at the sight of Loren in the corner.

"Greg," Ruiz whispered.

Loren's hands left his torso. Blood dripped from his fingertips and down his slashed shirt. Dark streams in the already darkening hallway.

Loren shook his head. "I don't want your rambling to be the last thing I hear."

CHAPTER FORTY-THREE

"I'm sorry. I don't understand."

Soriya Greystone placed the blood samples stolen from the coroner's office on the workspace in the center of the lecture hall. Professor Erikson stared at the five tubes of crimson, confused. Doubt riddled Soriya. Her judgment had not been the best in recent times, ever since the lightning struck.

Erikson appeared ill, ready to drop from a sudden breeze. Still on the bright side of fifty years old, his physical appearance inched closer to a frail man of seventy. He was all Soriya had, the words of Kok'-Kol and the warnings of Death repeating in her thoughts.

"I need your help."

"I heard that much," Erikson said. He pointed to the tubes resting between them. "And these would be...?"

"Blood samples from some recent murder victims. I need them analyzed."

"Don't you have labs for that?"

Soriya rubbed her neck. "Not me, per se."

Erikson looked her over, from her torn jeans to the ribbon running down her left arm. He nodded, lifting one of the tubes. "Why me?"

She hesitated, unsure about the next part. How much to tell the man? Did she start with the warning from a talking raven with an apple addiction? Did she mention the Charon ripping through corpses like Halloween candy?

"You knew someone close to me. Christopher Eckhart."

"Eckhart?"

Soriya reached into her pocket and removed the folded image. She laid the picture on the table, smoothed out the wrinkles and slid it over to the waiting man.

"I found this."

He lifted the photo and flipped it over. He read the words, the ones that led her to the university, to Erikson. "I haven't thought about this day in decades," Erikson whispered. "Christopher Eckhart."

"You worked with him?"

"A student of his." A laugh escaped him. "I put professor there, always did. Call it ambition but I knew where I was headed in life and let everyone else know it. Chris chided me for it—quite often, in fact. Called it arrogance over prescience. We argued about everything, but I stuck with my studies and earned the moniker eventually."

Soriya listened. Besides the wife and daughter Mentor left when he took over the job as Greystone, she believed there were no more connections to the man who raised her. Every word spoken sounded like gospel about the man, her teacher. He was her father in so many ways.

"I took this picture a lifetime ago," Erikson continued. "Chris was a friend. A dear friend who helped me survive this place when I was a student. Quite literally, in fact, though the details would pale in the telling."

"I doubt that," she said with a smile.

"Let's just say my interests tended to skew a darker way every now and again. Curiosity and that damn cat, only I turned out to be the cat in the end. Chris opened my eyes to things I never could have imagined. He was a mentor to me when I needed one."

"He was good at that kind of thing."

He held the image out to Soriya, who tucked it in her pocket. "I was sorry to hear about what happened to him. When he vanished all those years ago I was devastated. He talked about it with me beforehand but I never thought he would just leave. And then to end the way he did? Tragic."

Who was this man? Soriya wondered. She thought Erikson was an ally like those she had made during her time as the Greystone. Like Loren and Ruiz but to a lesser extent. Erikson, however, appeared to be more than that. The truth tucked in his voice, the words of memory. He knew. Somehow he knew it all.

"You never said why, though."

"I'm sorry?"

"Why me? Not that I—" Erikson stopped, a cough escaping. He turned away, wiping the liquid from his hands, darker than spit. Almost like blood.

"Are you all right, Professor?"

"Fine. Just fine." He wiped his hand on his pants.

"I need someone I can trust." Soriya lifted one of the samples. "I think there's a link between the victims that can explain how to stop their killer."

"I see."

"There's more," Soriya said, hesitating. If she was right, Kok'-Kol's words were about more than the current case. They related to her other problem and one she needed solved to handle the Charon. She opened the pouch along her right hip. "Something else you might be able to help me with."

She placed the stone before him and his mouth fell agape at its arrival. "A Greystone."

"You know it?" she asked, surprised. Relief and excitement filled her. Mentor trusted Erikson, told him the truth about the city and the world at large. Soriya would have liked Mentor in his youth, she imagined. The exuberance they shared at the true city and its prospects over its terror. If only he was still around. If only he had shared everything with her.

"I do," Erikson confirmed. He lifted the stone from the table, his fingers running over the rough surface. "Chris showed it to me, once upon a time, as they say. I marveled at its potential, at the good it could do for everyone but he held it tight. I tried to help, to convince him of more, to… Well, it was one of our last arguments, as you can imagine. He vanished soon after that. With the stone. Smaller than this one."

"It's merged." She held out her hand and he returned the object. "Two stones in one now. It's become uncontrollable. Dangerous."

"Most tools are," Erikson muttered. He ran a hand over his left pocket, rubbing the fabric.

"Professor?" Soriya asked, concerned at the pale look on his face, the sweat pooling around his brow. "Is everything all right? I know you were ill."

"I was," he said. "I'm fine now. I'll *be* fine. Thank you."

"If there is—"

He shook his head and moved for the test tubes of blood. Lifting them up, he scurried to the end of the table. "Let me get started with your samples."

He turned the corner for the back workstations and the equipment. Soriya stood silent, eyes on the stone. He knew about it, studied it with Mentor in the early days. He was there with her teacher, acting as a friend, acting as an advisor, much like Loren to her.

Working with others. Not exactly the Mentor way. It occurred nonetheless, his pulling in others from the world, sharing the truth about Portents. He needed to talk to someone, just as she did. The burden too great to handle alone, yet he ultimately did. He vanished, as the professor said. Walked away from family and friends.

To be the Greystone.

And then to be her Mentor.

What was she missing? What made him change? What pulled him away from the city and the world, only to take refuge in the shadows? Why couldn't she do the same? What pulled her back to the world, drove her to be so different from the man who had given her so much, constantly disappointing him with her need to surround herself with the life that infected the streets of Portents?

Erikson returned. He appeared different, more awake than before. No more sweat, his skin almost translucent in its pale hue, now seemed flush and that of a younger man. More vital.

Soriya shook her head, trying to focus on the stone. "I know it's a long shot to ask but even after so much time with the stone, I'm no closer to understanding it. Where the Greystone comes from. Why it exists. Its purpose. My purpose."

"Weighty questions for one so young."

"I'm an old soul, doc."

"Of course," he laughed. "I don't have much in the way of answers, unfortunately. Not to the degree you're seeking. My time with Chris and the stone was limited. Not my choosing to be sure.

"Pure will and focus are the driving forces," he continued. "Both required to channel the energies trapped inside. You say this is a merged piece?"

"The two stones into one, yes."

"Incredible." He picked up the stone again to study it.

"Too incredible," Soriya replied. "And destructive."

"Perhaps," Erikson said, drawing out the word. His fingers ran the length of the stone then circled around to the other side for the same act. "Possibly because it is incomplete."

Soriya blinked and shook her head. "I'm sorry. What are you saying?"

"Have you tried merging the other pieces?"

CHAPTER FORTY-FOUR

Loren's chest burned. His legs felt like they were on the other side of the building and not beneath his soaked torso. His shirt, once blue and red, now leaned more on the red side, almost black at the center of the deep gashes jabbed into his flesh.

The Charon did real damage. In a split second, one quick slice of the air, the beast ripped through his shirt and his flesh like a knife through butter.

The Charon.

The doors to the lab slammed against the barricade, pushing the hodgepodge of furniture away. Ruiz held firm but it was a stopgap at best. Ruiz left the shaking barrier and came for him.

"Come on." He lifted Loren's arm over his shoulder. Overhead, the lights flickered as the beast screamed behind the doors. Ruiz lifted hard and quick like a band-aid but Loren resisted.

"Can't. Ruiz—"

"That barrier is not going to hold," Ruiz said. He was sweating, beads dripping down the sides of his face. "We need to get out of here."

"How?" Loren pressed against his chest, putting pressure on the gaping wound, fighting the urge to weep at the slightest graze.

"What do you—?" Ruiz's hands went to his belt and found nothing waiting in return. "Oh, shit."

"No access card." Both of their coats were in the room.

"Or phone. Or Goddamn gun." Ruiz slammed his hand against the wall. Both saw the sidearm resting against the tile. Ruiz bent down to retrieve it. "How many—?"

"One."

"This is your backup piece," Ruiz said, tucking the cold steel in his waistband. "Where's your primary?"

"Long story," Loren replied, recalling the fallen pieces resting on the seventh level of a secret library.

The doors slammed forward, the barrier sliding away. Twin black chasms peered out at them, fangs snapping at the air in frustration. Ruiz dropped to Loren's side. "Yeah. Definitely no time for that."

"Ruiz," Loren started as the captain pulled at his arm once more.

"How bad?" Ruiz asked over a scream. It took a moment for Loren to realize it was his own.

"I'm... I'm fine," Loren stuttered, his feet pins and needles along the cold tile.

"Never get tired of hearing you say that," Ruiz shot back. The two started down the hall, Loren's left hand tight to his chest, his right dangling over Ruiz's shoulder.

"Stick with the classics."

Ruiz shuffled to Hady's office, jiggling the handle. Working phones would be questionable at best considering the electrical issues raging throughout the building. The Charon was playing with too many forces, too much power interfering with the natural world. Or some other shit excuse Soriya would spout as fact. Loren kept quiet, letting the captain make the attempt.

They made it halfway down the hall, the slamming of the doors against the collapsing barricade following their every step. Loren's painful cries helped in that regard.

Another handle fought against Ruiz. "Dammit."

"They're all locked?" Blood ran from his fingers. Loren closed his eyes. "Where the hell is everyone, Ruiz? All the personnel this place carries? Do you see—?"

Loren stopped. He opened his eyes and his answer waited for him. Ruiz's head was low, catching a glimpse between the drawn shades on the viewing room near the end of the hall. Loren could barely see anything other than the pain in Ruiz's eyes. Then he noticed the body just inside the door of the lab. Then another. And another.

"Don't look," Ruiz said, tugging them toward the access door. He lifted Loren's hand off his shoulder and settled him beside the exit. Dark splotches stained Ruiz's white button-down when he stood.

"Hady—"

Ruiz shook his head. "That is not Hady. You said it yourself. It can't be. Not anymore."

The frantic captain yanked on the access door handle, the red light of the security system flaring. Even with the dimming lights, the power to the facility failing with every cry of the barricaded Charon, the access door held.

"Come on," Ruiz yelled, his fists slamming against the swiping device. "Dammit!"

A chair clattered to the ground at the end of the hall. Both men peered through the growing darkness. The wall of furniture and the dead was collapsing. Ruiz spun, trying to find something. He fell to Loren's side, reaching for his hand.

"Supply closet. End of the hall."

It was the only open door, and had been since their arrival. Loren had somehow forgotten about it and so many other things of late. Like the dangers of the city and how to keep his friends out of harm's way, Soriya's own justification for leaving him behind. Not that he listened. There was more too, lost in their rush for safety. The Charon—Hady—whispered something to him, hadn't she? *What did she say?*

"We'd be trapping ourselves."

"Buying us time."

Loren looked down at his flowing wounds. "I don't think that will be an issue with me."

Ruiz stood, exasperated. "You want me to leave you behind, Greg? With that?"

The barricade exploded, the doors slamming out. The Charon stepped into the hallway, claws scraping along the tile. The beast screamed, black tendrils of hair flipping away from its sunken face.

"Okay," Loren gasped, reaching for Ruiz's waiting hand. "We can run now."

Ruiz lifted, pulling the wounded detective close and the pair raced down the branched hallway. The Charon screeched, chasing after them. Her claws cut the air, closing the gap.

"Shut up," Ruiz cried, seeing the door—their escape—so far away. Too far away. "And move your ass!"

The lights flared overhead, sparking as the beast slammed into the access door. Loren looked back. Hady was inches behind them, claws reaching for them and missing by less with each swipe. Her screams filled the air but Loren's ears were attuned to the prayers slipping from Ruiz's lips.

"Almost there," Ruiz whispered. "Almost there."

Hot breath blew along their backside. In front of them the supply closet sat just out of reach—their last safe haven. Their only hope at survival. *Almost there. Almost there...*

Then the lights went out completely.

CHAPTER FORTY-FIVE

"There are more Greystones."

She muttered the same phrase for minutes, trying to process the revelation. How had she not known? How could Mentor not tell her about the truth behind the stones? She knew of the two stones: her own and Mentor's. Why would there *not* be more?

Professor Erikson studied the stone closely. His hands shook, a sign of age or something more. Her need outweighed her doubts in the man, and she had found his help invaluable since her arrival.

"How many?"

"No idea," Erikson said without looking. The stone enthralled him. It had that effect on people. "But this is imperfect, jagged in spots. Pieces of a greater whole."

"For what?" The question left before she could stop herself. Erikson tried to answer but fell silent.

No one understood the full extent of the Greystone, its relationship with the Bypass, or how any of it related to her—her purpose, her destiny. All these answers mired in secrets kept by her teacher, and she was too tired to pursue them all, too burdened by the job at hand: the blood samples and the Charon hunting innocent people in Portents.

Had she truly forgotten them? Lost sight of the goal? Erikson waited for her, watching her. His own distraction kept him from realizing the stream running down his chin.

Blood.

"Professor?" Soriya called. "Your nose."

Erikson turned away. He reached for the nearby roll of paper towels, tearing some free to wipe away the blood.

"A regular occurrence of late, unfortunately," he said, his voice muffled by the towels.

"Are you sure you're all right?" Soriya started for the end of the table and he pulled away, backing off for the washroom.

He dabbed at his face, trying to smile. "The life of a dedicated educator, I'm afraid. I will be fine. Let me clean up."

"Of course."

The door to the washroom clicked shut behind him.

Soriya paced the length of the room, her thoughts a whirlwind. Images of Mentor danced in her head, laughing at her ignorance over everything. Did he know the truth? Did he not trust her, just like he didn't trust anyone else? Were her sacrifices not enough for him? Was this punishment for her choices to work with the city instead of in solitude, the way he always wanted?

Soriya groaned into her cupped hands, then ran them through her hair. She needed to snap out of it, needed to stop questioning everything. Focus on what was in front of her.

The case. The Charon. The connection between the victims and the reason behind their selection, by whoever controlled the Medusa coin. Learning who they were and why they were chosen would lead her to the killer. Erikson was the key to helping her find the answers.

Soriya stalked into the back room, re-energized. Putting the case to rest would give her clarity, would give her time to figure things out.

Equipment whirred across a series of tables. A computer fan worked overtime on the small desk, packed tight between lab tables. Centrifuges lined the adjacent table—perfect for running the samples she had brought. Shuffling by stacks of paper flooding from the printer, Soriya tried to find them.

The centrifuges were empty; no tests were running in the lab. She reached for the closest one, her foot kicking a garbage can tucked under the table. It toppled to its side and the contents spilled to the floor. Glass clinked along, coming to rest by her foot. A test tube.

One of the samples she brought.

"What the hell? Professor?"

The washroom door opened. She turned to confront her help when she noticed the papers on the printer. She pulled at the dossiers, one on top of another. Six names. Six men, all matching in age and race. "Jeremy Bennett? Jacob Gephart. Edgar…oh, no."

She turned to see Professor Henry Erikson's grinning face.

"You."

"Don't even—" The dark-skinned warrior dropped the paper, reaching for the hand-woven pouch worn at her side. It was empty.

Henry Erikson opened his hand. The Greystone rested against his withered palm. "Looking for this?"

"No," she whispered.

"Yes."

Light beamed from the surface of the stone and he clenched his teeth from the strain. Focus was required, with the great and terrible energy pouring through the stolen stone. The young woman rushed toward him. Too late—much too late.

Strength rippled from the ancient artifact and flew up his arms. He swung out, his right hand delivering a sharp backhand.

The blow slammed against her cheek and she soared out of the small room, crashing into the second and third row of wooden desks, snapping furniture.

Henry stared at the stone, the light of the sigil still beaming bright along the surface. He knew the truth about the weapon for many years—since Christopher Eckhart, a name not heard for decades. Not until news of his death reached the papers.

Henry worked with him in those early days, studying the strange behavior emanating from the tool currently locked in his grasp. The news about Eckhart, the list of names and the coin, and now the stone itself was serendipity—all coming together for him, bringing him to the end of his journey and the final sacrifice.

Helping him achieve immortality.

Henry walked over to the young woman. She fought to free herself from the wreckage of desks and chairs wrapped around her. He watched with intense enthusiasm at her struggle, his heart pounding with anticipation.

The coin was like a drug in his pocket—always requiring another hit, always sooner than the last. But the stone was power, true power. And it was in his grasp at last.

"I had my doubts, child," Henry said, inching for the woman. "When you came I thought you recognized me from the church. That my work would be undone. Instead, you offered me this. The key to my salvation. The tool needed to complete my work and save my life. Forever."

"You're insane," she spat. She fought to stand.

"Nonsense," Henry replied. "Letting mortality rule you is insane. I'm enlightened—or I will be, soon enough."

She leapt at him. He caught her clumsy assault, her fist locked in his free hand. The stone filled him with strength and he tossed her aside as if she were weightless. She collided with the wall, falling to her knees. She held her chest tight, wheezing from the loss of breath from the force of the impact.

Henry refused to give her the chance to regroup. He reached back, feeling the rune along the surface of the Greystone fill him. Then he unleashed hell in a furious strike, driving her to the ground until she stayed there, unmoving.

He smiled as the energy swirled then faded, the light dissipating from the surface. He let out a long breath, content. It was all coming together. The path was clear. This was all meant to happen, the sacrifices, all the pain and the disease riddling his body. The ultimate test.

The stone proved he was worthy. Worthy to finish the journey. One last death.

Then life eternal.

CHAPTER FORTY-SIX

Natalie Bennett worried. Not exactly a unique situation in her day-to-day activities. Worry was a state of mind with which the twenty-six-year-old was familiar.

There were reasons for concern in her eyes: work—the diner offering less and less time for someone so distracted with problems at home. Loyalty only went so far. Being unable to put in more time, with the constant stress from home, made her boss wary of keeping her on yet he did what he could to offer her as many shifts as possible.

Fill-in work helped. Natalie was close with the other waitresses at the small diner. They threw her the occasional shift, but nothing much. Everyone needed the money.

Which brought her to the bills—*always* the bills. She hated math in high school and she sure as hell hated it more now. Long division and polynomials may have been wastes of time in her eyes but they had solutions at the end of the day. Her checkbook told a different tale. If she trusted herself to use anything other than pencil inside the Bennett family ledger, it would be all red, all the time.

When did everything stop being fun?

Probably when the dishwasher broke, was her guess. Damn the convenience and damn it to hell for vanishing in a cloud of smoke from an overblown motor that would never be replaced. She always hated doing the dishes, too, finding herself embroiled in the task now.

Natalie sighed, dropping the scrubbing brush into the sink. She turned off the water and stared at the flickering fluorescent overhead. It had been too much for too long, draining her from head to toe.

Jack was sick again with another cold, one she denied for too long to keep from bringing on a fever. How could she know? Jack disliked school almost as much as she had at his age. Not the classes, though—her son was intelligent whether or not he wanted to admit that for fear of being handed the dreaded checkbook. Jack's problem came from his classmates, especially the fairer sex. Natalie chuckled. Seven years old and already problems with women.

You're screwed, kid.

She thought his complaints were another excuse to escape the social trappings of a second grade field trip. She packed him up and shooed him out the door, refusing to engage his insistent whining. Her lesson came swiftly when Jack showed up at the diner two hours later with her father, his cheeks rosy and his temperature spiking. She left her shift immediately to help him out despite her dad's so-called ability to handle things.

Dad.

Jack wasn't the only one ailing. Something was going on with her dad. Not yet fifty but the way he slept, no matter the time of day, seemed to be the habit of an older man. Even when awake, something pulled at him. Like he was lost in another world, despite—or perhaps because of—the one unraveling all around him.

He had been there for Natalie and Jack right from the very start of their rocky journey to now. At the time Natalie could never have envisioned moving back home but their mutual worry for each other made it the perfect situation. Her mother had passed. Her boyfriend turned father too soon ditched without so much as a "Smell ya later." Both losses—one thought of more fondly than the other for sure—made it hard for the survivors.

That was what they were after everything—survivors. Only now something was wrong with her dad and she didn't know what to do.

She couldn't even manage the dishes.

Natalie left the sink with a huff. The sound of running water met her upon leaving the kitchen and the caked-on egg of another rushed morning behind. The shower. Another early night for her dad.

He's just slowing down, whispered a reasonable voice. It was followed by worry and doubt. *He's too young to slow down.*

Blistering pain shot up her left foot. A pile of action figures scattered under her weight and she struck out at them in retribution.

"Jack," she yelled down the hall. "Please pick up your toys!"

The door on the right opened. Jack's head poked out, a nervous smile on his face.

"But I'm busy, Mom." A cough escaped his lips on command. She recognized it.

Natalie's hands moved for her hips. "If I pick them up, what do you think happens?"

"I shower you with gratitude for being mom of the year?"

"Nice try," Natalie replied with a wry smile. "Your room or the trash, young man. Make the call. Before your grandfather trips on one. Again."

Jack offered a quick nod before disappearing, and Natalie was alone once more in the hall. She took care to avoid any more calamities. Her toes were still throbbing.

The television continued to blare in the living room. Considering the small distance between speaker and easy chair—less than ten feet by her estimate—the volume was unnecessary. So was the rhetoric spouting from every newscaster on the screen. Another back and forth argument over the handling of what appeared to be a murder spree in the city.

Not too far from them yet another world away. No, the city seemed darker and more dangerous by the year. But what could they do? They were stuck, their lives pinned beneath the wreckage of bills and obligations. Let the city fall into chaos as long as it stayed north, out of Tolliver's Grove.

She clicked off the television and dropped the remote on the chair. Natalie reached for her book on the table, her one escape from the day. It felt heavenly in her hands, and the chance at escaping the worry and the exhaustion for a few minutes was too tempting to pass up.

Until the doorbell rang and the moment fell into memory.

"There's no chance of me sitting today, is there?"

Natalie tossed the novel aside, knowing she'd have to renew it from the library a fourth time. The sun faded in the distance, the sky above starting its transformation to dark pink hues.

Natalie opened the door, pulling the oak hard as it ran against the thick carpet of the living room. "Yes? How can I...?"

She stopped, greeted by a shining badge and a short woman.

"Detective Myers," the petite woman said confidently. "I'm looking for Jeremy Bennett."

CHAPTER FORTY-SEVEN

The lock clicked into place on the door to the classroom. Henry Erikson peered inside at the unconscious woman in the rubble of broken desks. The stone, warm to the touch, continued to pulsate up his arm. His pain faded, and the coin drifted further from his mind.

The sickness remained, he knew that. There was no overcoming it—not yet. Not until he finished the task set before him. But now he had the means to complete it without compromise, without the monster tucked in his corner. This was his victory, his final day of pain and misery.

Everything else stretched to eternity before him.

He would be immortal.

Nothing would stop him now. The stone made it all possible, as if Christopher Eckhart was looking down upon him with a silent helping hand. Henry wondered how different things would have been if Eckhart had shared his secret life completely, if he would have trusted Henry with the world beneath the surface of Portents. He had tried for years, serving his teacher and friend with advice and science to counteract the chaos that surrounded their lives. It was never enough and his pushing forced Eckhart away in the end.

The stone was an apology of sorts. No more reliance on the Charon and its destructive nature. Henry found the collateral damage with each occurrence too costly. This time, this final instance, everything fell to Henry Erikson.

He could not fail.

Henry pushed off the wall and started down the corridor. He bounced ahead, a skip in his step, lightness in his core, one he had not felt in a long time. One more death, one more sacrifice, and everything would be better. He would make it right with his life.

With the work, he would make the deaths of six strangers fade into memory under the weight of his accomplishments. Thanks to the stone in his hands, he would change the world.

"Henry?" a voice called. "Henry Erikson?"

Henry turned down the hall to see a uniformed officer approaching. He was tall, over a foot taller than him, Henry guessed. He strode along the hallway, hands near his jingling belt, which held his sidearm in full sight.

"Yes?" Henry stopped in the center of the hall, tucking the stone behind his back.

"Officer Pratchett," the man said. He pointed to his badge. "I need you to come with me."

"Why?" Henry looked through the officer for the waiting door.

"For your own protection, sir."

A sharp, toothy grin crept out. "Oh, I believe I am protected already."

Light grew behind his back, the stone pulsing through him. Strength ran up his arms. Easier this time, the stone growing more accustomed to him, his need, and his drive.

His control.

"What are you...?"

Henry's eyes burned white in the stone's thrall. Grabbing hold of the man's extended arm, Henry twisted it away, causing the officer to cry out. Pratchett fought for release, turning away from Henry's rising fist.

The punch slammed into the officer's cheek. The force of the blow drove his body into the wall. A low moan slipped from his lips. Pratchett's unconscious body slid to the floor in a heap.

Henry fought for breath. He couldn't stop smiling. Violence was never his answer. Yet here he was brutally assaulting an officer and a young woman in less than a ten-minute span. Why did it feel so right? Why did it feel so good?

The light from the stone faded, the strength returning to its source for later. He was near the end of his journey. Everything was within reach. *Only one more.* His chest continued to heave, exhilarated from the exchange. He leaned close, removing the officer's gun then started down the corridor, stopped by the shadow of his aide at the end of the hall.

"Professor?"

Henry sneered. The fear on the boy's face excited him. After watching the lout over the course of the semester, worried about nothing more than a recommendation letter and the phone number of every girl that passed by, available or not, all confidence in the face of Derek Carruthers faded from view.

"Professor, is he…?"

Henry held out the sidearm. He leveled it on the frozen form of his assistant and cocked the hammer. "I wish you hadn't seen that, Derek."

CHAPTER FORTY-EIGHT

The Bennett home was simple in its layout. The front door opened to the narrow living room, a couch splitting the space, twin end tables on either side with matching lamps. An office turned exercise room connected the far side of the room. A hallway branched off to the right of the entrance, leading to two of the three bedrooms. The lone bathroom jutted off the left side of the main hall with the final bedroom beyond it just before the exit to a small patio to the fenced-in yard. Everything on one floor, together.

A true home—something that always made Samantha Myers uncomfortable. The coffee cup in her hand helped distract her from the feeling, though her constant sipping did little for her nerves.

The house was more than just a collection of photos and knick-knacks gathered on every shelf, or the fact that they even had shelves—something Myers was still working on and imagined would be completed by the time the department threw her ass to the curb for insubordination. Something deeper resonated in the way the couch cushions sank perfectly, the way the water ran from the dish rack into the sink and in a small drip down to the floor. Or the way a rag sat within the window frame to keep the water from collecting. Things to denote a family with staying power. A family that had come together for a long time, that built something over time. Together.

Myers wanted to run and fought the urge.

"Detective?"

Myers sipped her coffee, turning back to Natalie Bennett, who sat with her hands folded at the kitchen table. "Hmm? Sorry. It's a lovely home."

"I asked if I could get you anything else while you're waiting?"

"I'm set." Myers put the coffee down and checked her phone. No word from Loren. Hours slipped away since their talk. Had she been cut out of the loop? Trusted the wrong person to handle Hady Ronne? Part of her knew better. A greater concern existed in John Pratchett. He had the shorter drive—only to the university—and still she had heard nothing from him. Sure, the man lacked a sense of direction and probably ended up at the burnt tree adorning Olcott Curve…but what if he didn't?

She lifted the cup. "This coffee is amazing. What kind of brewing system do you have? I'm a ten dollar Mr. Coffee woman myself but I think I buy more than I brew. Might be the ten dollar aspect of the purchase."

Natalie tilted her head and smiled awkwardly. "Should I ask to see your badge again?"

"Probably," Myers laughed, joining her at the table. "Sorry. Been a long couple of days."

Natalie stared into her own cup, her hands tight to the sides. "Is this about those murders downtown?"

Myers hesitated, unsure what to say or how to say it. She was still figuring things out herself, the story from Herman Kampe following her every thought. *There were seven of them. Seven sons.* What the hell did it all mean?

Natalie noted her silence, brushing her hair out of her face. "Dad has a thing for the weather girl on channel four. Never misses a night."

"Man's got to have hobbies."

Natalie winced. "I prefer ones not seen by my seven-year-old."

"No husband?" Myers closed her eyes, biting her tongue. "Sorry. Boot in mouth syndrome. No cure."

"Maybe more amazing coffee?"

Myers handed over the cup. "Worth a try."

"No." Natalie topped off the cup denoting the *World's Number One Grandpa* on the side. She handed it back to the waiting detective. "The answer to your question. Jack's dad left when I shared the good news. We've stayed here since. I was stupid. Too young."

"Doesn't make the guy less of a dick."

"True." Natalie toasted the proclamation with a clink of her cup.

Myers cocked her head to the exercise arena in the next room. "And your dad?"

"Work-related injury," Natalie sighed. "Blew out his knees a few years back. He's been home since. He's been great for Jack. For both of us." She stared off, listening to the sound of the water fading down the hall.

"What is it, Natalie?"

"Nothing," she said with the shake of her head. "A mother's curse. Always worrying."

"I suppose."

"Why my dad?"

A good question. The same one Myers had since stepping inside the home. If five others connected to the same bloodline were targeted, there had to be something to it, didn't there?

"I'd rather wait until—"

"Until what?" Both turned to the sight of a middle-aged man enter the room. He wore a stained white T-shirt and gray sweatpants. Jeremy Bennett patted his hair with his wet towel, curious at the presence of another woman in the house.

"Dad," Natalie said. She stood and took the towel from him, dropping it to the counter. "You hog more water than a teenager."

"Increased surface area and decreased mobility. The cost of age."

She poked his stomach. "And late night snacks."

"Guilty."

"Dad, this is—"

Myers stood, badge in hand. "Detective Sam Myers."

"The police?" Jeremy asked, suddenly concerned. "Nat, what's going on? Did Jack—?"

"Jack's fine," Natalie said. "Though going to him right away brings up new concerns about what you two have been up to while I'm working."

"I'm here for your protection," Myers chimed in. Still no word from Pratchett; the young detective was starting to feel like that meant more than it should.

"My protection?"

"Someone is targeting your family," Myers answered.

"Jack?"

Myers shook her head. "No. Your brothers."

"Brothers?"

"Dad was adopted." Natalie patted her father's arm. "He doesn't have any siblings. Step-siblings. Whatever."

"I'm talking about biological brothers. Six of them."

Jeremy fell back a step. "Six brothers?"

"I'm sorry to be blunt about it. Five have been killed. I believe the other murders this week have been to conceal these five."

"Meaning what exactly?" Jeremy pulled away from his daughter, staggering to a kitchen chair. "You're saying I'm next? Absurd."

"Possibly. But I have to follow up on every possible lead. Mr. Bennett, does the name Ellie Tamblin mean anything to you?"

"No. Should it?"

Myers finished her cup of coffee and placed it on the table before going for the jacket left over the chair. "I have a photo here."

She handed the image to Jeremy, who almost dropped it. His eyes widened, his cheeks flushing at the sight of the woman in the picture.

"You've seen her before?"

"In a dream," Jeremy muttered, still staring at the woman in the photograph. She wore a sparkling dress that swirled around her in mid-spin. Her smile overshadowed everything else about her.

"Dad?"

Jeremy handed her the photo. "She had the same dress. In the dream. It was just like this one. Blue. And those eyes? Green. So green."

"Like yours," Myers said.

"What are you saying? Who is she?"

"Your mother."

"Why me?" Jeremy asked. Natalie joined him at the kitchen table, the photo between them. "Why now?"

"That's what I've been trying to figure out," Myers said. They continued to stare at her. No, *through* her. "What is it? What's wrong?"

A loud click echoed through the room and her heart stopped. Myers turned, her hands raised away from her sidearm. A man, thin and sickly, stood in the center of the living room. He held a gun to them in one hand and some kind of stone in the other.

"I believe my brother was directing his questions at me, Detective."

CHAPTER FORTY-NINE

Soriya slept. In the void of unconsciousness, the young woman did something she had not done in ages: She rested. Troubled and fitful, Soriya drifted into the deep dark of her mind. The city was lost, the world out of reach, and she let it stay that way. The comfort of the blackness soothed her battered body.

The job was too much, the burden too heavy. She tried for so long, pushing herself so hard to be better. To be greater. To be Mentor.

"Little one."

She heard the voice and closed her eyes tighter, letting the darkness consume her. She didn't want to disappoint anyone else. Not after all her failures. Someone else needed to take up the fight.

"Little one."

The voice called again and he stood before her.

"It can't be," she whispered.

Mentor crouched beside her, his gray eyes consuming her. "The stone tests you."

"It's winning," she snapped, curling tighter on the floor of the classroom. "I can't do it. I can't be you."

"No one asked you to be."

Her eyes flared. "You did. Every damn day."

"Then you never understood the lessons," he said. His hand reached out. "Get up."

"No."

Mentor shook his head. "Doubts are normal. You are better than that."

"Your pep talks have always sucked," Soriya cursed. She shut her eyes tight.

"How about this, little one?" He leaned in close to whisper. "Henry Erikson has the stone."

"He knew about it. You told him about the Greystone. About everything."

His eyes saddened. "A mistake. Erikson was a friend but had ambitions—dangerous ones."

"I figured that out," she groaned, pain returning to her body as her vision cleared.

"Then you know the danger," Mentor continued. "With the stone and the Medusa coin in his possession, the balance has tipped. If the last brother falls, so does Portents. The Charon will be unleashed on all. Without restraint."

"What the hell can I do about it?"

"Stand up and fight back," he commanded. "Be who you are."

"Why?"

He smiled. "Because I believe in you, Soriya Greystone. Always and forever."

Soriya reached through the haze, the darkness fading around her as she fell back into reality. Her hand went for Mentor's and wound up in another's, one covered by a thin black glove.

"I didn't realize being a Greystone allowed for naptime," Death said, pulling her to her feet.

"*You.*"

"Me." He let her loose and stepped away, dusting off his clothes. "You talk in your sleep."

Soriya huffed, wondering how much was a dream. Kok'-Kol mentioned past connections, two of them—one that would help, one that would harm. She was wrong about the role Henry Erikson played in the affair, and wrong about Mentor's own role. She had someone else to thank.

"You answered," she said. "Didn't you?"

"Some." Death shrugged. "Not all."

"About the Charon?"

He nodded. "The coin put her in a cage and upset the natural order. With her task complete, the cage breaks."

"And Portents pays the price."

The man in the suit fixed the bowler cap to his head and turned for the door. "You should get to it then."

She sighed, watching him depart. "I know you."

"You always have."

"I mean the real you," she said. "Before this. All that talk about Enkidu and Uruz. Old campaigns and older friends. Of a life wasted looking for immortality. I know you very well…Gilgamesh."

He stopped. "A name from another life."

"You found it. All that searching and you did it. Immortality."

"It cost me everything. Everyone."

"You're here to set things right." The feeling followed her since his arrival at the church, since he let his presence known to her when there was no reason to do so.

"I can't."

"You can," she yelled. "You can make a difference here. You can make a choice."

He wavered, unable to look at her. "Time is running out, Soriya. Don't let it."

There was a knock at the door. Soriya turned to see Pratchett looking through the small window near the top of the frame, his face bruised and battered, his left eye swollen shut.

"How do I find him?" Soriya asked, ignoring the pleas from the hallway. Gilgamesh was gone. "Now I know how Loren… Wait."

She rushed away to the back room, kicking aside the debris left from their short but destructive fight. Papers flew around her, caught up in the wind, and she snatched them each in turn. The names came fast but all lined up with the story behind the coin. Edgar Rusch. Jacob Gephart. Willis Freely. Donovan Michaels. James Becht. All unknown to her, their lives more of a mystery than their deaths. Only the number mattered. Those five, Henry Erikson, and the final dossier from the pile.

"Jeremy Bennett."

Seven names, seven sons. All tied to the coin, all required to unlock the power within. And only one left on Erikson's list.

Soriya clutched the paper, seeing the address marking the bottom of the page. She started for the door then stopped at the sight of Pratchett twisting the handle for her attention. He tapped his badge against the small window on the door. She didn't have time for his questions.

Soriya picked up a stray chair and slammed it against the large windows in the back of the room. Glass shattered from her assault and she tossed the chair aside.

Pratchett stared wide-eyed from the hallway, screaming for her attention. Soriya saluted the officer and jumped out the open window to the empty grounds of the university campus. Questions could wait. Henry Erikson needed to be stopped and she was the only one left to stand in his way.

It was time to be what everyone expected her to be—only better. It was time to be the Greystone.

CHAPTER FIFTY

I'm dying.

It repeated on Loren, the powerful thought ripping through him worse than the wound taking over his chest. His own mortality. The end rising up and taking over. It couldn't happen, not with so much left unfinished: Beth's case, the dozens missing in Portents, not to mention their current situation. He couldn't leave Ruiz to face this alone, though the idea grew more tempting with each tug of the tourniquet the captain wrapped along Loren's torso.

"Quit it," Ruiz chastised, holding Loren steady. The lone light bulb hanging from the ceiling lit up the space in the center of the room. Loren wished it would blink out with the rest of the lighting in the building, as the concern on Ruiz's face terrified him.

"It hurts," Loren said, shifting from Ruiz's ministrations.

"Squirming doesn't help."

"Neither does your bedside manner." Loren peered at the growing shadow under the door. "Or the noise from the waiting room."

The Charon paced, ready to blow the door down. Her screeches filled the air, joined by the wounded Loren as Ruiz tightened the rag turned tourniquet on the man's wound.

"There," Ruiz said, stepping back. "Don't try to—"

Loren stood, and immediately his legs gave out. He tumbled to the ground, knocking away empty cleanser bottles, causing them to rattle around the small closet in all directions.

"—Move," Ruiz finished, rubbing his eyes. "Idiot."

Loren took the waiting hand, struggling to sit. The tourniquet held, the bleeding slowed, but stars continued to dot his vision. Sweat pooled across his forehead yet his skin felt like ice. He coughed, drowning in pain.

"I'm dying here, you know," he sputtered. "Show some respect."

"Earn some," Ruiz replied. He smiled, and Loren joined him. Then the Charon's claws scraped along the locked door of the supply closet, and their grins faded.

"Does she have to keep doing that?"

"Lets us know she's still there. Almost prefer that." Ruiz settled beside Loren. He pulled his knees in close. The aging captain took out their lone weapon, the backup piece Loren bought after graduating from the academy. His reward, a cheap one considering how little he had earned in the first twenty-three years of life from a dozen or so crappy jobs. Ruiz slapped the revolver, spinning the chamber to see what remained, before knocking it back into place. A single bullet.

"That won't do anything," Loren warned.

Ruiz nodded. "It's all I have."

Loren turned away. "Can't believe this is how it ends."

Ruiz glared at him. "Cut that shit out, Greg. We'll get out of this."

"Maybe." Loren knew better. His head fell back, hitting the edge of the metal shelving supporting his weight. He thought of Soriya, wondering when she would hit the scene to save them, hoping she would. He'd spent so many years relying on her to bail him out of stupid situations. Was it really any surprise now that she left him behind?

No white hats rode to his rescue. No eleventh-hour saves coming from the mysterious woman he called friend and partner. Only Ruiz and the monster at the door.

Loren sighed. This was supposed to be different. *He* was supposed to be different—better, more prepared, more assured. His fresh start, a chance to have a life, one he denied for himself for so long after the loss of his wife. She was what mattered then and she still did, her killer on the loose, lost in the shadows of his memory. He hoped for more, though—friends, colleagues, a life—refusing to fall into obsession again.

"Dammit."

"What?"

"I've wasted so much time, Ruiz. After Beth—"

"Greg."

Loren refused to listen. "It's true. I lost everything with her. Then I came back and saw it as a new beginning. But the past keeps blocking the future. I have no friends. No life at all." His eyes fell on one of the few people that kept him from his solitary life. "Who the hell is going to care if I die here?"

"You know the answer to that, you ass."

"Thanks."

"Hey," Ruiz snapped. He stood, pacing the room to match the tapping of the claws of the Charon outside their gate. "At least you're out there. At least you're trying. Better than hiding from everything."

Loren shifted, his chest in agony. "Michelle?"

Ruiz stopped, head falling. "I promised I wouldn't be my parents. Always steeped in silence and secrets. She deserved better. To go out like this—"

He trailed off and Loren let his last words linger. He huffed, banging his head along the shelf. "Like this."

"What?"

Loren snapped his fingers.

"What is it?" Ruiz asked again.

"The banging."

Ruiz spread his arms in disbelief. "She's trying to get in here, remember?"

"Why?" Ruiz continued to stare at him. Loren shook his head. "Stop with the look. Think about it. Think about the church."

"Edgar."

Loren pulled him back before the sadness returned. "No doors."

Ruiz's eyes widened. "The shadows, Soriya said."

Both peered around the confined space of the supply closet. The lone lamp dimmed and faded but still maintained a small cone of light in the center of the room. Shadows penetrated every corner, deep, unforgiving. Frightening space surrounded them.

"Why not here? How can any barricade hold her back?"

"I don't—"

"She said something to me," Loren said, transfixed by memory. "When she pulled me close."

"What was it? What did the Charon say?"

"Not the Charon. Hady. She whispered it to me and I couldn't hear her over everything. But it was there. She said, 'I'm sorry.'"

"Wait," Ruiz said and both paused.

The noise had ended. No pacing. No scraping claws along the tile and the door. No screeching in anger. And no shadow stretched along the base of the frame.

"She stopped?"

Ruiz shushed him. He inched for the door, revolver in front of him.

"What the hell are you doing?"

"You're bleeding to death. Time is not our friend here."

Loren nodded, trying to smile. "But you are. My friend, that is."

Ruiz reached for the handle, refusing to turn around. "Let's save the tender moment for after this is over."

"Fine," Loren whined. "Leave me hanging."

Ruiz grinned. "Baby."

"Stubborn ass."

Ruiz stopped at the door. His hand rested on the knob. He took deep breath after deep breath, trying to steady his shaking body. Loren did the same, struggling to face the door. If this was it, if the end had truly come for them, there was no way in hell he wasn't going to face it head on.

"Okay." Ruiz flipped the lock, the clicking loud against the silence of the room. "Here we go."

The hallway was empty, the few remaining lights overhead steady with a deep hum. Scratches marked the door and the tiles below. The ones in the door almost reached through. But the Charon was gone, called away by something else.

Someone.

Worry for his own well being faded, Loren's concern suddenly growing for the others involved. Soriya. Myers. Pratchett.

And everyone else in the city of Portents.

CHAPTER FIFTY-ONE

The same mistakes haunted Samantha Myers. Trapped in the living room of the home, the young detective stood defiant in front of the gun pointed at her and the two adults of the Bennett family. Natalie hugged close to her father, his eyes wide and his mouth agape at the newcomer.

The man had the same eyes as Jeremy—Myers noticed them right off. The same dim sparkle surrounding the bold pupil in the center. There was a youthful vigor to him, excitement and exuberance, none of which inspired confidence in the woman standing in front of the barrel of the gun. His hair was thin in multiple places, a patchwork. His frame wiry, his bones threatening to poke through at every joint. He appeared to have been sick. Very sick.

Sick equaled desperate equaled dangerous. Simple enough equation, and one Myers read too late. The same mistake. A misjudgment. The wrong call. She was always on her own, her need for control overtaking common sense. She realized now she should have called backup upon discovering the two final brothers out in the world. Instead, in spite of her discussion with Pratchett she took it upon herself to follow through with this lead. She had been unable to allow anyone else the chance to steal whatever control or glory or other horseshit excuse she could conjure up to justify her stupidity.

"I was hoping for more," the man said. His eyes flitted around the small ranch home on the south side of the city, disdain in every glance.

"Mom?" a voice called. The gun in the man's hand tracked to the hall then fell back on Myers. She sighed at her thwarted attempt to grab her own weapon, the moment lost. Jack, Natalie's seven-year-old son stepped into the living room, and the young mother crouched with her arms outstretched.

"Jack, come here, baby."

The boy raced across the room, eyed cautiously by the man with the gun. He fell into his mother's arms and hugged tight to her chest. Myers stepped in front of them, her five-foot-nothing frame doing little as a shield, but it was all she had to offer.

"Stay behind me."

The man huffed at the dramatic display, waving the gun around like a toy, as if nothing stood in his way.

"Out of everyone, when it came down to the last, I expected more," he said. "I expected better of you, brother. You had a family, connections. Not the loner, the academic, the priest, or the closeted lover. But what do you really have here? A cramped home. Jobless. Barely able to dress yourself, unless you consider those stains honorific of some great deed?" He paused, letting out a deep laugh. Mania was buried behind a calm veneer. "To think of how much energy I wasted building this confrontation up in my mind. I never asked for this to happen. Any of it. However, I will see it through. *I* will. Not some witless pawn."

Myers listened to the man's rambling and felt nothing for him. Nothing for a man holding a gun to an innocent family. Nothing for a man that had basically confessed to dozens of murders. For what? She didn't know.

"It's Erikson, right?" she asked, inching forward. His gun shuffled, tight in his hand, pushing her back. "Henry Erikson?"

"Very good, Detective."

"What did you do to Pratchett?"

"The gangly fool of an officer?" Erikson sneered. "He'll be fine. Eventually."

Myers clenched her fists. "I'll add it to the list of charges. Now drop the gun."

"Not quite yet," he said. "That's far enough as well."

She stopped inching forward. Her sidearm begged to be drawn. She wanted nothing more than to take the shot, to take the chance and bring this to an end. His hand was shaky, sweat building along his brow. Whatever he was doing to keep it together was wearing off. She just needed time, a window of opportunity. It would only take a moment for her to make her move and end it all. However, the Bennetts behind her made it impossible to take the chance.

Myers' head swam. Another question gnawed at the inquisitive detective. Erikson mentioned an accomplice. Who? Were they still out there, committing murders in his name? And how were they being done? Erikson held a pistol, Pratchett's from the looks of it, but none of the other victims had suffered a gunshot wound. There was nothing mundane about their deaths. They suffered worse things. Darker things. What was she missing?

"You're supposed to be my brother?" Jeremy asked, changing the focus.

"He speaks!" Erikson laughed. "Impressive."

"You killed people."

"Not by choice," Erikson snapped. "Never by choice."

"Then why?"

"To take back control. To take back my life!"

Jeremy puffed his chest, holding his family close. "You're no brother of mine."

"Oh, we are brothers." Rage settled in Erikson's eyes, a fire reflected on the deep black of his pupils. Then they softened. "You've seen her, haven't you? Our mother? Eyes like emeralds and a shimmering dress?"

Myers shared the startled glance with the two adults of the Bennett family. Jeremy managed to reply, "How?"

"The dream," Erikson said. "An awakening for each of us. You stayed in the dream but I answered its call."

"*Erikson*," Myers interrupted. "Last warning. Drop the damn gun."

He laughed, loud and long at her bluster—for that was what it was. She had no play, other than to rush him and hope he missed on his first shot. Then what of the accomplice mentioned? What happened to the Bennetts should that person seek them out and take up Erikson's mad crusade? Still, the laughter unnerved her.

"Very well, Detective." Erikson put the gun down on the back of the couch. "Why waste a bullet when I have this?"

He opened his hand to reveal a small, jagged object.

"A stone?"

Erikson's brow furrowed, and he extended his arm. "You should study up on Portents more. If you had more time, that is. Goodbye, brother."

ᚾ

The stone lit up before them, white beaming from its dull surface. Myers watched intently, confused and curious. The light formed a symbol, one Myers found unrecognizable. Wind picked up, slamming against the house. The windows shattered around them and Myers turned to grab hold of the Bennetts.

"Run," she screamed over the howling wind. "Now!"

Fear carried them across the room to the mouth of the hallway. Not enough, however. Lightning swept the room, coursing through the shattered windows in every direction for their position. Myers pushed the Bennetts forward, feeling the lightning sear the wall behind them, cutting through plaster and wood.

They screamed, Natalie's cries louder than the rest as the second strike connected. She started to fall, caught by the petite detective and carried along the hallway for the bedroom to the right. They dove into the room, toys lining the floor and walls in every direction. Jeremy held tight to his grandson and Myers cradled Natalie, who cried out in pain.

"What was that?" Jack asked in amazement.

"Jack," Natalie whispered through gritted teeth.

"Natalie." Myers helped her to the wall, propping her up. "How bad?"

The mother's pant leg was gone, her skin like burnt toast. Natalie tried to put pressure on the foot and couldn't, the pain too intense. "Less than good. What do we do?"

An excellent question, one Myers should have anticipated before getting into this situation. She reached into her pocket, her cell phone dropping into her hand. She held it out, thumbing the pass code before giving it to Natalie.

"Call 911. Then call the last number in the history," she said as she pulled out her sidearm and cocked the hammer. "Greg Loren. He's a friend. Tell him where you are. Do it now."

Myers moved for the door, held back by a small hand. Jack looked at her with worried eyes. "What are you going to do?"

She smiled. "Buy you time. As much as I can. Take care of your mom."

Part of her wanted to pull Natalie up and run for the back door, to escape from the madness. Lightning striking at them under the command of a stone? This wasn't what she was trained to handle, and more importantly, it wasn't what she could control.

Unfortunately, running didn't end the threat. It would have been the smart move, but not one she felt comfortable making, not with another player yet to be revealed. The missing gun—just like before. Her error in judgment hung over her like a shroud. She needed to end this and keep the Bennett family safe.

When she reached the living room, gun at the ready, Erikson stood beside the couch. Awestruck, he stared at the stone in his grasp.

"The focus required," he muttered. "Astonishing."

Only her arrival shook him back to reality. "I've never understood the fascination with pet rocks. I'm more of a troll fan."

Erikson grinned, holding the stone toward her. "As final words go, Detective, I rate you high on originality."

"I'm the one holding the gun," Myers said, her words shaky at best considering the small flames still flickering along the carpet.

"Close your eyes, Detective. It won't hurt. Much."

Myers' finger fell on the trigger. She could end this with a single shot. She could take Erikson down and hope to track down the accomplice before another life was lost. Her momentary hesitation was enough to take the decision out of her hands.

The front door shattered, crashing into the living room. Soriya Greystone stood in the frame, shadowed by the moonlight at her backside. Her eyes flared, her fists balled up in front of her.

"Erikson!" she shouted. "This ends. Now."

CHAPTER FIFTY-TWO

"Knocked out by a middle-aged nerd. Embarrassing to say the least." Soriya stepped deeper into the living room, edging closer to the man at its center. Henry Erikson put his back to the couch, covering both women, eyes carefully watching each movement. It was not his eyes that concerned her.

It was the Greystone in his grasp.

"The stone is mine now, child."

"Getting real tired of people calling me that," Soriya said. She continued to circle the room, noticing the concern on the face of the woman in front of the hallway and the gun shifting between targets. "Detective?"

"Myers," she snapped. Her eyes thinned, recalling their first encounter at the coroner's office. "You're no better than him in my book, lady."

"Lady?" Soriya shrugged. "A step up, I guess. Jeremy Bennett?"

"You know what this is about?"

Soriya offered a silent nod, her focus firmly on the stone. Small flames flickered along the ground, the scorch marks along the wall clearly indicating a struggle. The wind continued to whip through the living room. He had used the stone, controlled its power to a degree that had eluded her since the lightning struck. The stone bent to Erikson's will, as did the other tool at his disposal.

"Where is it, Erikson?"

"Clever." He patted his left pocket. He reached inside and removed the small coin resting within. His body shook from the contact, visible chills running along his arm.

"The Medusa coin."

"What?" Myers asked.

"It controls death," Soriya answered without looking. The coin was intoxicating, even obscured by Erikson's thin fingers. Marred by age and neglect, the ancient object appeared just as stimulating to her as it did all those years ago resting in the seventh level purgatory that was the Library of the Luminaries. Locked away and hidden, kept safe from the world. Now unleashed for one man's purpose.

"With Jeremy Bennett's passing I will be the last of seven sons. Seven sons caught in a well of death since birth like the martyrs of old. But death will not take hold of me. With this and the sacrifice of my estranged family, I will not die. I will live forever."

"Seriously?" Myers cried, incredulous.

Soriya shook her head, waving the uninformed officer down. "That's not what's going to happen here, Erikson. The coin comes at a cost. Like a drug. Each death gives less and takes more. Doesn't it?"

She could see it in the way the artifact helped him in the classroom not two hours earlier. He left the room weary and broken only to come back vital and full of life. Whatever effect the coin held on him was wearing off, though. Maybe it was the delay between sacrifices. Maybe it was a mental trick played behind Erikson's wide eyes. One thing was clear: Erikson was dying, the disease that kicked off his search for immortality raging through his system faster with each passing second. She needed to get the coin away from him. No, she needed to do more.

Destroy the coin. Or all is lost.

"It doesn't have to take anymore, Erikson. No one else has to die here."

"Exactly," he shouted. "That's exactly what I'm trying to do!"

"No," Soriya replied. "You can't keep it caged. If you do this, if you take Jeremy Bennett's life, everyone dies. You, me, everyone."

"Not me," Erikson said, defiantly. "Never me."

"You can barely stand," she said, but he refused to listen, to hear her words, or heed any warning. He had written the end already, one that would allow his own story to extend into infinity.

"A small price to pay," he muttered. He held the stone over his palm. "I have enough left to see this through."

"Don't!"

Too late. The jagged edge of the stone sliced the frail skin along his palm, blood streaming over the coin. Crimson soaked the surface, the smirking face upon its surface lapping up the sacrifice.

Myers lowered the gun at the sight of the coin glowing in his hand. "What the hell is this now?"

"You need to get out of here, Detective," Soriya warned. The shadows behind them whirled and they turned away from Erikson. What little light shone from the twin standing lamps in the living room faded, swallowed by the growing swirl of darkness building in the room.

"Not a chance. Now tell me what the hell is going on?"

Erikson smiled, his teeth gleaming against the black. "You asked for Death. Welcome her."

A form stepped through the shadows. Massive tangles of black moppy hair covered the withered face and the scabbed-over chasms of darkness that served as the beast's eyes. The creature entered the living room and screamed, its cries directed at the man holding its existence in his hand.

"The Charon," Soriya whispered. It looked more monstrous than she ever imagined, growing more horrific with each passing glance.

Erikson raised the blood-soaked coin over his head. "Kill them all."

CHAPTER FIFTY-THREE

Myers couldn't move. Soriya's timely arrival had bought the detective a chance to learn about Erikson's accomplice and hopefully end the threat not only to the Bennett family but also to the city. She tried to tune out the rants of both players in the drama. Talk of immortality and controlling death made little sense to the grounded law enforcement officer.

Until Death walked into the room.

Darkness swallowed the light and the beast, *the Charon* as Soriya had uttered, stepped forward with a scream. Shadows melted behind the creature's arrival, the mysterious accomplice revealed. In more ways than one.

The question of how the other victims of Erikson's rampage met their end, the mysterious and devastating injuries to each man and woman caught in the path of the beast, became clear to Myers. She swiftly understood how Erikson, who appeared frail and fading beneath the veneer of his mania, could accomplish such a deed. He couldn't, but the Charon could—a mythological monster that wore a striking lab coat over its desiccated figure.

And an ID badge.

"Holy shit," Myers said, recognition dawning on her face. Her gun lowered in the presence of the beast. "Hady Ronne?"

Soriya threw a nod, backing away from the creature. "Not anymore, Detective."

Myers shook her head, defiant. She stepped closer to the screeching beast, padding through the room. "Doctor Ronne? It's me, Sam. Samantha Myers."

"You need to back off."

"Listen to me, Hady," Myers continued. "You're not yourself. Let me help."

"That isn't—"

"Kill them!" Erikson shouted. "Now, dammit!"

Myers shuffled ahead, undeterred. The beast stood its ground. "Ignore the lunatic with the coin collection, Hady. Guy couldn't be a bigger nerd. Unless he collected comic books. Now those guys are scary."

"Off topic," Soriya whispered.

"Right," Myers said. "You're like us, Hady. More me than '80s ribbon girl here but all the same. You help people. You catch the bad guys. You don't work for them. No matter what creepy hoodoo they work on you."

The creature screamed, claws scratching at the ground. Myers stopped, hand still open and extended, just like her hope at reaching the woman lost inside the killer, trusting her to make the right choice.

"Detective."

Myers needed to make this work. She needed the win. It would be a chance to balance the scales after her loss in New York—her mistake, always there, never fading. No matter her talent for the job or her control over it all, the mistake remained, and Myers couldn't afford another one. She couldn't let Hady get lost in the mix, either.

"Do it now!" Erikson ordered.

The beast did not move. The claws of the Charon scratched harder at the floor, steam flowing with each breath. Tendrils of hair flew away from the withered and decayed face of the beast. Even through the black chasms that served as eyes, Myers saw it—the reason behind the hesitation, the truth behind the Charon's inaction since arriving: doubt. And more than doubt, recognition. Of her deeds, of Myers.

"Hady," Myers said, a disarming grin on her face. "Don't let Erikson define you. Fight this. Help me. Help—"

She didn't see the strike until it was too late. The Charon's arms shot up in a wide arc. Myers was too close to avoid them. They struck as one enormous hammer, the blow connecting with the woman's chin.

The world spun and time sped out of control. Everything was out of her control. She met the far wall of the living room, smashing through plasterboard to the guts of the home. Wood beams cracked as her body made contact. She fell hard to the floor.

"Detective!" Soriya cried out, her voice distant. Her dark skin was a shadow across Myers' vision.

"Damn," Myers exhaled, all her breath gone.

The world blurred then faded, her last sight of the Charon inching toward her, claws reaching for her chest.

CHAPTER FIFTY-FOUR

"Just get here. Please," Natalie Bennett whispered before ending the call. She held the phone in her hands, staring at the blacked out screen. She tried to stand, but collapsed back to the soft carpet of her son's room. Her right leg was seared, her black yoga pants shredded where the lightning struck her. Lightning. *In her house.* Shot at her like a bullet from a gun. Less than two hours ago the young mother held concerns about grime collected on her dishes. Now she had people shooting lightning at her.

What the hell happened to her day?

Her right leg was useless. Any weight placed on the scorched appendage brought a wave of agony. The door to their yard stretched less than twenty feet away, the highway not much farther than that. She imagined leaving the craziness of their home behind them, but she was trapped. She couldn't move.

Natalie pulled Jack close. The boy of seven tucked himself against Natalie's side, brushing along her wounded leg. She sucked in air at the touch and Jack fell back. Fear rested in his eyes and she fought through the pain to pull him even closer.

"Help is coming, Jack. Help is coming," she said in the dimming light of her son's bedroom. She ran her fingers through his overgrown brown hair, wondering when he last combed it properly.

"Mom?" Jack asked, resting on her shoulder.

Natalie closed her eyes, taking slow, calming breaths. There had to be a solution, a way out of the house. If Jack and her dad helped her up they could stagger to safety.

But what about the detective? Samantha Myers bought them precious time, sticking her neck out for them without any concern for her own life. They couldn't abandon her, could they?

Jack looked concerned, his cheeks flushed. Her hand fell on his forehead, new worries stretched across her forehead in thin lines. "You're burning up, baby. Are you okay?"

He didn't reply, his eyes distant.

"Jack?" she asked, her leg screaming with each subtle shift. "What is it?"

Jack pointed to the door. "Grandpa."

"Dad, are you—?" Natalie Bennett turned to her silent father, suddenly feeling selfish. Her own concerns had taken over, but what about her dad? In two hours he had learned about his mother, his birth mother, and that his family was much larger than he ever knew. The string of murders took his brothers from him without ever giving him the chance to meet them. Did they share his interests? Did they all laugh at the same jokes, play the same games? Did they have happy, fulfilling lives? Hell, did her dad?

Natalie reached for him. Jeremy Bennett was gone, the door to the bedroom left open from his departure.

"Dad?"

CHAPTER FIFTY-FIVE

"We're on our way," Ruiz screamed before dropping the phone to his lap. A sedan cruising in the left lane down the Knoll forced the desperate Latino to jerk the wheel right while slamming hard on the brake. Skirting in front of the sedan, the geriatric gentleman behind the wheel tossing him the finger, Ruiz hit the gas and jumped through the traffic light before it could change to red.

Ruiz let out a long breath, a reprieve for the next block. The minivan flew forward on King's Lane, heading southeast for Tolliver's Grove. Traffic picked up the farther along the Knoll they went, everyone rushing away from downtown with the fading sun. Stop and go for what could end up being hours and no way to avoid it on the major thoroughfares.

Too far away.

Ruiz pushed the thought away, laying on the horn before weaving into oncoming traffic to avoid a collision. The momentum carried the van off the lane and to a side street, narrowly missing a school bus and a tractor trailer.

A patrol car would have been helpful. Some flashing lights. Some pressure on the clueless pedestrians surrounding him. *Why the hell couldn't Loren have picked him up in a requisition vehicle instead of taking the bus?*

Loren.

He sat strapped in tight to the passenger seat, bleeding on the upholstery of Michelle's car. It was definitely Michelle's car, never his. He joked to keep his mind focused, to avoid the result of his decision to bring Loren along. The man was dying. Why did he have to fight to come along? Dying, yet thinking only of the case. Damn him.

"Myers?" Loren croaked. Ruiz nodded, finding the phone between his legs to key in the address. God forbid voice command actually worked for once but he couldn't take the chance. Another red light blurred by to the sound of honking horns and screaming drivers. Ruiz ignored the noise, letting the GPS take over in its dulcet tones.

"Where are we?"

Ruiz tossed him the phone. "Don't talk. You sound…"

"Like I'm dying?"

Loren didn't need the admission. He surely felt the sweat clinging to his pale skin as much as Ruiz saw it from the corner of his eye. The man was bleeding to death and instead of a hospital they were racing to face the creature that sliced him open. Not exactly procedure but at least the young woman on the other end of the line had already called for backup.

"Knock it off," Ruiz said, swerving down Pike for the ramp toward Gatiss and the Grove beyond.

Loren lifted the phone, the question still hanging over them. Ruiz sighed. "Natalie Bennett. Daughter of our next potential victim." He pounded on the horn, slipping the van between two commuter buses, his knuckles white against the wheel. Gatiss opened up for a second before filling from the expressway circling the downtown area. Ruiz hit the horn, shifting between lanes without success. "Get off the damn road!"

"If only minivans came with sirens."

His fist slammed against the wheel. Ruiz hit the accelerator, forcing the van to the exit ramp for another way around.

"Right now with the minivan jokes?"

Loren grinned, blood pooling around his teeth. "Might be my last chance. Ruiz—"

"No." The man shook his head, refusing to look. The ramp gave way to Lowtown, never a safe place to be when the sun went down but it stayed light on traffic. The phone chittered over their silence, recalculating to keep up.

"This isn't up for debate," Loren muttered before coughing hard along the dash.

"To you."

"Hell yeah to me," Loren replied. He held his soaked bandages, wincing at any touch. "I need you to do something for me."

Ruiz grabbed the phone from Loren to double check the route. He needed a new screen or an eye exam, he wasn't sure which. "You do it. I'm tired of carrying your ass."

Loren fought back a laugh. "Tell Michelle—"

"Wait. What?" Ruiz slammed on the brake before the light on the corner turned red. Pedestrians rushed across the street, throwing nervous looks at the out-of-place van and the men inside. Ruiz ignored them, turning to Loren with a wide stare. "You're about to use your dying wish speech to talk about my wife?"

"You can't deny our love," Loren joked. "No, you idiot. You have to tell her."

"Tell her what?"

"Everything."

Through it all, Loren cared. Not for his own life but for Ruiz and his marriage. For the city and people dying because of a monster unleashed. With his dying breath Loren fought for everyone else. What had Ruiz done? When pressed by Michelle about Loren's lack of presence at the house since his return, how had he responded?

With lies. With excuses meant to maintain the distance between work and family. Between safety and danger, as if Loren was a walking magnet for the death that seemed to surround them.

Or was it Ruiz that was the magnet?

He didn't deserve the man's friendship. Not today. Maybe not ever. But he would. Ruiz swore to that in the shadow of Portents. He promised to make things right. He just needed a little more time.

Fate answered with the light turning green and the van powered ahead, deeper through Lowtown to Tolliver's Grove along the horizon. From the city into the fire.

Ruiz turned to his friend with a small smirk and nodded. "Right. One problem at a time."

Loren understood, pointing ahead. "Like if this piece of crap can go over forty?"

"You're not gonna die, Greg. You're too much of a pain in my ass," Ruiz smiled, slamming on the accelerator. City blocks turned to blurs of light and shadow while the Grove burned bright in front of them, getting closer with each passing thought, with each passing moment.

A little more time. That's all I need. For everyone's sake.

CHAPTER FIFTY-SIX

The Charon reached for the unconscious detective. *Myers. She said her name was Myers.*

Fingers like tendrils slipped from the lab coat, spreading wide. Light grew over her chest. It pulled from her open lips and through her closed eyes, coalescing above her, where it started as thin streams and grew into a glowing orb of color. Myers didn't move, didn't try to fight back, the blow to her head taking everything out of her. She couldn't stop what was happening to her.

Only Soriya could stop this. She had seen another form of Death perform the ritual on a young girl on the fourth floor of Saint Helena's Orphanage almost two decades earlier. Now, the Charon was killing Myers right before her eyes.

"Back off," Soriya screamed, rushing through her fear of the creature.

She leaped at the beast, all her weight tossed into one assault. Colliding with the side of the Charon, both figures toppled over and slammed into the exposed wall of what had been the Bennett living room.

The light broke, the orb giving way to the streams that had created it, then filtered back into the detective. Breath returned to the woman, slow and steady. Soriya immediately regretted the momentary distraction.

The Charon swatted Soriya aside, the blow snapping hard against her arm. She rolled with the attack, skirting back to her feet.

"I always knew there was something creepy about you, Hady," she said, rushing back into the fight.

Thin claws scratched for her but she avoided them, slipping under the swiping fingers of the Charon. She struck upward into the beast's abdomen. Her hand pulsed from the blows, like hitting concrete instead of flesh. Her momentum carried her out of reach of the Charon's reprisal, the monster from hell stomping at the ground to trap her.

"You have no chance," Henry Erikson shouted from across the room. "I control the stone. I have the coin. You don't have to die here. Give me my brother and you and the detective can walk away. I give you my word, as a friend of Christopher Eckhart."

Mentor. Definitely the wrong card to play. Fury rippled through her lithe frame, building through every muscle. All waiting for a chance to explode.

"No." It was definitive, the collective anger that had been brewing for months. She would be the Greystone, now and forever.

The Charon screamed, swiping the air. Soriya ducked the first assault and leapt over the second, lower strike. Her right leg shot out, slamming into the black chasms that had stolen Hady's beady eyes.

The force did nothing to rock the creature and when the rage-filled Soriya landed, the Charon was ready. Emaciated and sinewy hands caught the dark-skinned protector of Portents off guard and pulled her close.

Erikson's eyes widened with anticipation. "Then die. It ends the same."

The effect was immediate. Burning, smoldering flesh filled her chest and her vision clouded, but not enough to avoid the sight of the Charon drawing closer and closer. Its jaw distended, screaming in her face with rows and rows of fangs.

Soriya winced, pulling back. "Dammit, Hady. Brush your teeth once in a while."

Her heart slowed, and the clouds hovering over her eyes turned black as the world around her went dark.

Suddenly, the light began to grow. The final light. The ending light.

No. This isn't how it ends. No way in hell.

The young woman fought through the darkness and the swirling colors pulled from her very being. She fought with every ounce left in her and screamed back at the beast.

"No!"

Pink ribbons snapped the air, spreading like wildfire around the Charon's maw. They spun faster, twisting tighter. Then they pulled, driving the beast's head back. Tendrils released Soriya and she fell to the ground.

Breath returned but time refused to give her a moment to enjoy the feeling. She cartwheeled back, the Charon's claws sinking into the ground where she once stood. Jumping forward, she kicked hard at the blinded face of the creature.

"Stop!" a voice called out.

The Charon ripped at the ribbons, and the lifelike extension of Soriya released the creature and returned to their place along her left arm. Saliva spilled from its open jaw in anticipation at the end of its mission. The man stood at the edge of the living room, scared and alone. Both forces paused at the approach of the newcomer and Soriya realized how little time there was left to make this right.

Jeremy Bennett pleaded, his hands open. "Please stop this."

CHAPTER FIFTY-SEVEN

"MOVE IT!"

The minivan hopped the curb, nearly colliding with a bus. Ruiz swerved, his cursing more to himself than those around him as the van lurched toward the corner storefront, the patrons within holding their cell phones high, hoping to catch the act on video—or to cash in on a lawsuit.

Cars stopped, screeching brakes running the length of the block, to give the possessed van space on the one-lane nightmare that was the Grove. Ruiz tried to focus on their fast-approaching destination and the dozens of people jumping from the shadows like a damn obstacle course during his academy years.

"Wow," Loren said, his voice little more than an exhale. "I—"

The van dropped down to the street once more to the sound of angry motorists fading into the background. Ruiz turned to the sight of his friend's eyes roll back in his skull before closing completely.

"GREG!" Ruiz shouted to no avail. No movement from the passenger seat. "Loren!"

Ruiz reached across the aisle and slapped Loren in the face. Dusty eyes shot open and Ruiz felt his chest loosen from the tension. He turned back to the road in time to see a car braking.

"Dammit," Ruiz breathed, feeling the right side tires of the van threatening to leave the safety of the road and never return. The out-of-control vehicle clipped the side of the car before continuing up the road, the GPS chirping at their approach of the Bennett home.

Now that the road was clear, Ruiz checked over his friend, catching Loren's wide eyes, still shaking off his momentarily lapse into what was most likely an early grave.

Ruiz pointed at him. "Don't do that again."

Loren shook his head, settling back in the seat, each shift a moment of pure agony written all over his face. "Sorry. Just didn't think your driving could actually get worse."

"I'm…" Ruiz checked his rearview mirror. The driver of the clipped car stopped in the middle of the road, writing down his license plate number while screaming at his wife over the damage. "I'm a great driver."

"Sure thing, Rain Man," Loren said. The van pulled forward and Loren clutched tight to the armrests on both sides. "You know you're not driving stick, don't you?"

"I'm not even going to answer that," Ruiz said. The GPS on his phone blurted out directions and he slammed on the brakes, forcing both of them forward in a quick lurch. "Sorry."

"Made my point."

Ruiz checked the address, not that any police work was necessary to identify the Bennett home. The damage inflicted to the ranch home at the corner of Loyola and Clearing made it clear this was the correct location. The windows on the front of the house were shattered, the door battered and broken, its screen whipping back and forth in the frame.

Ruiz kept the van idle in the center of the street, yet his mind was anything but. Two entrances to the home, one visible from the road with another most likely leading to the garage and backyard to the rear of the property. One bullet in his gun—his *only* gun. No help was coming from his companion. Myers was another question mark. What was her position in the house? How many civilians were caught in the middle of the situation?

The only tools on hand were what he could see from the street. One bullet in a piss poor backup piece Loren should have upgraded years ago.

Through the window leading to the living room Ruiz saw him. The man held tight to something small in his left hand that Ruiz couldn't make out. Ruiz identified the item in his right hand—he knew it from a dozen cases over the years, dating back decades to his first encounter with the mysterious object.

The Greystone.

"What the hell?" Ruiz reversed. The van flew back, up the driveway to the home across from the Bennetts. Spotlights beamed up the driveway, helping Ruiz guide the monstrous vehicle up the narrow path between homes. The van stopped inches from the garage.

"Ruiz?"

"Not now, Greg."

He didn't bother to look. He didn't need to see Loren's worried face or hear the concern in his voice. There was a madman threatening innocents across the street. One that needed to be stopped.

Ruiz shifted the van to drive, then paused. "Oh, Michelle is going to kill me, isn't she?"

Loren, his skin paler than the moon on a clear night, reached out, stopping short of his shoulder and nodded.

"Do it."

"Like I need advice from you right now."

"Buy domestic next time."

"Shut up," Ruiz snapped. His foot left the brake and slammed hard against the accelerator, launching them forward. "And hold the fuck on."

CHAPTER FIFTY-EIGHT

The end had arrived. Henry Erikson felt it under his skin, the chill of the Medusa coin balanced by the heat of the stone in his other hand. Control, full and total control, was within his grasp. He had wrestled with the moral dilemma of it all, the small sacrifices of six men he never knew, for the sake of his own life.

No longer.

His research had saved lives, but his brothers could not say the same. Their worlds were small, petty and self-involved, creating small circles of connections but never seeking to better mankind, only advancing their own meaningless lives. Family and faith were nothing compared to his own achievements and the potential for more in the future.

Jeremy Bennett didn't see things that way. "Why?"

"A simple question." Henry grinned at his brother, this man he had never come to know over the last forty-eight years. A man he shared nothing with, except for a single dream that plagued them both to answer. Out of all of them, only he reached through the dream with his reply. "Yet here we are."

Chaos surrounded them. The young woman from his lab fought bravely against the Charon. The Greystone bearer's efforts, however, were futile. The beast could not be injured, would not be slowed, not from its objective. The final sacrifice. The confused man stood sadly before him, trying to understand something bigger than anything he could ever imagine.

"People are dying," Jeremy said. He looked to the unconscious detective behind him. His compassion sickened Henry worse than the cancer working through him like an all-you-can-eat buffet.

"People are always dying," Henry snapped.

"But your own brothers? Your *family*?"

"What family?" Henry shouted. "How dare you speak to me of family? I gave up everything to do more, to be better. For everyone else! You call yourself my brother? My family? You are a stranger to me. A necessary sacrifice."

"You're wrong," Jeremy replied, sadness in his eyes.

"You saw it too. The chance. The opportunity to take back control. To live forever."

Jeremy nodded. "You mean the dream."

The epiphany, Henry thought. More than the list and the coin provided by the shadowed stranger in his darkest moment. The dream provided the conduit for Henry Erikson. To understand the beginning to counter the end. To defeat the inevitable.

Ellie Tamblin was a fool. A pretty fool that found herself in over her head with a man she thought loved her as much as she loved him. She was wrong and her reward was a pregnancy unlike any other.

The birth was difficult. Tests would have predicted this but Ellie feared them and the judgment that came with them. She was unmarried and so young. Her parents threw her out, the shame of her condition too great for them to bear. They provided her passage to an estranged relative. Ellie took the train ticket and envelope of cash and made a life away from everyone, trying to hide what had happened to her. There were no tests. No doctors visited.

Until the birth.

Doctors were clueless to the woman's condition. They tried, with the help of the nurses, in the late hours to do the impossible. For what they all witnessed was nothing short of a miracle.

Ellie, her emerald eyes screaming with pain, crying out for the parents that disowned her, gave birth to not one child that night, but seven. Each took something out of her, the accumulation of the pain and the strain devouring the shimmer in her eyes. They took everything out of her. Those seven births.

Those seven sons.

When it was over there followed a moment of pure joy. Her smile washed over all of them in turn. She held them close; seven newborns huddled against her body, all crying their relief at entering the world. Her heart filled with love for them. All of them. In that one peaceful instant the world had righted the terrible wrong done to Ellie Tamblin and given her the greatest gift of all.

In the next moment she was dead.

Suddenly and without warning, Ellie flatlined. Her body gave out, the strain of the pregnancy and then the troubled birthing process had been too much for the young woman. The nurses and the doctors were unable to do any-thing in the end. The seven sons lay swaddled next to their mother, her eyes wide with love for them—and empty with death.

In that instant the seven sons made a connection, a doorway that could never be closed. They tried, burying it behind their lives, their brief existence in the world. Still, the urge remained, the connection linking them to death. Some accepted it, some ignored it.

Henry Erikson fought against it.

"We saw death," Henry said to his brother. "Looked it in the eye. It called to us. It still calls to us. This is how we beat it. How I beat it."

"A fair assessment."

Henry fell back as shadows grew behind the confused Jeremy Bennett. A figure stepped out of the wall of darkness. He wore a tailored suit and bowler hat, a man out of time. *No, not a man at all,* Henry realized.

"Who are you?" Jeremy asked, staggering deeper into the living room, surrounded by threats.

"Death," Henry said to the newcomer. "I've been waiting for you."

"And I've been waiting for you, Henry," the man in the suit said.

"The prize," Henry muttered, his opportunity within reach. He raised the stone at his brother and light pooled into the mystical object.

"Better hurry," Death said. He extended a hand to Jeremy. Henry's brother hesitated. Both men did.

"What are you doing?"

"Making a choice and hoping it isn't too late," the man answered. His hand lay open. "Jeremy?"

"Who are you?"

"Today?" The man in the suit smiled. "A friend."

Jeremy took his hand and the pair pulled away from the living room.

"No, I won't let you," Henry screamed. He raged, the full fury of his words at Death's involvement channeled into the stone. The light threatened to crack the weapon, every ounce of will and focus flowing from the angered man. "You can't choose him. This is for me. For—"

A minivan smashed through the front of the house, screeching to a halt in the center of the room. Brick shattered, crashing and ricocheting off the front of the van and flying through the room. Henry's connection to the stone severed as it launched from his grip, a stray piece of debris striking him and knocking him into the back of the couch and to the carpet.

Blood ran down his forehead, a gash from the flying bricks, long and deep. He didn't care. Henry Erikson didn't care about anything other than the end. Not the cloud over his vision from the blow. Not the sickness burning in his veins. Henry found his gun on the cushion beneath him and picked it up. His moment was not lost, not yet.

He would have his ending, no matter who had to suffer.

CHAPTER FIFTY-NINE

The world slowed. White noise filtered through the background. The floor shook around the room. The plaster fell in streams from the conflict. Where once the Bennett living room stood, chaos reigned.

A chaos Samantha Myers woke up during, her head splitting and blood collecting at her lip. She tried to wipe it clean, groaning at the effort. She blinked hard repeatedly, yet the world refused to focus before her. Nothing worked under her direction. Arms, legs, fingers, toes. Nothing.

What the hell happened? There was the entrance of Soriya Greystone, "vigilante of the stars," and in the eyes of Myers a clear threat to the safety of the city. Then Erikson unleashed hell in the form of a creature wearing a signature lab coat.

Hady. Hady was the killer yet wasn't at the same time. The scantily clad black woman with the pink ribbon adornment joined the chorus with Erikson in calling Hady Ronne the Charon. Like the River Styx guy, only not a guy at all, and with a penchant for slaughtering innocents.

That Charon.

No wonder my head hurts.

Not just her head. Her chest burned, heat driving deep beneath the surface. What happened after the impact from Hady's—no, the Charon's—blow? She remembered her body slamming into the wall but nothing after that moment.

Myers groaned. She needed to move, to get up and figure things out. To do something, anything but lie down as the room exploded around her. Or at least it appeared to have exploded.

Her fingers were finally back in the game. She wiggled them along her sides, overjoyed at the subtle bending of each digit. Toes and feet followed suit, crashing sounds booming in her ears. She ignored them all, refusing to distract from her injuries and her immediate need to recuperate.

"Come on, come on," she muttered. Her voice sounded like a damn synthesizer.

Her arm shifted, her hand pushing off the ground and allowing her to roll over to her chest. Her aching, burnt chest that screamed with the arrival of the floor. Carpeting helped. A little.

The flood of colors faded. Slow shifts of her head revealed the rubble of the wall surrounding her. The debris from plaster and broken studs, wallpaper, and scorched fixtures. None of it registered. All she could see as her sight returned was a small, gray object resting next to her.

A stone. Erikson's stone.

She shuffled, breath catching in her throat with each movement. Her body roared in agony, but fought to move forward by pure determination. That, and her desire not to be heard by anyone else, specifically gun-toting maniacs and mythological creatures from the underworld.

The stone had the power to call down lightning. What could do something like that? And why did it seem like the sort of question Soriya Greystone would be able to answer? She *did* call the stone her own but she probably said the same about the lab samples stolen from the coroner's office.

Myers turned away, scanning the living room. She stopped at the object resting at its center. A van was in the living room. *How the hell was there a van in the living room?* Ruiz appeared trapped on the driver's side, blocked by the exterior brick carried through from the impact. Loren sat in the passenger seat, but *sat* wasn't the right word. *Strapped down* was more like it. Pale skin, his lips discolored, and the way he held his chest? He was hurt. Bad.

Crashing sounds rocked the room. Soriya and the Charon formerly known as Hady Ronne slammed around the premises, smashing furniture and causing destruction with every second. A distraction and not the reason Erikson was at the home.

No, his target stood at the mouth of the hallway—Jeremy Bennett. The man Myers had come to protect. He pleaded with his brother, his eyes screaming for more time.

The gun in Erikson's hand said otherwise.

When did this get so complicated? The time to question the world surrounding her was over. Not a second remained to consider and plan and try to recover from the pain rocking her chest and splitting her skull. It was time to act. Not for herself—little could be done on her own. She needed to make a choice, the right choice, to trust in the right person, before it was too late.

Detective Samantha Myers reached for the stone beside her and hoped there was enough time left to make a difference.

CHAPTER SIXTY

Time slipped away, the clock ticking fiercely behind the scenes of the unfolding drama, one that threatened to upturn the entire dynamic of life and death. Erikson's success meant only the latter, not just for the people in the room but also for the city at large.

The Charon hungered for fresh victims, getting more ravenous with every life taken. Its cage shook, threatening to break open. Soriya grappled with the beast, crashing headlong into the personal gym set up adjacent to the living room. She slammed against the ground and rolled into the treadmill in the back of the space. The Charon pursued, enraged and salivating at the kill. Lights blared then faded in its presence, the darkness building in Soriya's eyes, but she pushed through it, refusing to let the creature win.

She kicked, connecting with the Charon's jaw then slipped away from its swinging claws. During her roll, Soriya snatched some free weights in her path, tossing them at the monster one after the other. They drove the Charon back and Soriya pressed the assault, leaping feet first and crashing against the rock wall that served as the Charon's abdomen, sending it toppling over the treadmill to the ground.

Turmoil rocked the living room. Gilgamesh had arrived and pulled Jeremy Bennett away from the front of the house.

Right before the minivan crashed through the wall.

Brick and mortar shelled the room with debris and the young woman ducked to avoid the larger chunks.

Ruiz was behind the wheel, trapped from the impact. Loren stared at the ground in front of him, unable to lift his head. He was pale. *Hurt. He's hurt. I was supposed to protect him.*

Their separation during the investigation was meant to buffer him from the danger. Her fear pushed him away and he still found his way into danger. Just as he always would. They both felt the need, the drive, toward the work. The need to solve the mysteries set before them, to help everyone at the expense of their own lives.

His decision to leave the city was almost a blessing…and now? Now Greg Loren might not live to glimpse another sunrise. In fact, none of them might.

Erikson stood once more. No stone this time—it was somehow lost in the vehicle's dramatic entrance into the home. Now he held a gun, Jeremy Bennett caught in his line of sight. Another innocent. The last one necessary.

Time was up.

The Charon roared behind Soriya. Its flailing limbs had unleashed hell on the gym equipment to free itself from its entanglement. The monster that had been Hady Ronne rushed at Soriya and there was nothing she could do to stop her. To stop Erikson. To save everyone.

Then help arrived.

"Soriya," Myers cried. "Catch!"

The Greystone flew from the injured detective's hand. Soriya rushed at the soaring object, catching it in mid-leap and letting the momentum of her jump carry her across the room. She kicked out with her legs, forcing her body up before skidding to a halt with the Charon in quick pursuit.

"Goodbye, dear brother," Erikson said, the gun shaking in his weakened hands. "Your sacrifice is appreciated."

"Don't do this," Jeremy said, standing tall. Gilgamesh stepped away, letting the moment play out.

"Erikson!" Soriya screamed.

He didn't turn. His finger fell on the trigger. "You're too late, child."

Time rushed away from her. The stone sat in her hands, the uncontrollable weapon of destruction that had ripped an apartment complex from the skyline because of her lack of control. So much changed that night. Her confidence shaken, her strength shattered. All in an instant.

A single moment. Just like this one.

The Charon screeched, charging at her from behind. There was time enough for one assault, one move. The Charon or Erikson. Her life or Jeremy Bennett's.

To Soriya there was never really a choice. She turned away from the beast and lifted the stone.

"Soriya!" Loren shouted.

Propped against the passenger door, the window open, the detective held tight to his backup revolver. His vision faded, the room turning to shadows. His chest was on fire, a cold burning that swept throughout his body. His left arm dangled at his side, the bones having been shattered in the crash. The pistol, a lead weight against his right hand, threatened to spill out of the open van window to the floor below. It took every effort to keep it locked in place, every inch fighting to let go of the pain.

The Charon barreled across the living room, knocking aside furniture, on the hunt to the woman in the center of the maelstrom. Soriya took aim at the creature's keeper, the stone pulsating so loudly Loren heard the thrumming in his ears.

He took aim, squinting through the darkness that was his field of vision. The Charon pounded ahead, screaming.

Find the bastard and end him. Ruiz's words echoed over the humming of the Greystone. Loren couldn't. *It's Hady. It's still Hady.*

He fired, the kickback knocking Loren against the seat. The bullet slammed into the shoulder of the Charon, which screamed at the impact. The beast toppled, crashing to her right, claws missing Soriya by inches.

The young woman turned to him, her eyes as bright as the rune glowing on the stone before her. Loren forced a smile as he closed his eyes.

"Do it."

Light burst from the stone, every ounce of spirit and will from the young woman who had worked her entire life for the safety of Portents and everyone in it.

Flames sparked on the Medusa coin, bursting along the surface of the ages-old obol. The change was instantaneous. The Charon bellowed in pain, blood beginning to pool from the bullet wound in its back. The creature stumbled toward Soriya, swiping one last time, a desperate and ineffectual ploy, before the broken form of Hady Ronne collapsed on the scorched carpet of the Bennett living room.

"What have you done?" Erikson yelled. The fire burned his palm, searing his fingers.

"Let the coin go, Erikson," Soriya said, focusing the stone's energy on the coin. "You can live."

His hand shook, the fire building along the coin. The face of the gorgon faded behind the growing flame. Erikson, lost to his plight, was unable to see anything except the coin, his life-extending drug now in danger of being lost. He dropped his gun and held the coin with both hands, trying to smother the flames.

"I can't," he pleaded. "Not like this."

"Erikson," Soriya said once more, her hand reaching out for him. "Please."

The broken man, riddled with disease and regret, looked to her with tears in his eyes. "You call this living?"

He hugged the coin tight, the flames spreading all over his body.

"No," Soriya said, the rune gone from the stone. Too late.

All she could do, all any of them could do, was watch as Henry Erikson let the fire consume him. Master of his fate to the end.

CHAPTER SIXTY-ONE

It was over.

Silence filled the destructive chasm that was once the Bennett's living room. No one moved. No one spoke. Every player in the drama paused, shocked into position from the events of the last few minutes.

Jeremy Bennett whispered a prayer to his fallen brother, now a heap of bone and flesh in the center of the room. No one deserved an ending like that, not even one so bent on killing for their own personal gain. The last surviving son of Ellie Tamblin wondered if more could have been said, if he had done enough to change the course of events for the day, yet he knew nothing said would have been enough. Not from the madness in his brother's voice, or the pained and tortured look in Henry Erikson's eyes.

The world spun, the room transforming into a wheel of light. Jeremy braced against the wall, thankful what remained of the plaster held to the pressure. His chest heaved, pain running through his left side. Jeremy closed his eyes, then forced them open, wide and knowing.

The man in the suit was gone. The others remained, offering little more than quiet glances and shuffling steps toward their next goals. Jeremy slipped out, staggering down the hall.

Natalie hopped out of the bedroom first, her weight on her left foot and balancing against the adjacent wall. Jack snuck ahead of her with a broad smile. He grabbed tight to Jeremy's hips and squeezed, the old man fighting through all manner of aches to hold his grandson. Natalie joined them, careful to keep her wounded leg away from Jack's eagerness.

Jeremy savored the moment, running his hand through his daughter's hair. Natalie was the first to break the hug, her questions too great to ignore. She was always in a hurry. Jack joined in on the ramblings, adding his own commentary along the way, most sentences using the word *awesome* multiple times.

The old man said nothing. He simply smiled to his family, running his hand along Natalie's cheek. He pulled away, his slow steps carrying him to the back door and the patio.

The night air was sweet with the scent of early blooming mums that circled the small patio. Jeremy took a deep breath, struggling to hold it in place, to keep the cool, fresh air locked in his chest for a moment longer. To hold it for a second more.

Nights were always among his fondest memories. Campfires with his wife and daughter. Staring out at the night sky from their sleeping bags. The sound of the crickets lulling them to sleep. Memories drowned out the torrent of sirens approaching from all directions.

Jeremy Bennett sat down on the patio swing. He rocked, the chains above squeaking with each rotation, and peered out into the city skyline in the distance.

"It's time, isn't it?"

The shadows separated and from them stepped the man in the suit. He rested on the railing, twin eyes of crystal blue shining down upon Jeremy.

The old man shook his head, turning back to the brightening night before him.

"It comes so quick. Too quick."

Jeremy turned to his company, ignoring the pale skin and the grooved circles adorning his flesh. He saw him as a friend, someone he had known for years.

"Nothing to say?" Jeremy asked the man in the suit. "I suppose I wouldn't either."

Jeremy fought to keep his eyes open one moment longer. To see Natalie playing in the backyard, running from side to side with so much energy. To watch Jack grow up one more day. But his eyes were too tired, the exhaustion settling over him. The pain down his arm and covering his chest were too considerable to ignore.

He closed his eyes. "Will I see her again? The woman from my dreams? My mother?"

"Yes."

A tear escaped, racing down his cheek. The world surrounding him continued to brighten, glowing against the darkness now.

"I think I'll rest my eyes for awhile."

A hand patted against his, warm to the touch. A soothing voice called to him through the bright light.

"Jeremy?" The Suited Man's voice was distant. So far away now. "I'm glad it was you."

Jeremy Bennett smiled and stepped into the light.

CHAPTER SIXTY-TWO

Erikson's bones lay unmoving in the center of the living room. Soriya crouched over them, sifting through his remains and charred flesh. It sickened her but necessity outweighed everything else. She had to know if the coin remained intact. Obols of power, ancient tools and weapons, tended to outlive their masters. The coin could not be allowed to survive. Remains shifted and crumbled, the heat stinging her fingertips, but there was no sign.

The Medusa coin was no more.

Around her, the world held its breath. Jeremy staggered away from his loving family for the back door of the home. Gilgamesh was gone. The others remained, quiet and solemn in the aftermath of their struggle.

Until Myers stepped behind her, gun raised. "Drop the damn stone!"

Soriya held firm to the Greystone but raised her hands over her head. Her body ached from the pitched battle with the Charon, the simple act of lifting the stone an effort.

"Detective," she started, hearing the click of the gun.

"Do it," Myers demanded. Soriya shook her head, facing the bleeding officer. The gash along her brow was deep, blood soaking her cheek. None of it seemed to bother her. "You killed a man. You interfered in an official investigation. Obstruction of justice, at the least. I'll see you charged for this, you damn vigilante. Don't think for a second I won't."

Soriya saw through the anger. Myers had given her the stone. She had thrown it to her at the last second, trusting her judgment to end the threat. To save Jeremy Bennett. To save everyone. She had made that choice willingly, just as Erikson made his own choice in the end to accept his fate.

The fate that awaited all in the end.

"Finished?" Soriya asked.

"Not even close."

"Myers."

Ruiz stood outside the van, finally able to extricate himself from the debris blocking the driver's side door. His left arm tucked close to his side, thin cuts running under his shredded shirtsleeve. He fought through the living room for the other side of the vehicle.

"Captain," Myers said. "This woman—"

"Help me, Myers," Ruiz interrupted. He tried to open the passenger door, Loren unconscious against the open window. Myers tucked her sidearm away to join Ruiz. "Help me with Greg. Please."

"Loren," Soriya whispered. His last act saved Soriya's life. Without him she would be dead, cut down by the Charon, leaving Erikson free to complete his ritual.

Loren saved them all.

The pair pulled him free from the minivan, Myers taking the bulk of the weight despite her own injuries. Sirens blared in the distance. Ruiz fought back tears, trying to find a pulse on the limp Greg Loren.

"Please," he muttered. "Please don't be too late."

Myers stopped at the threshold to the darkness, turning back at the standing Soriya Greystone. "How can you just stand there? He's dying!"

Soriya nodded. "He's not dead."

With tears running along her swollen cheeks, Soriya turned to the silent party in the room. The young woman and her son huddled at the mouth of the hallway, surveying the wreckage of their home, unaware of the totality of their loss.

Soriya looked at Natalie Bennett through wells of sadness. "Death didn't come for *him*."

All stopped moving, silence filling the room. Natalie held tight to her son, eyes locked on the woman in the center of the room. Her words echoed, and for Natalie Bennett they clicked.

Her hand rose to her lips, her eyes wide with terror. She left her son behind, her pained steps hopping down the hallway and out of the house.

All heads bowed low, a silent prayer escaping their lips, as Natalie Bennett's wails for her father filled the air.

CHAPTER SIXTY-THREE

Emergency vehicles sat on the lawn and across the length of the street. Two uniformed officers kept traffic moving, though it was pointless as anyone traveling by the corner home on Loyola and Clearing stopped to see the show.

A detective from the Sixth, the closest precinct to the incident, sat with the Bennett family on what remained of the porch, while an EMT treated Natalie's leg. The detective listened to the details, her questions light considering the other resources at her disposal. Her purpose was clear and she was skilled at it: to keep Natalie and Jack Bennett talking and not thinking about the man being carted away in the body bag.

Jeremy Bennett. The final victim of the tragic affair.

Or so Captain Alejo Ruiz hoped.

The gurney left the gaping hole in the front of the home, Greg Loren strapped tight and surrounded by trained technicians attempting to keep him breathing. Ruiz walked beside them, trying not to trip on the rubble created by his addition to the Bennett home.

"Is he—?"

"We have to go," barked one of the EMTs. Ruiz slowed. He was in the way. He knew better, but Loren looked so pale. So far gone, despite Soriya's proclamation.

"Wait," a voice croaked through the respirator. The gurney stopped and a hand reached toward him. Ruiz rushed to his side, his worry growing with each passing moment.

"Greg, don't try to talk."

"She—" Loren started to cough as the technicians lifted him into the back of the ambulance. He joined an unconscious Hady Ronne.

"What?" Ruiz called from outside. "What is it?"

"She needs you," Loren whispered through the flurry of activity surrounding him. He pointed to the woman sitting across the street on a bus stop bench. Alone. Even with everything happening, with death knocking at his door, Loren worried for everyone else. Especially Soriya Greystone.

Ruiz nodded, an EMT jumping out of the back of the ambulance.

"Sir?" he said, cocking his head away from the departing vehicle. "Now."

Ruiz stepped back and the doors closed. The ambulance rushed down the front lawn a moment later. Grass sputtered up under the tread of the tire, and the emergency vehicle cut a thin hole in the growing traffic on the corner. Sirens blared and the ambulance turned toward the expressway.

"Save my friend," the solemn captain muttered. "Please."

They had been through too much over the years and the guilt at calling him back to Portents weighed on him. Ruiz suddenly felt exhausted, the day catching up to him. He needed to call his wife; he needed to tell her he was okay. And about the damn car—a conversation he could definitely postpone as long as possible. Michelle had to wait, though. Others needed him first.

He stopped at the second of the three ambulances that had arrived at the scene. The third carried Jeremy Bennett, slipping into the shadows of the city without pomp and pageantry, without the quiet tears of his surviving family.

The second treated everyone else. Where Ruiz only shared minor cuts and bruises from the van's impact with the immovable home, others needed more. Samantha Myers winced at the antiseptic used to wipe at the deep scratches along her forehead. The EMT handed her a pad to clean the wound, noting the glare from Ruiz.

"I just need a second," Ruiz said. The technician nodded, rummaging through the supplies for bandages.

"Captain," Myers started, patting her wounds, testing to see what hurt most. "I know I—"

"You did good work today, Detective," Ruiz interrupted.

They turned to those grieving on the porch and the devastation that would follow the Bennett family for quite some time. A chill drove down Ruiz's arm. More scars from the day's events would follow them all from now on.

"It doesn't feel that way."

"It should," Ruiz said with a small smile. "Get some rest."

She nodded. He started to leave when she called him back, the question hanging over them. "Loren?"

Ruiz's eyes fell away, though they caught her nod at his silence. The EMT returned to continue treatment, Ruiz leaving her for the silence across the street. The chaos of the Bennett home fell into the background. He joined the young woman on the bench, the dim streetlight throwing her eyes in shadow.

"You were right," Soriya Greystone said.

He sighed, hands tight to his knees. "That's debatable."

"No," Soriya replied, shaking her head. "The city doesn't… Portents needs to be left in the dark. One man found out more than he should and people paid the price. I made a mess of the whole damn thing."

"You stopped him."

She held the stone in her grip. "Barely."

"But you did."

"After how many died?" she snapped, keeping her voice a whisper to avoid more attention. Officers passed by the bench, curious looks to the captain. "I wasn't out there. Where you always wanted me. In the shadows. Doing the job. Doing it better than I have. The way Mentor wanted. The way everyone wanted."

Ruiz stayed silent. He had given the argument to the young woman. She held the weight of the city on her shoulders. And he helped heap it on, always wanting an answer to the dangers plaguing Portents, surrounding his family. There was no financial incentive for Soriya Greystone, no reward for the work she provided the city. She did the job because it was right, just as he used to believe.

But that was before he knew about Portents. After that, he did everything he could, used every resource available, to keep it buried. He used Soriya, and it wasn't right. He used her because of his own fear over what would happen if he wholeheartedly accepted the truth of the city.

The city had changed and fighting it did nothing to stem the change. Rejection of an idea did not negate the thought and even proved to accelerate it in some instances.

When he started at Central, Ruiz wanted to change the world. He wanted to make the city safer. Soriya did that without being asked, without question to her own safety. Yet all she had were questions and doubts of her worth.

Because of Mentor. Because of him.

"What do *you* want?" Ruiz asked.

"What?"

Ruiz smiled. "Expectations are great. Desire, though…pure need wins out. What we want. What we need. Maybe you're right. Maybe you need to be better. Hell, I know I feel the same about a lot of things after today. But you have to do it your way, Soriya. No one else's."

Ruiz settled against the bench and looked at the devastation across the street. The physical and emotional destruction of the Bennett home and family. He saw the many deaths of the last week. Hidden away, tucked beneath the surface by a friend and ally, controlled by the fear of another.

Fear could no longer drive them.

"I should have stopped this, Ruiz," Soriya said to the darkness. "Long before it started. You were right."

Ruiz shook his head. His right hand fell on her shoulder, hoping to help ease the burden with a touch and a kind smile. With a firm pat, he let his scarred hand fall back to his lap and stared out at the city stretching into the night.

"I was wrong," Ruiz said. "Very wrong. The city doesn't need someone like me. Someone who hides behind protocol and red tape. Someone who hides because they're afraid to face the truth of what is going on around them. Portents needs you, Soriya."

She was gone. Ruiz let out a small chuckle and settled against the bench, unsurprised. The pain down his right arm lifted and the late night air filled his lungs. He hoped she heeded every word. It was all true, including the whisper uttered into the night sky.

"Don't let her down."

CHAPTER SIXTY-FOUR

Portents needs you, Soriya.

She heard every word, tucked in the shadow of a large oak across from the Bennett home. Sticking around wasn't her strong suit. Ending conversations was another skill she lacked. It didn't mean she wasn't grateful for the kind words from Ruiz.

Through all their arguments, all the anger over the years on how to handle cases and the threats that seemed to plague Portents, to see Ruiz come around and extend the olive branch—to show his support for the work ahead—almost made the pain of the last week, the trouble of the last three months, bearable.

Almost.

His support would never be unconditional. There would be limits—she knew as much. Trust had to be earned but to earn as much as she had from the man meant more than words could describe.

It could have gone a different way with Erikson, the Medusa coin, the Charon...*everything.* The shattered lives of the Bennett family spoke to that. The remains of their home littered the lawn, Ruiz's minivan still deep in their living room. Mother held close to son, the pair in mourning.

They were not the only ones, though. The Charon claimed the lives of dozens of innocents during Erikson's quest for immortality. It never should have happened—not under her watch and not in Portents. The Medusa coin never should have left the Library of the Luminaries, should have never ended up in the hands of someone like Henry Erikson. He never would have been able to gain access to the library. Someone did that for him, Soriya knew. Just as with Nathaniel Evans and the innocents targeted.

Someone was playing a game with the lives in her city.

Soriya held the Greystone to her side, slipping away from the scene. She kept close to the shadows, the long walk out of the Grove for downtown necessary despite her aches and pains. She needed to work through it all. More than anything she needed to find the answers plaguing her every turn.

About the person manipulating events in her city.

About the Bypass.

And about the Greystone and the power contained within. A power firmly back in her control, her renewed focus, her drive channeling its energies back at Erikson to end the threat. She saved the city. She did that; it was her choice. Fear remained about the stone, about the missing pieces of the puzzle alluded to by Erikson. But fear would not stop her from finding the truth.

Fear would no longer control her, nor would she be controlled by the decisions of the past, the desires of others. Her life was her own, stretched out before her, splitting off in multiple directions like the great city of Portents, every avenue a choice.

She held the stone out and smiled. The secrets hid beneath the surface, the answers to her questions. More important than that was the answer she had all along. The truth of the power within her. More than the stone and the Bypass. More than Mentor and the never-ending lessons. The power was hers and hers alone.

Soriya raced into the night, losing herself in the city. *Her* city. She was the Greystone.

Now and forever.

CHAPTER SIXTY-FIVE

Ruiz hated hospitals. Ever since his childhood, everything about the sterile environment disturbed him. Now he knew better. For as much as he hated being stuck in their beds, at the whim of their nurses and doctors for endless tests and more endless periods of waiting, he discovered something about hospitals he hated even more.

Visiting them.

It could have gone the other way. He could have been the one bleeding to death. He could have been the one lying in surgery for eighteen hours to try and stem the bleeding from multiple wounds and lacerations. Concern spread throughout the wings of not having enough blood on hand. Emergency donors stepped to the plate to knock that one last worry off the list.

All Loren needed was a miracle.

And he delivered.

One week after their confrontation with the Charon, Loren was alive and well. Alive, anyway. *Well* was a word he would use, but this changed things. It certainly had for Ruiz, who had visited every day, avoiding eye contact with everyone wandering the halls of the recovery ward. Seeing the other patients became the worst part of Ruiz's visits. Not much of a problem when you're strapped to a bed with IV tubes and monitors, but when you're forced to face the unlucky souls next door, it was a different story.

A tragic one, at that.

Ruiz left for the night, his seventh in a row, with a heavy heart. The night air soothed his troubled soul, but nothing swept the pain and misery from memory. He kept his head low, turning away from the parking structure and his waiting rental car. Out of pocket, of course. Insurance didn't cover running headlong through a home to save lives. Go figure.

He passed by broken men and women—those grieving, those concerned, those with loved ones locked inside the hospital. There were others, of course: the jubilant, the excited, those with a second chance, a new lease on life.

It was the city of Portents in a nutshell. Every time they walked away from things, it seemed to be because the city took a breath and gave them the moment. No choice entered the equation, only random happenstance—the whim of Portents.

No more, Ruiz thought. That thought had been building over the week, going over events, the questions behind what happened and what might have happened. So many questions that brought so many decisions.

Decisions that changed everything.

The car could wait. The questions demanded more time, included a revisit to the decision made earlier that day. Second-guessing turned to its third or fourth iteration, spinning in circles. A walk would help, though the thoughts would remain. Ruiz circled the block, almost crashing into a woman at the corner.

He fell back, apologies at the ready. Ruiz stopped when he realized who she was.

"Michelle."

His wife fought to smile. "You're avoiding me."

"I'm not."

"You are."

Ruiz threw her a look of aggravation. He leaned against the wall of the hospital. "What are you doing here?"

"Checking in on my husband." Michelle joined him, reaching for his right hand. He pulled it away. "You remember him, right? It's tough because he hasn't been seen at home in a week for more than ten minutes at a stretch."

"Michelle."

She stopped. Neither of them wanted to fight anymore. "How is Greg?"

Ruiz asked himself the same thing. Behind the jokes and the complaints, he worried for his friend. The man who had saved him, saved them all in the end. He worried about the lack of fear in Loren's eyes, about the lack of anything other than the need to laugh.

He hoped those worries were unwarranted. Hope was all he had left.

Ruiz peered back at the hospital, trying to smile. "He's watching Superman cartoons and eating Jell-O."

"Sounds like Greg." Michelle laughed.

"He'll be okay," Ruiz said, seeding hope. "A few scars, that's all."

Michelle reached for his hand once more. He pulled it back, tucking it close. Her fingers grazed his side, then fell on the burned limb. Gently, taking her time, she lifted up his sleeve. Her eyes welled up at the sight of the mark along his forearm and the scars left by the event at Evans Tower.

"Seems like you're both carrying your fair share lately."

Ruiz pulled down his sleeve and pushed off the wall. They walked up the block, circling the building back to the parking garage.

"It shouldn't have happened. Not to him."

"You can't blame yourself. You didn't—"

"I pulled him back. Into this place. And then what did I do? Nothing."

"We invited him—"

"I never invited him, Michelle," Ruiz snapped. "I couldn't. Not because of Beth and all the hell he had been through to get back here. It was because of me. Because of my own selfishness. What the hell kind of person am I to deserve such a good friend?"

Michelle said nothing. He earned the lack of response after all the self-recriminations at his actions, his pulling away from everyone and everything that once meant so much. She stayed silent.

They both realized the truth: Loren would have made the choice no matter who was in the room with him. Be it Soriya, Ruiz, or a complete stranger. That was who Loren was and always had been, even if he failed to see it from time to time. Loren made a decision and God granted him a second chance. It didn't make Ruiz feel any better.

"I tried Hady."

"You what?" Ruiz asked louder and angrier than intended. His words shocked her, causing her to take a step back. He filled his lungs with a deep breath. "Michelle."

"I heard she was hurt in this whole thing," Michelle said, confused. "I called to see if she needed anything."

Ruiz ran his left hand through his hair, cuts and scratches causing him to wince at the slightest touch. "Did she?"

"There was no answer. I left a message but she never called me back. What's going on?"

Ruiz turned away from his wife, unable to answer the simple question. But that was how they always started out, wasn't it? After everything, even with one of his oldest friends down the hall at the hospital, Ruiz had said nothing to the woman he once called a friend. He kept a close eye on her recovery, one that was "uncanny," in the words of the hospital staff, as the bullet wound delivered by Loren closed and sealed in record time. She left on the third day of her stay at the hospital, while Ruiz trailed her to the door without a word.

There would have to be questions asked, of course, about the Charon and the deaths. The conversation needed to happen, but not yet. Not until he thought things through.

He should have told Michelle, at least warned her to leave Hady alone for awhile, until he answered his own gnawing thoughts. He didn't, though, fearing follow-up questions from his inquisitive wife, always too damn smart for her own good. Always pushing for answers to secrets hidden away.

Hidden by him.

"I'll talk to Hady. When I can."

"Alejo," Michelle intoned, refusing to move.

"How are the kids? Are they—"

"Home," she said in frustration at the diversion. "Zoe is with them."

"Zoe?" His oldest. Eighteen, though he didn't know how the hell that happened on his watch. She started college two weeks earlier. Where had the time gone? How had he let it pass so fast? "What about school?"

"She took the day off."

"She didn't have to do that."

"Family comes first," Michelle said, fingers circling her wedding ring. "That was our promise. Our vow."

"I remember."

She offered a sad smile. "It's been…well, it's been difficult to say the least. I get it. The girls get it. There has to be a line for you, but it's become a wall."

"I know."

"It's time for a change."

"I was thinking the same thing." He smiled at her, holding out his hand.

She hesitated. "Alejo."

"I took a leave of absence, Michelle."

Her eyes widened. "What?"

The paperwork cleared that morning. The commissioner didn't want to approve the request but it was his to take.

"For how long?" Michelle asked. He took her hand and held her close.

"As long as it takes. Maybe forever."

"This is—"

He nodded, kissing her cheek. "I'm tired, Michelle. Of the secrets and the politics and the distance."

"You were the one—"

"And I'm through with it," Ruiz said, remembering Loren's wish for them. *Tell her everything.* "All of it. If you'll still have me."

"Forever," Michelle replied. She squeezed his hand tighter. "Another promise."

The two walked through the darkness of the city. They turned away from the hospital and their waiting cars, leaving behind their responsibilities and everything else.

"Forever is a long time."

CHAPTER SIXTY-SIX

She found the bag under her teacher's cot. Tucked in the back corner, behind a pile of unwashed laundry long since forgotten. The bag fit her needs perfectly, sturdy with a woven canvas dyed forest green. Her few possessions—clothes, books both her own and his—slid inside the deep duffel. When filled, Soriya Greystone slid the thick strap over her shoulder and left the small domicile.

It was time to leave.

The decision did not come lightly. Yet with each argument, some more physical than others—the footprints throughout the chamber evidence in this regard—the final choice seemed clear. Hiding beneath the city was not the answer. It worked for Mentor. When he left his wife and daughter, when he took up the stone and then a student, a life disconnected from the people they protected, it was his choice.

A choice that never worked for her.

Staring at the Bypass, the orb of green light floating serenely before her in the center of the large chamber, she knew there was more to the final choice. The shadows continued to fluctuate along the surface. The light remained shimmery yet stunted. Despite her newfound control over the power locked in the merged stone, despite her renewed faith in the mysteries contained in the Greystone, the Bypass continued to change.

Balance is the key. Yet balance was achieved. Something else hid in the background, waiting in the periphery since the return of Nathaniel Evans. Perhaps even longer. Something was coming. Something that had been in Portents longer than she cared to admit.

The bag settled along her back and she hitched it up tighter. The answers would not come from constant meditation and belief in the all powerful Bypass before her. Her answers were out in her city.

The darkness held her for so long she almost hesitated at the stairs. She believed she did the right thing: keeping Loren—everyone—at a distance. It was the way Mentor would have wanted. She tried so hard to make him proud, to learn the lessons and act on them just as he would have done. But he made choices and she only followed them. Angry and defiant, she broke the rules, but they were his and his alone.

She needed her own path. It took almost losing everything to realize that. Loren, thankfully recovering from his injuries, would be proud of her. If she ever had the courage to face him again, that is. She tried to keep him safe and almost lost him in her ignorance, but never again. She couldn't let that happen again.

She needed him, like Portents needed her. Out there, in the light, connected and questioning the world as it happened, not after the nightmares were unleashed.

It was time for a change in the hope of fixing everything.

Soriya Greystone moved for the stairs, rising with each step toward the city she loved. Portents—a city she would die for, knowing it deserved no less to keep it safe.

CHAPTER SIXTY-SEVEN

Greg Loren walked down the second floor hall of the Rath Building as if for the first time. His left arm sat in a sling, his recovery knitting back the majority of his wounds. Pain lingered and would for quite some time, with only two weeks having passed since his encounter with the Charon. When he took a sharp breath or made a sudden movement the aches returned, a reminder of what happened.

Of what could have happened.

But he was still standing. After pacing around his apartment the last week, binging on missed television shows between naps on the couch, Loren needed to move. He needed to be back at work.

Not that any work waited for him. Not yet. His time off stretched a few more weeks but there was no reason he couldn't stop in for a visit, to know some things refused to change even when the world crashed down around them.

Not everything stayed the same, however. His arrival brought the standard array of looks and mutters from the officers on the floor. The gossip mill working overtime since his injury no doubt. Instead of the glares that followed and the silence that joined their condemnation, cheers sprang forth through the floor.

"Glad to see you're up and about," an officer from the first floor said, passing Loren for the open elevator.

Another patted his back as he passed. "Welcome back, Greg."

I need to start learning everyone's names, Loren thought at the onslaught of praise and acceptance showered over him. Pratchett was waiting for him when he rounded the corner.

"Detective," the tall officer said through the welt along his cheek. The bridge of his nose still swelled, purple skin peeking out of the oversized bandage.

"Pratchett, how are you?"

"Fine." His jovial attitude seemed muted. Loren hoped it would not be forever. "Just fine."

"Good."

More well wishers walked through, nodding their appreciation to both men. Loren couldn't help but smile at each of them, his grin growing in kind. Pratchett joined him.

"Change always is, right?"

Loren nodded, chuckling.

Pratchett pointed to the open office door across the hall. "Well, maybe not all change."

The tall officer left Loren with his thoughts and the open door to his office. Only it wasn't just his office any longer. His name hanging on the plaque beside the door now included another.

Samantha Myers.

He stepped into the frame, looking over the chaos unfolding in the cramped space. The second desk alone took up most of the walking space allotted in the office but Myers went further. Stacks of reports consumed both of the work surfaces, paperwork pouring out of the open filing cabinets along the right wall.

"How do you stay organized in this mess?" the woman's voice called out and he smiled. Myers dropped the phone, pulling reports into one gigantic pile only to watch them slide out from the bottom into a larger mess.

"There's a system to it," Loren said. "Heavy caseload?"

Myers sighed, slumping into her chair. "I've become a dumping ground."

"Mathers?"

She nodded, blowing her hair out of her face. Her gash was healing, most of it covered by a thick bandage. "Clearly upset with my transfer to nights."

"Especially since his was denied," Loren said with a grin. It faded at the sight of the closed door at the end of the hall. Ruiz's office.

"How is he?" Myers asked, reading his thoughts.

"Ruiz will be all right."

They spoke a few times since Loren's release from the hospital. Ruiz gave him the news about his leave of absence and about everything he shared with Michelle in such a short time. He eased her into things at first, of course. A smart move, both looking to find a level of comfort in the new dynamic.

Ruiz sounded more awake now, more alive than he had in quite some time. His family sounded happier as well. Ruiz even invited the poorly groomed detective over for dinner next week. Loren looked forward to it.

"And you?" Myers rubbed her eyes, shaking her head. "I probably should have asked that first."

"Still walking." Loren raised his sling before the pain returned. "Slower but still."

Myers nodded, clicking her tongue. She tapped a tune with her feet. She waited impatiently and Loren let her, enjoying the way she squirmed under the silence.

"We going to talk about it or what?" she asked, exasperated.

Loren grinned, pointing to the placard beside the door. "The partner thing?"

The announcement came as a surprise, one he was glad to hear about ahead of time from the interim captain, an old hand from the Ninth. Loren was unfamiliar with the woman, their one exchange limited to Myers' new status in the department. Loren hoped to last a week before pissing her off.

A nice dream.

"No." Myers cocked her head for the door and Loren closed it. "I mean, we could talk about it if you want, but me being in here making a disaster of the place pretty much sums up that update. I meant the other thing."

"Portents."

"Bingo."

He fell against the wall, hoping not to slip on the papers scattered across the floor. His wife's case stared back at him from the corkboard on the far side of the office, her smile saddening to see. He slipped his hand into his pocket, wishing for some gum. *Filthy habit.*

"So," Myers started, fighting for the words. "How does this work exactly?"

"It just does. Except when it doesn't. Then—"

"Then everything goes whackadoo crazy and we clean up the mess."

"See?" Loren smiled. "No explanation needed."

"You don't see the problem in that?"

"Myers…"

"The problem with her?" Myers finished.

Loren turned away. He hadn't seen Soriya since the Bennett home, or spoken to her since their trip to the Library of the Luminaries. Since her decision to push him away, to try and protect him instead of work with him to help the city. To trust in each other the way they always had.

Loren knew she was out there still, that she would be there for him when needed, but it seemed different. Changed, for both of them, like they each had their own path to follow, their own purpose to find in Portents.

"Soriya helps," Loren said, staring into the darkness of the city. "She stopped Erikson."

"She's not a cop."

Loren understood the argument, the same one from Ruiz for so many years. "Sometimes that's a good thing."

Myers shook her head. "She does what she wants. She knocked out a damn lab tech to steal some samples from the case."

"To get answers."

Her voice fell quiet against the rustling wind outside. "Loren, that kid…"

Myers trailed off, not needing to finish. The kid was part of the staff at the coroner's office. A staff that didn't see the morning sun thanks to the monster hidden among them. The one none recognized until it was too late.

"It's not your fault, Myers. Or Soriya's."

She leaned on the desk. "You trust her."

He nodded. "Even when she doesn't share the sentiment."

"You shouldn't."

"Come on, Myers," he cried, aggravated at the continued assault from his new partner.

Myers opened the drawer to her desk then paused. "I found something. About your wife."

Loren stopped, eyes wide. "What?"

"The day she died—"

"How dare you?" Loren screamed, pain shooting up his arm and down his chest. He took a breath. "I know you have boundary issues, Myers, but for Christ's sake. You had no right to—"

"I know," she said, a silent apology slipping from her weary eyes. "But I did it. And I found something."

She held up a photograph. In four years of searching, Loren never viewed the snapshot before.

"Is this...?" he mumbled, trying to form the question, to understand the image in front of him.

"I went through the eyewitness statements." Her voice stayed steady and calm. To calm *him* more than anything. "I tracked them down. Every single one. There had to be something else, something missing from the scene, and there it was. You questioned someone named Fredericks four years ago."

"I remember."

"But not his brother."

"His—"

"His brother was with him at the scene and he snapped that photo. Then forgot about it. Until I found him." Myers stopped, taking a breath. "Quality was garbage but I had it cleaned up. I have others too but that one..."

Loren held up the image. "The shadow in the window."

The gnawing feeling from his dreams, from his memories of that night. All his notes, all his recollections, all pooled toward the thought that someone was there. That there was an answer to the greatest mystery of his life in that shadow.

"Only it wasn't a shadow," Myers said.

No, it wasn't a shadow in the window at all.

It was Soriya Greystone.

CHAPTER SIXTY-EIGHT

The sound of squeaking sneaker soles faded with each passing moment. Myers continued to wait, the report crumpled around her tense fingers. When the noise was replaced with silence, the file fell free, coming to rest on the mass graveyard that was once her desk.

Loren had been stunned by the image and the revelation that came with it. His reaction was expected, but what came after was a surprise.

Nothing.

Not a word uttered, not even a curse word or ten at the betrayal of Loren's closest ally outside of the department. The still recovering detective held tight to the photo of Soriya Greystone hidden in the shadows of his apartment four years earlier—watching from above as the love of his life left the world. Then he tucked it into his pocket and left

He needed time. His eyes spoke to that more than anything. She could tell that in his mind the answers were already there. The truth behind his wife's still open case. The reason why it remained an unsolved murder. Each answer leaned darker until he could no longer look back at the office and his new partner, shuffling down the hall for the elevator.

Loren needed to understand this news, to figure out the reasons behind the photo. And to come to the conclusions Myers placed in his head.

Exactly as she intended.

Satisfied at the time elapsed since his departure, Myers reached inside the top desk drawer, retrieving a small burner phone. She held it for a long moment, teeth running along her bottom lip. Flipping it open, she slammed her finger down on the number 7 to activate the saved entry. It rang twice before she hung up, then closed the phone and slipped it back into her drawer.

A breath escaped her. The choice made in her mind. So many choices made over the last few days. Building to this.

When the landline rang out, the booming tone startled the detective. Myers cleared her throat, settling further into the hard wood of the chair. Feet shuffled out in the hall and she hesitated, letting the loud ring continue for what felt like ages.

"Loren?" she asked, nervously. But Loren was gone. Myers closed her eyes and lifted the receiver. At first there was nothing, dead air on the line, then an audible smile escaped into Myers' ear.

"It's done," Myers said.

"The photo?" the voice on the other end muttered back. Myers shifted away from the office door, looking at the open window and the darkness of the city beyond.

"Yes," Myers replied. "Just like you told me."

Myers' breath caught in her throat. Everything led to this. Every choice made since her arrival. Mathers. Ruiz. Loren. The case. The night shift. Her new partner. All building for a purpose.

"And?"

"He believed it," Myers said, her badge glinting in the corner of her eye. "Why wouldn't he? I earned his trust. I told you I would."

Myers stared out at the city, listening to the voice on the other end. Level and calm against the pounding of her heart.

"Right," Myers replied in the silence that followed from the voice on the other end of the line. "I'll wait for your instructions."

The phone rattled into place on her desk, her eyes stuck on the open window. She snapped the switch on her lamp and shadows filled the rest of the room. Returning to the window, hands running the length of her face to her hair and back, Myers stared out into the darkness of the city.

Letting the darkness of Portents stare right back at her.

CHAPTER SIXTY-NINE

Traffic ran the breadth of the thoroughfare. Exhaust wafted down the sidewalks, flowing into open doors and windows on both sides of the street. The sun sat behind thin clouds moving rapidly over the skyline.

Horns honked. People yelled. Anger mixed with frustration. Others cheered, laughing about stories too personal or too impolite to share. More still roamed the streets of Portents, their heads low, tucked against the portable devices that occupied their waking world.

Soriya Greystone loved every aspect of the world around her. The angst, the joy, the crowds, everything. Sitting in the corner of the outdoor patio in front of Jumpin' Java, she watched the city of Portents come to life.

She squinted at the bright shining orb in the sky, peeking out from behind the wave of clouds, unstoppable in its efforts. It hurt, the intensity of the light, but she refused to look away. Just as her smile refused to fade.

This is what she needed, what she always wanted. So many years burrowed underground, working from the shadows, hoping to make a difference without any chance to connect with those around her. Always watching from a distance, pretending it was to keep everyone else safe. Pretending fear played no part in the decision.

Both hers and Mentor's. His edicts ruled her life, even after his death. His way of life became hers, the rules passed on from one generation to the next. From one Greystone bearer down the line, without pause. It started to keep her safe but became more about protecting that feeling than her safety. Keeping them together despite his absence.

Soriya needed more—not to live in the shadow of the dead. Fear no longer drove her actions. Fear of not being good enough for him, fear of not living up to the standard set by those that came before. She would live but she would live on her terms, her way.

She sipped her coffee, hot to the touch. It burned going down and she put it back on the small, round table. A woman in a wide-rimmed bonnet passed by, men staring at her as she walked. An older man tried to parallel park without success, slowing traffic for two blocks. Officers patrolled the city, wary eyes watching all. Just like her. Knowing this time, no threat went unseen.

Her promise to Portents.

"This seat taken?"

Soriya turned to the shadow looming over her table. He wore a light blue polo and khakis. His pale skin, once marked with deep grooves, was now clean except for a number of small cuts along his cheeks.

Gilgamesh still wore his bowler hat, though.

"I was wondering when you might show up." Soriya offered the chair across from her. Once seated, she pointed to the dried blood marking his face. "You look like crap, Death."

"I know," he laughed, running his hand over his face. He winced when he grazed each cut. "It feels amazing. And I think we can drop the Death moniker now. It's Gil."

Soriya held up her cup, looking him over. "Sticking with that one?"

He ran his hand along the brim of his hat. "Why mess with success?"

A waitress walked up to the table at Gil's arrival, waiting for their laughter to fade. "Can I get you anything?"

Without looking at the menu at the center of the table, Gil's blue eyes gleamed at the young woman. They were no longer sharp crystalline but they still glowed. Especially to the waitress.

"A triple espresso macchiato with nonfat milk," he said without pause. She noted it without looking away. "To go."

She left them, Soriya's mouth agape. She shook her head. "You picked up the lingo quickly enough."

"I had plenty of time." Gilgamesh took a deep breath, settling in the chair. "Decaf?"

Soriya nodded. "Black. I'm adventurous enough with the company I keep."

The man once known as Death grinned. She meant every word. Not only with him but for Loren. Hell, even Ruiz. She was there for them, no matter what happened. She always would be.

Soriya needled her cup, taking a long sip of the delicious blend.

"Ask." Gilgamesh's drink arrived and he offered a quiet nod of thanks to the young woman who lingered a moment too long before her awkward stare caused her cheeks to flush. She retreated from them. He turned back to Soriya, rolling his finger. "Ask the question."

"Jeremy…"

"Will be fine," Gilgamesh said, his tone understanding. "Trust me."

She did and probably always had, in spite of her fear. "You knew, didn't you? How it would all end. The seven sons."

"I hoped." He took a sip, letting it settle over him, like a warm blanket. Satisfaction filled his lips. He placed the cup on the table and nodded. "You did too. On some level."

There always had to be an ending to the story of the seven sons. An end to Gilgamesh's story as well. One way or the other there would always be an end to things. And hope, that when the pages ran out, when the tale was told, that the ending met with approval for all that remained. For the sake of the city.

For the sake of everyone.

"What's next for you?" Soriya asked, letting the somber tone fade behind them. "Time to join the working world?"

"Pass," he replied with a grin. "I hated my last job."

"Maybe hit up the local dating scene? I think I see some interested parties." Soriya cocked her head to the waitress.

Gilgamesh laughed and shook his head. He lifted his cup high. "Coffee first. Then we'll see where the day takes me." He looked out at the city around them, living in the moment, once more able to savor each one knowing they could all end in an instant. "Portents truly is a beautiful place."

Soriya beamed with pride at her home. "It is."

"Keep it that way, Soriya." He stood to leave, but his eyes remained on her. Sad eyes. Worried eyes.

"I will," she said, leaning closer. "Why? What do you see?"

"There is a darkness coming, Soriya. A circle about to close on you and those closest to you. You have to be ready. For the city. For everyone. If the Bypass falls…"

"It won't," she answered. "Ever."

Gilgamesh nodded, a thin smile on his lips. He turned to leave, her voice holding him in place.

"You could help."

"And I may before the end," he said. "But this is your challenge, Soriya. Your test. Prepare yourself."

"I will."

He left without another word, though more could have been said. More hints at the growing darkness, one she felt that night at the Bennett home. The same feeling that haunted her with Nathaniel Evans. The idea that something else was out there. Waiting for her. Waiting to strike.

Gilgamesh melded with the crowd, just one more member of the city. Living his life among them, with them, not lording over anyone or serving anyone. Truly living for the first time.

Like her.

Prepare yourself. She heard the warning in the back of her mind. Then she smiled.

"Tomorrow."

Soriya settled in her chair and savored a sip of her coffee. It warmed her entire body, the sun washing over her from above. She closed her eyes and listened to the city surround her.

CHAPTER SEVENTY

Loren tried to call her when he left the hospital. He would listen to the initial ring then hang up before a second attempt and a third. All with the same results. How to start the conversation always tripped him up.

The office was his next venue. Face to face offered a more personal experience, but he couldn't. He made it as far as the front door to the converted elementary school before turning away. It was too soon, the shrill screams and the fading lights still waking him throughout the night. A call confirmed his suspicions anyway.

Hady Ronne's office was empty.

None of it was her fault. Thanks to her, Loren was still alive, as was Ruiz and who knows who else. If someone else had been possessed by the Charon, walking around as an avatar of Death, the damage could have been much worse.

If only he could tell Hady that.

No one had seen her since the hospital. When she discharged herself from their care she slipped into the night like a wraith, fading into the shadows. After a few days people stopped asking about her, stopped caring, and fell back into routine. All without a clue as to the story behind the story being told.

Ironically, Loren thought about her more with each day. Because of the truth. Because he knew without a doubt that he would be dead had it not been for her strength and restraint in the end. The beast did not win out. She did. Plus, he felt slightly bad about shooting her in the back. Slightly

At the end of the month, with the rushing wind tossing the vibrant colors of the leaves to the ground in torrents, Loren decided to take matters into his own hands. He took a cab to her home in Traveler's Cove—a Queen Anne style with eaves clinging tight along every edifice. A large home considering its single occupant but its size gave it breathing room from the rest of the neighborhood. Privacy, most likely necessary for the secret she hid from the world, either knowingly or not. That was still a question to all.

No lights beamed within the home. Not a surprise considering her penchant for dark places. Shutters rattled along the home in the wind. Loren opened the creaking gate and shuffled up the front walkway to the door.

He knocked twice, a deep booming that shook birds loose from a nearby tree, unnerving Loren, who cursed under his breath. His nerves surprised him, much more than the lack of any answer to his arrival. He peered around the neighborhood. Night kept most eyes away, the evenings of many people lost to television and sleep. Then Loren tried the handle of the door, waiting for Jacob Marley to scream at him for the tight grip. He twisted and the oak shifted forward.

"Hady? It's Loren."

He waited, catching the echo rise to the vaulted ceiling of the foyer. No response. He didn't expect one. The truth was clear long before arriving at her front step.

Loren flipped the light switch, closing the door behind him. His newly replaced sidearm fell into his free hand and he inched deeper into the home. Nothing sat out of place. Nothing touched. Nothing moved. Only a thick layer of dust to denote the passage of time.

Hady hadn't been here.

Loren searched, keeping the lights to a minimum. Nosy neighbors were an inevitability in the modern world. With them came questions the detective did not want to answer. Not yet.

From the living room, Loren turned to the kitchen. Nothing. An immense area for a single resident, the same as every other room in the home.

The second floor turned up little else. No sign to prove his theory faulty, nothing to tell him that she had packed up after the ordeal for an extended vacation or a leave of absence, much like Ruiz. One would have been expected but this was more. The fully stocked closet—black, black, and more black—plus the untouched luggage tucked away painted the picture clear for him.

Hady Ronne was gone. Missing.

Matching the growing number of cases throughout the city of Portents, Loren noted the similarities with the other scenes. The pristine condition of the home. The lack of concern from anyone. The few cases that managed to poke through to the proper authorities were the oddity but alluded to a massive undertaking going on behind the scenes.

Dozens of people were missing, Loren's friend Dominic included, one of the reasons he pushed to visit Hady. Loren made copies of each file and continued to investigate during his absence, filling his hours with their histories and any other links between every occurrence. A distraction to the photo of Soriya sitting on his coffee table, begging for an answer. A necessary distraction for now. One intricately connected by a single point.

A sign.

Loren found it in the dining room of Hady Ronne's vacant home. Tucked in the corner, under the shadow of the empty hutch, it marked the wall close to the floor. The sign matched the one found in Dominic's apartment and a dozen others. One that matched notes he found four months ago in the Bypass chamber on a map kept by the man called Mentor.

A thin circle of black, its consistency like ash. A sign from whoever took Hady, whoever held the answers to the city's secrets. Secrets Loren would bring to light, a promise made in the empty home of the woman who let him live, who gave him his second chance, one he would see returned. Secrets including the truth behind the sign itself and the name attached to it.

A Circle of Shadows.

CHAPTER SEVENTY-ONE

Brendan Wilcox fought for each breath. Coughing and wheezing, the young man of twenty-three tried to rest, unable to find comfort in his full size bed or his mountain of pillows. Photos of family and friends crowded his nightstand, blocking the little amount of light offered by his table lamp.

Flowers joined the images of better days. None filled him with gratitude at the thought behind them. They only reminded him of what was coming. Of how long the coughing and wheezing had been part of his life. At how long it had been since he felt healthy.

Since the cancer took over his body.

The doctors discovered it early. Back in the days of optimism and treatment plans, of which there were many, plans were already in the offering for what Brendan would do once in full remission. The chemo failed to take. Surgeries failed to remove the tumors completely and that which was removed was replaced. It seemed despite optimism and hope, another plan was in the works for Brendan Wilcox.

There was no saving him.

The young man, with dreams of opening a bookshop and coffee bar to share his love of both with the world, never gave up hope. He lived every day. He smiled and played and loved just as hard as everyone. Harder even. For his family. For his friends.

But time caught up to him. It always did.

When the latest bout of treatment failed to improve his condition, Brendan took to his room to rest. A long day of filling his family with as much false hope as they did in return took its toll and he wanted nothing more than a night of reading and sleep. Alone.

Lying in his bed, eyes closed to the world, Brendan was not as alone as he would have liked. Company rested at his bedside, watching the troubled breath wheeze in and out of his body, looking over the young man solemnly as he struggled to find some peaceful rest against the will of his body.

A tear slipped down Jeremy Bennett's cheek, luminescent against his pale skin. He grazed Brendan's hand, memories of his daughter filling him, fighting through the pain of her life with the tenacity of the young man in the bed. Fighting for everyone else as much as herself.

He missed his daughter, the constant battle as a parent, as well as the fun of being a grandparent, his time with Jack far too short. Jeremy Bennett thought of them often since he entered the white light. He carried them with him and would forever.

The same promise offered to Brendan Wilcox in the darkness of the young man's bedroom.

Light grew over his body, the coughing and wheezing intensifying then silencing. Streams of color collected in a luminescent ball, hovering for a long moment over the tired frame of the young man, then disappeared, dropping the room back into shadow.

Jeremy Bennett patted the boy's hand lovingly and stood. As he stepped into the hallway the light coalesced beside him, the young man walking in stride. Brendan Wilcox looked back to his body then took Jeremy's hand with a smile.

Jeremy returned the sentiment, eyes of emerald crystal beaming at the young man. They started down the hall, a bright glow showering them from the far end. They walked in tandem, cherishing the happiness of their lives. The joy of the journey. Then they stepped into the light to start the next one.

The beginning of forever.

ABOUT THE AUTHOR

Lou Paduano is the author of the Greystone series of urban fantasy adventures, which follow Detective Greg Loren and Soriya Greystone as they hunt myths, monsters, and legends in the city of Portents.

He is also the author of the conspiracy thriller series, The DSA, a serialized tale about a clandestine government agency trying to discover the true power behind humanity's future.

He lives in Grand Island, New York with his wife and three daughters. Sign up for his e-mail list for free content as well as updates on future releases at loupaduano.com.

AVAILABLE NOW

BOOK ONE - SIGNS OF PORTENTS

Portents is a city like no other—and one that Detective Greg Loren can't wait to escape. Since his wife's death years earlier, Loren has looked forward to the moment he can leave the city of Portents for good—and never look back.

But fate has another plan for Loren. Called back to duty, Loren finds himself embroiled in a series of murders that has shaken the city. Together with Soriya Greystone, a young woman with unearthly powers, Loren must work quickly to find the otherworldly being that is killing citizens of Portents one at a time. Loren is tasked with deciphering the mysterious signs left at each of the crime scenes…even if it means traveling to worlds not his own to do so.

BOOK TWO - TALES FROM PORTENTS

Six tales of monsters, the dead rising, and the terrors of Portents.

The beasts Detective Loren and Soriya Greystone battled in Signs of Portents were just a hint of what lurks in the city. Tales from Portents explores the city's immersive history, including stories of Loren's descent after his wife's death—and his opportunity to have her rise from the grave. Among the pages, Soriya battles gremlins, navigates lessons with Mentor, and meets the werewolf Luchik. Follow new characters with expansive histories as they come face to face with the horrors of Portents—both human and otherwise.

GREYSTONE CONTINUES IN…

The shadows are growing around Portents.

Detective Greg Loren attempts to recover from injuries sustained during his hunt for the Medusa coin but is pulled into more darkness as the full extent of Erikson's attempt at immortality is discovered.

Soriya Greystone works to connect with the city she protects, stumbling on fluctuations caused by the evolving Bypass and an ancient cult attempting to bring back the god Anubis.

On top of the dangers surrounding the pair, the Founder returns to the city and brings death with him.

Danger is around every corner and Portents grows darker as war inches closer to the surface in this collection of tales from the Greystone collection.